DECADES OF DIRT

Murder, Mystery and Mayhem from the Crossroads of Crime

Speed City Indiana Chapter

of Sisters in Crime

Edited by

MB Dabney and Barbara Swander Miller

DECADES OF DIRT
Murder, Mystery and Mayhem from the Crossroads of Crime

Edited by
MB Dabney and Barbara Swander Miller

Copyright 2015

Published by
Speed City Press

Other Anthologies
Sponsored by Speed City Indiana Sisters in Crime
And Published by Blue River Press
Racing Can Be Murder
Bedlam at the Brickyard
Hoosier Hoops and Hijinks

www.speedcitysistersincrime.org/

ISBN: 978-0-9963092-0-2

DEDICATION

This book is dedicated to the members of the Speed City Indiana Chapter of Sisters in Crime. It is because of your hard work and dedication to the principles of Sisters in Crime that this book is possible.

CONTENTS

ACKNOWLEDGMENTS

We would like to thank all the members of the Speed City Indiana Chapter of Sisters in Crime for your support, help, encouragement and inspiration as we labored to give birth to this anthology. We could not have completed this book without your faith and commitment.

A special thanks goes to Norm Campbell, Diana Catt, Jeanne M. Dams, Elaine Orr and Brenda Stewart for their help and assistance as the manuscript was taking its final shape. In addition, we would particularly like to thank Andrea Smith and Cheryl Shore, the two members whose tenures as chapter president spanned this project. Your steadfast encouragement and support were both essential and greatly appreciated as we worked to give life to *Decades of Dirt*.

Lastly, we want to thank all the authors for their wonderful stories. There's a lot of murder, mystery and just plain mayhem in the coming pages, and it was a pleasure reading it all.

Michael Dabney and Barb Miller.

INTRODUCTION

This collection of short stories, varied in style and content, is unified by the historical source of inspiration for each tale. Most, though not all, are set in Indiana from the nineteenth through the early twenty-first century, but each was triggered by some real incident or situation that fired the imagination, and the passion, of the author. More than one deals with the searing pain of discrimination. The failures and foibles of humanity are explored, sometimes with humor, always with insight. We see a Native American at the settlement the English call Jamestown and an African-American family coping in various ways with bigotry and hatred. We watch nineteenth-century grifters get their comeuppance and a pop idol stage a comeback – perhaps – and an international issue get settled, temporarily.

All the stories deal with crime, but that word has many definitions and the authors play with most of them. And watch out – you may have to change your point of view, the direction you're looking, even your ideas about right and wrong, before a story reaches its surprising conclusion.

I hope you will find in these pages new authors to savor. I know you will learn some things about the country we live in. I know you will find intriguing ideas, fascinating characters, and, in the words of an English friend of mine, some "ripping good yarns!"

Jeanne M. Dams
April 2015
South Bend, Indiana.

Blood of the Hunting Moon
S.M. Harding

Powhatan Confederacy, Pamunkey Village, 1621

The mist crawled along the marshland, slinking along the river with wispy tendrils. Mattachanas shivered, though the late summer morning was warm. *Something bad comes.* She rubbed her upper arms seeking heat that wouldn't rise. She'd felt the anxiety since the Green Corn Moon, building each day until she felt the pressure like the Big Wind storming in from the sea.

The dream had finished last night. Finally. She had debated who to tell. *I need to tell someone with the power to do something about it. My Uncle, our Chief, will act.*

Even later in the day when her Uncle took her out on the bay in clear skies and on calm waters, she felt the dread. It was as if the warmth of the sun was gone.

"The fresh air should make you feel better. What is wrong?" Opechancanough asked. "Is the child you carry trying to be a warrior already?"

"No, Uncle, our child is a girl, my mother assures me." She trailed her hand in the water, but the water felt like ice. "I have been dreaming."

He put the paddle aside, let his gaze skim across the water. "Your mother is a dreamer, and your grandmother."

"I dreamed the Pale Men before they came, but my Mother thought the dream had another meaning. When we first saw their boats, I knew it was the Pale Men. But it was too late."

"Dreamers don't always understand the dream."

"That is why I ask your help, Uncle."

Gaze still on the horizon, he nodded.

"I dream of two Pale Men," she said, closing her eyes. "They are angry, they yell at each other, make fists. One is huge, like a bear, but with an orange beard. His hat is like a mushroom."

Opechancanough sucked in his breath. "The English trader, Ezekiel Stone. And the other one?"

"I cannot see his features clearly, but he has a scar here." She touched her forehead.

"You are sure he is English?"

"Yes. He had hair the color of autumn grasses." She gathered herself. "He strikes the big man with a tomahawk. The Trader stumbles and falls and lies on the ground without movement. The blood from his heart flows like a river, and it floods the land and drowns the People. All of the People but a few who remain on the highest ground. The Old Chief's Advisor is the first to die."

"Nemattanou?" He uttered the name from surprise. "He is my trusted advisor, too. His guidance is from Spirit. In these times, I cannot afford to lose his wisdom."

"He will drown in the blood. You must do something, Uncle."

He looked at her briefly, then shifted his gaze to the water. "The English built their village in a marsh and would have died had it not been for our generosity. Now they demand more and more from us, as if we owed them. But your own husband crossed the sea and saw for himself how these English live. They are more than the leaves in the forests."

"My husband has told me the greed he saw, the stink he smelled and the constant noise the people made. He does not want our land to become another England with King James telling us how to dishonor this land."

Opechancanough nodded. "I will take this information to Council. We can forbid Ezekiel Stone to trade with our people. He cheats the People and what he trades is poorly made. But we must walk carefully." He picked up the paddle and turned to her. "You must pray for clarity. Ask the Spirits to guide you to understanding why my Advisor will be the first to die."

* * *

A light frost caught the sunlight on the corn stalks and rimmed them with a glow. Mattachanas looked around the village with a sense of wonder that the people could go about their morning business so calmly. Around the homes covered with tightly woven mats, children played; men headed down the path to the river weirs; women busied themselves at the cooking fires. She pulled her shawl around her shoulders. They hadn't had a night of horrible dreams.

The same dream, again and again, as if it were a lesson to learn like the winter stories told to the children. To guide action. What action? What, Spirit, must I do? The only answer was the raucous call of a crow.

"The dream came again to you," Tomocomo said, coming up behind her and putting his hands on her shoulder. "You didn't stop muttering and tossing all night."

She leaned against him, rested her head on his hand. "I am afraid, Husband. I want our daughter to grow up in the land of our ancestors, to walk these forests in peace."

He rubbed her shoulders, easing the tension he felt under his hands. "We share that dream for our daughter."

A man trotted into view, saw Tomocomo and ran up to them. "Where is our Chief? There is news."

Tomocomo gave his wife a final rub. "He is praying at our temple." He led the other man to a path into the woods.

Mattachanas rubbed her belly. "It begins, little one. The dream unfolds."

Tomocomo returned for the midday meal. "The Trader Stone was found murdered yesterday."

She nodded. "As I saw?"

"I do not know. He was camped in the Uttamussak woods, not far from the main temple. The English think he was caught looting the temple and killed by one of the People. They send soldiers to look for the killer."

A cold hand squeezed her heart, took her breath away. Tomocomo steadied her, led her to their house and settled her on their bed. "You must take care of yourself so that our daughter will emerge into this earthwalk safe and at peace."

"She will come into a world at war, Husband." She pushed herself onto her elbows. "I want to see the place where the trader left his body."

Tomocomo searched his wife's face. "Tomorrow. Today you rest."

* * *

"This is the place I saw in the dream," Mattachanas said, looking at the clearing in Uttamussak woods.

Rusty blood pooled by the fire ring and a tomahawk, its haft broken, lay close to the rocks. Tomocomo walked over and picked up the pieces. "This is not ours. It is one of the cheap ones the English Trader exchanged for pelts."

"He was killed with his own weapon?"

"The Trader wouldn't have used it, he knew better. But it must have been close at hand."

"So the fact that it is not Powhatan, that it is cheap trade goods, could be dismissed by the English."

He nodded. "Even though no warrior would ever use such a poor weapon."

She closed her eyes, saw again Yellow Hair swinging the tomahawk above his shoulder and bringing it down into the chest of Orange Beard. She opened them. "Husband, Yellow Hair used this hand." She stuck out her left hand. "None of our warriors use this hand in battle – do they?"

He shook his head. "The wound in the body would show that, but the English would never let us examine it." He shivered. "Not that it would be healthy to do so."

"We need an English friend who can do so. And quickly, before they place him in the earth."

"There is one man Opechancanough trusts," he said. "His homestead is not far from here. Go to the main temple, see that the bundles are safe. I will find George Thorpe and ask for his help."

Mattachanas watched Tomocomo trot into the woods. Though her limbs felt detached from her mind, she forced herself to turn and follow a deer trail to the temple.

The longhouse sat in another clearing, new bark covering its barrel roof and sides. Even though it was well tended,

Mattachanas felt a heaviness in the air, a feeling that all was not well. She entered the room and saw the bundles opened on the floor, their sacred contents scattered. She muffled a cry. She fell to her knees and quickly gathered the objects into their proper bundles and wrapped them again. She murmured a quick prayer and hurried from the site.

The trip upriver was silent, Tomocomo bending with the paddle, eyes only on the river ahead. Brooding, Mattachanas thought. He'd heard something he found upsetting. He would tell her when he was ready, when he'd turned the problem over like the ground in spring.

He set the paddle across his knees. "There was a witness, an Englishman. He said the Indian who killed the trader is called Nemattanou."

"No!" She felt as if the earth had tipped and clutched the sides of the dugout. "It is impossible. I saw the murder. There was no one else there but the two English. Nemattanou was not there."

He looked at her. "The English do not believe in dreams or visions. We know they are sent by Spirit, but to the English, we believe in things that cannot be seen and so they do not exist." He picked up the paddle again and headed to their landing.

Even though Mattachanas was weary and her mind filled with racing questions, she immediately took the bundles to the Head Priest to be cleansed. "They were on the floor, open, Grandfather," she said to the old man.

"Open? Did they think we had the yellow metal in them?" His eyes were wide and black with anger. "That is all they think about – the gold so that they may become rich. Pah! What can you buy that the Creator has not given us already?" His scrawny arm swung, encompassing the clearing and the forest beyond. "They are fools and they have committed an offense I will never forgive."

Mattachanas bowed her head. So much sorrow in the People turning to anger. She handed the bundles to the old man, bowed and made her way home. She knew she should fix a meal, but she didn't have the energy. Tomocomo had gone to see Opechancanough and the Council and wouldn't come home until late. She realized tonight was the full moon of the Hunter and promised to be a cold one. She sat on the edge of the bed, knowing how much she desired Tomocomo's strong arms around her. Comfort, safety. She snuggled under the bearskin, imagined Tomocomo next to her and fell into a dreamless sleep.

Tomocomo woke her with a gentle hand cupping her cheek. He sat on the edge of the bed, and she could see a shaft of sunlight. "Your mother is here to take care of you – just for a part of this moon. Your time is drawing near and the Chief wants me to find out as much as I can and sends me with presents to George Thorpe."

"So long?" she asked, sitting up. "The Farmer is not even a day away."

"I am to be the Chief's eyes and ears down river. I can watch Fort James and be ahead of any soldiers they send. He trusts me to give warning if the People are in danger."

"If the Old Chief's Advisor is in danger, then all of us are."

"The Old Chief's Advisor left for the western mountains last night with two warriors. He will be safe there until this is over."

Two warriors and an old man in the mountains in winter. Safe. These men have a strange notion of safe. "Let me fix you food, for now and to take..."

"Your Mother has already taken care of me. More than anything, I want you to take care of yourself and our daughter until she comes to this earthwalk. I want to return to find you both well." He stroked her cheek, nuzzled her hair.

Then he was gone.

Her Mother's presence in her house made her feel like a child again, being fussed over and tended from sunrise to sunset. She decided not to fight but to surrender as gracefully as she could. She knew her daughter's birth would be soon and she wanted to swaddle the baby in peace.

Four sunrises later, Tomocomo returned and met with Opechancanough. Mattachanas waited, feeling impatient but knowing her husband would come when he could.

It was between meals when he appeared at the door. "What a life you are leading – that of a princess!"

She struggled to sit up, but he sat on the bed and gently pushed her back down. "Rest. The soldiers come. Everyone in the village will say they haven't seen the Old Chief's Advisor since the new moon when he left to visit relatives in the south."

"The storm that comes will not simply blow itself out. They will not give up, Husband. What did the Farmer tell you about the witness?"

Tomocomo stared at the wall. "He said: the witness is a storekeeper in Jamestown, but he also trades with the People for corn, squash, beans. He went to the Trader's camp to see if he could buy some provisions for his store. He arrived in a boat and as he was walking to the camp he heard voices quarreling. He approached cautiously, hid himself behind a tree. Then he saw the Indian raise the tomahawk and bring it down on the trader's chest. He hid in the woods until sunrise, then went to get the authorities."

"This happened at night?"

"He said it was late afternoon. That is how he could recognize the Indian."

"It was night." She shook her head. "The Old Chief's Advisor would never have raised his voice in anger. Too, he would have heard a Pale Man approach, not to mention smelled him. The breeze always comes up off the river. It could have been any one of the People, from any nation. Perhaps that was the only name the Storekeeper could remember."

"The English have no reason to doubt him. They will hunt only the Old Chief's Advisor."

"Did the Farmer look at the wound?"

"He did – and barely in time. He said the strike came from the left but that it means little. A backhanded stroke would have looked the same."

"But it gives truth to my dream." Mattachanas closed her eyes, trying to conjure a solution. "Something stinks about this death. The Storekeeper just happens to be present at the time of the killing and just happens to be able to point his finger at the Old Chief's Advisor?" She opened her eyes. "I would like to see him, Husband, this Storekeeper. Have you thought that he could be the killer? How else would he know about the tomahawk which was left behind? How else could he name someone who is innocent? I saw only boot prints at that site."

"The men who took the body away probably trampled any other footprints that might have been there."

"The sacred bundles, Husband. The Trader may have opened

them. He felt no respect for the People. But it gives reason for anger in the People, so the English will say."

"The Farmer said they found one of the carved figures in the Trader's pocket."

"The Trader committed the sacrilege? The carved figure gives proof for our anger toward him. Unless the one who killed him planted the figure like a seed of suspicion." She looked at him. "Do you believe the Old Chief's Advisor killed the Orange Beard?"

"No. He was here in camp. Besides, he had no reason. He would not have found the bundles disturbed and just left them there. His first act would have been to bring them safely to the priests for cleansing. As you did."

"And this Storekeeper?"

"I will see what I can learn."

* * *

The birth was an easy one, or so her Mother assured her. But her reward for pain was the most beautiful little girl Mattachanas had ever seen. She was not sure every woman in the village shared her opinion, but it mattered not a wisp of smoke to her. She yearned to show her husband the wonder, but he was still at Jamestown, being the eyes and ears of the Chief.

Two sunrises later, her husband appeared at the doorway. She smiled at him. "Come see Spirit's gift to us."

He knelt down by the bed, and carefully pulled back the blanket and gazed into his daughter's dark eyes. He looked at his wife. "The Chief sent a messenger and I came as soon as I heard. You are well?"

"How could I not be?"

They began their first day as a family with grandmothers and aunts tending them, and Mattachanas luxuriated in the feeling of safety and well-being. She knew those feelings were fleet-footed. When her husband rose with her each morning for the next three, she began to wonder if he was to return to the English settlement.

As if he had read her mind, he said, "The English get suspicious of my presence. The Chief said I may stay with my new daughter for now."

"That is good. She needs to feel your love to grow strong and brave." She stirred the pot, glad to be outdoors and active. Her Mother was close by but letting Mattachanas tend to her family. "What did you learn down river? What of the Trader? The Storekeeper?"

Tomocomo shifted slightly, stealing a glance at his wife. He sighed. "Our friend the Farmer said that the Trader made many enemies in the time he was in the area." He leaned closer to the fire. "The Farmer saw them two nights before the Trader was killed. The Storekeeper was very angry because he thought the Trader had cheated him. They were both inflamed by drink, the Farmer said, or they wouldn't have been so loud in a public place."

"They were overheard by others?"

He nodded.

"So the Storekeeper had reason to kill the Trader and he admits to being there when the Trader was killed. We know the Old Chief's Advisor was here at that time and had no reason to kill Orange Beard. Does the Storekeeper have a scar on his forehead?"

He nodded again. "Wife, none of the English will listen to us. They will not listen to the Farmer, though he has spoken on our behalf. If Pocahontas hadn't died, they might have listened to her or her English husband. John Rolfe is rich. The Farmer said when they capture the Old Chief's Advisor, they may not even put him on trial."

"Trial? Like the gauntlet?"

"A gauntlet with words only. But it might allow us to present what we have gathered."

"Then if the worst comes to be, that is what we must do. Our Chief must press for this trial of words."

* * *

The moons of Beaver, Long Nights, Wolf and Hunger passed, and Mattachanas watched her daughter grow like the first tender sprouts of spring. Tomocomo had stayed in the village all winter, leaving only for short hunting trips. He returned from one of those trips at the new moon of the Crow. She could read worry on his face, his furrowed forehead, his dark eyes darker. The anxiety she'd kept at bay wrapped its fist around her heart.

Tomocomo saw her and strode to where she sat by the fire. "I must see our Chief." He glanced around, leaned in to her. "We heard that a Tuscarora hunting party found the Old Chief's Advisor, captured him and took him to the English."

"No." The word sounded like a wail to her ears. Her mind was blank – except for the image of the river of blood flowing.

"Quiet, please. Until we know if it is true, we need to appear calm. We cannot act in panic." He touched her shoulder and walked toward Opechancanough's house.

A messenger arrived at dusk and met with the Chief and Council. Mattachanas heard the buzz of worry that circled the village like bees whose hive had been disturbed. She rocked her daughter, singing the song her Mother had sung to her and waited for her husband.

It was almost sunrise when Tomocomo returned. He slumped onto the bed, rubbing his face. "Our Chief is angry and the priests fuel his anger. He counts this as the last in a long list of wrongs to the People that began when the English burned the head village, killed the people and drowned the Old Chief's children."

"The last?"

Tomocomo nodded. "If anything happens to the Old Chief's Advisor, we go to war."

"We must do something, Husband. We must present what we have learned at the word trial. We must find someone who will speak for us."

"There will be no trial. Their new Royal Governor has put words on paper to execute the Old Chief's Advisor. It will happen at full moon."

"But this man must hear what we have learned."

"I will talk to the Farmer tomorrow, but I have little hope that he can gain a fair hearing. John Rolfe has not returned from the islands in the sea where he gathers seeds for tobacco. There is no one."

"Then we must go and speak."

"They will not let us speak to their Governor," he said. "They do not have the openness we have. I will do what I can, but I have little hope. We will start the war and the English will finish it."

At sunrise, they stood in the fog at the landing on the river. It swirled around them, making the familiar alien. Tomocomo finished putting supplies in his dugout and turned to Mattachanas. "I have arranged with clan members far upstream to come for you. They live in a small village far from where the English live and travel. Begin to prepare now. They will take as many as you can convince to go." He pulled her into a fierce embrace. "I will fight. For our Chief, for our people. For our daughter and you."

"I know you will act bravely."

"The first life I will take is the liar, the Storekeeper who began this with his cowardice."

"I will pray for your safety."

"And I for your safety – and our daughter's. That is the important thing. Our people must not disappear from this earth for then no one will take care of our Mother." He tightened his embrace then stepped back.

"May Spirit guide your every footstep, Husband."

"And yours, Wife." He stepped into the dugout and pushed off.

Mattachanas stood and watched her husband until he was swallowed by the fog.

* * *

Mattachanas gathered as many of those who would come, not many for the others did not believe the English would make war upon them again. Her husband's clan members came and transported them far to the west where the river barely existed. Where there was no fog that crept up from the river to cling on hair and skin.

In her dream last night, the mist crawled along the marshland, slinking along the river again. Her husband appeared from the fog, seemed to be one with it, swirling into his physical being. She'd moved to reach his arms, but he shook his head.

"No, Wife. I am passing."

Mattachanas saw then that he was as white as the fog, understood the hole in his chest that did not bleed. She dropped to her knees, the pain to her heart stopping all thought. She looked to his dark eyes. "Husband..."

"I came to tell you that our justice is complete. Before the war began, I killed the Storekeeper with his own weapon. His blood was enough, if only someone would have listened. Our Chief, the English. When the drums of war sound in our ears, everything else is silenced. Teach this to our daughter and to all our children."

Mattachanas heard the drums in her own ears more than the scream from her lips as Tomocomo was swallowed by the fog of the river.

AUTHOR'S NOTE

We often make the assumption that the "New World" was new. North America was new to its European invaders, but not the indigenous peoples already living here. Thus began the continuing genocide of Native Peoples in the Americas. I know, it's something we rather not think about, but it has existed from the first English and Spanish incursions. Jamestown was the first permanent English settlement in North America and very indicative of what would be the fortune of other Native People.

I wanted to tell the story of Jamestown from the eyes of those who faced Eurocentric arrogance and suffered from it. My protagonist and her husband are fictional characters, but the rest of the cast is real, or as real as I could make them. The Pamunkey Reservation, established in 1658 by the Crown, still exists in King William, Virginia. It is almost two square miles and supports around eighty tribal members.

S.M. Harding

The Thorntown Three
C.L. Shore

They say the road to Hell is paved with good intentions. I reckon I got on that road. But I turned off the road, and I did it with style, too. I'm twenty-three years old and my mother says I'm an old maid. For a while it seemed I could be a rich old maid. A kiss changed everything, though, but not like you'd think.

Even though Thorntown is a small town, it buzzed with talk after the Lincoln election, just like the big cities. The rail line kept us connected with the outside. I started helping my family make ends meet by serving beer at the Thorntown Inn when it looked like the crops would not be fetching the money my pa needed to keep things going. Barney was one of the town officials that came in several nights a week for a beer after the working day. Usually, there were three or four of them. They sat at a table, drank, and talked for an hour... or the entire evening.

Barney took a shine to me. "Hey, Red!" He'd called to get my attention. I liked his smile. "Bring me a draught, will you? If you make it quick, there might be a little something extra in it for you." When I brought the beer, he'd pinched my cheek. Usually I hated that kind of thing and would give the guy what-for. I do have the redhead's fiery temper, after all. But Barney's pinch was a little different.

"Name's Lizzie," I said. "But Elizabeth, to you!" I winked at him then, something I'd never done before.

Before long, we were keeping company; very cozy company at that. My ma and pa turned a blind eye, hoping to get me to the altar, I reckon. I still served beer, but on the nights I was off, I went with Barney to the Inn and drank ginger ale at the table with the men. Truth was, I'd rather have beer. But the ale allowed me to listen to the conversation without losing my wits, which the gents at the table did regularly. Most of their conversation centered on politics, and the election particularly.

Some folks felt that having a president from the Midwest would be a wonderful thing, seeing as Indiana is right next door to Illinois. The Indianapolis newspaper said Lincoln was the first Westerner to become president and it would be good to have him in Washington.

Others were not so sure about that. Quite a few, like my man Barney, were downright against Lincoln. As a woman who couldn't even vote, I didn't care all that much at first. But evidently there were people who did, and some of them wanted to change things. One of them offered to pay me money to help change the course of history.

I liked the sound of that.

In December, we heard that South Carolina had left the Union. Beer flowed, and the conversation was loud.

"Lincoln should've said he favored slavery for expansion only. In the new territories," Hiram, Thorntown's mayor, signaled for another beer after finishing the first. "Then we might have avoided this mess."

"You know slavery would not survive with that plan, for long." Barney dismissed Hiram's complaint with a wave of his hand.

"True, but such a stand may have pacified some. Now he's forced the issue. The union is disintegrating. And we'll fight. Many of us here, at this table, will be called to go to the lines."

I have to admit, his statement got to me. I hadn't thought of war. I wondered if Barney would have to go and fight for the Union.

Barney laughed. "You know, many Hoosiers have roots in Kentucky and even farther south. Our state was settled from the south to the north."

"What are you saying?" Hiram thumped on the table top. "Of course, we all know that."

Barney took a swig of beer before answering. "I'm just saying that many of us have roots in the South, and maybe family in the South. I'm just saying that many Hoosiers have sympathies toward slavery."

I reckoned there was some truth to that. My pa's brother, Richard, lived in Tennessee, and he had a few slaves.

As the days grew shorter, the drinking started earlier, and the conversations got even louder. A week before Christmas, a stranger entered the inn and approached our table. His coat was expensive, I could tell. I'd wondered if he hailed from Chicago, or even New York. He said his name was Jeremiah, and he talked in hushed tones with the local men. The usual laughter was gone. After about ten minutes of exchanging whispers with the group, Jeremiah turned to me and asked if I would help.

"Help with what?"

"Lincoln's going to stop here on his way to the White House. We want you to help offer a little hospitality."

"Hospitality? The next president?" His request didn't make sense to me. Surely the president wouldn't be coming to the tavern.

"Yes, you'll be part of a welcoming committee. Board the train, bring in refreshments, tidy up a little, that sort of thing. And we'll want you to keep an eye out for anything that looks official and important. If you see something – we want you to pick it up."

"How will I know if it is important?"

"Well, you won't know, for sure. But take anything you think might be important."

"What if I get caught?"

"You won't. You'll be doing this while Lincoln's addressing the crowd. If anyone says anything, just say you thought the item was trash."

"So... that's it? Just go on board, bring some food, tidy up a bit?"

"That's it. We'll have another woman with you – but she won't be in on the plan."

"I'll think about it," I said. I felt excited, but also a little uneasy inside. Excited because I'd be close to the man who's going to be president. Uneasy, because I'd be stealing. I looked over at Barney. He gave me a serious nod of the head.

"There'd be a little something in it for you," Jeremiah offered. He quoted me an amount that would keep my family fed all winter. My jaw must've dropped. As if to prove his ability to pay, he handed me a ten-dollar gold piece. "Down payment," he said, meeting my eyes. I fought the urge to stare at the coin.

"You have yourself a deal," I said, choking out the words.

"Excellent." Jeremiah tapped the table, but not too loud. The men raised their beer glasses.

I didn't tell my pa anything, but put the coin in a drawer with my stockings. Oh, Pa would get the ten dollars, but I wanted the deed done and all money collected first. As the days wore on, I heard more and more conversation. Mention of cities like Buffalo and Baltimore. I caught the word "assassination" once.

When Barney gave me a ride home in his buggy, I asked him about that word. "Is someone going to kill Lincoln?" I watched his face carefully in the moonlight, but couldn't see much expression. I did see him shrug.

"Maybe. But not here in Thorntown." He patted my knee. "We're just going to collect information. That's what you're getting paid to do." He gave me a lopsided smile. "Don't worry. What you're going to do is pretty tame. You and me and Hiram, Jeremiah calls us the Thorntown Three."

After the New Year was rung in, I met with the dressmaker in town. A young married woman, Annabelle, was going to be doing the honors with me. We were fitted with black dresses featuring fashionable bustles and lace collars. Only thing different between them was the extra pocket built into the side of my skirt, especially made for hiding things. Jeremiah had explained this to the dressmaker, and I guess she didn't think a thing about it. She was making good money. I guess that is all she cared about. The dress fit me perfectly and I took it home the last Friday in January.

February first dawned bright, but cold. Only a few more days until the President arrived. Lincoln would appear in Thorntown as one of the first stops on his whistle stop tour chugging toward Washington and the White House. His first stop of the day would be Lafayette; Thorntown would be second and Lebanon would follow. According to the telegraph received by the welcoming committee, we were to expect Lincoln's train about noon.

In spite of the frigid weather, Thorntown's small station was filled with people in heavy overcoats. The tracks were lined by people on horseback, in buggies and farm wagons, and on foot. I felt sorry for those standing. The icy ground surely numbed their feet. Barney and Hiram hustled Annabelle and me into the station, which was a good thing. We were not allowed to wear coats or shawls, Jeremiah's rule. He felt Lincoln's guards would let us board the train more quickly if we weren't wearing bulky clothing over our black dresses.

Noon came and went, and there was no sign of Lincoln's train. The horses' breath formed a low-lying cloud near the tracks. Those people standing shifted back and forth on their feet. Between my corset and my nerves, I felt a little light-headed. At a quarter till one, we heard a faint whistle. When I heard that high-pitched sound, it was all I could do to keep from screaming. Soon after the whistle's blast, we could hear the steady chug-chug-chug of the train coming down the tracks. The engine came into view, sporting red, white, and blue bunting. Only three cars followed it.

Annabelle was standing next to me. I'm not bragging or anything, but she was a very plain woman. I'd heard she was very active in the local church Ladies' Aid Society. She was very kind to me, not hoity-toity or anything like it. We'd practiced our curtsies at least a dozen times that morning. She caught my eye. "I can't believe it. We're meeting the new president." Suddenly, Hiram ushered us to the platform, where the local baker provided Annabelle with a tray of baked goods. I carried a hammered tin pitcher of water and three silver cups on a tray. I could easily set it down to pick up something of interest, as long as there was a small, flat surface.

The crowd was moving toward the rear of the train, since that's where Lincoln would address them. Hiram, the mayor, boarded with Annabelle and me in tow.

It was dim inside the car, compared with the bright sunshine reflecting off the snow. My eyes adjusted and there he stood: Lincoln. Tall, and downright skinny, dressed all in black, he looked like his pictures. I thought he appeared very tired, with dark circles under his eyes. Annabelle and I performed our curtsies. He smiled a little at that, and I thought his expression was a kind one. Was he really this evil person that Barney and the others thought he was? He seemed so normal. I felt some pity for him; he was walking into the White House at such a terrible time, with the country torn apart. I thought I'd turn and run, if I were him.

He shook hands with Hiram who welcomed him, then said, "These ladies will help you tidy up and leave a little refreshment for you."

Lincoln nodded, and the two of them walked toward the rear of the train. There were three other men in the car; two of them followed Hiram and Lincoln. One seemed very interested in the cakes that Annabelle carried on her tray. When she set it down, he had already made his selection, popping it into his mouth in no time.

Lincoln must've been visible to the crowd, because a cheer went up. I took a few steps toward the rear of the train. Hiram had stepped down from the transom. I could see him in the front row of the crowd. Just behind him, I saw Barney. He was wearing the bright yellow scarf we'd decided on so I could pick him out in the crowd. The cheering went on for a while before settling down. Lincoln started to address the crowd. I wasn't paying too much attention, but I did hear him say something about "our nation." I busied myself looking for anything that Jeremiah might be interested in. I looked around for the pastry-eater. He had wandered toward the transom, too, hanging in the background while finishing the sweet. Annabelle was busying herself tidying up in the car right behind the engine.

I returned to the middle carriage, which looked a lot like a parlor on wheels. A tiny desk sat against the wall on its east side. I saw a newspaper there, and a pair of spectacles that had been set aside. I left it for the moment. There was also a ledger. After glancing at it, I decided it was too big to stick in my hidden pocket. Besides, after a quick glance, it appeared to be a diary of the trip itself. The last written line referred to Lafayette.

I walked in the direction of the rear of the train, but stayed within the middle car. Nothing of interest seemed to be visible, so I set down the tray and crossed into the last carriage. The men accompanying Lincoln kept their eyes on the crowd; they paid me no attention. Near the rear of the car, I saw a sheaf of papers on a small table, just inside the door to the transom where Lincoln was addressing the crowd. A pen, ink pot, and a pair of spectacles were there, too. Looked to me like Lincoln might have been writing something just before he arrived at Thorntown.

My heart beat at a hundred times a minute, at least. I'm glad my corset was not pulled any tighter, because I'm sure I would have fainted.

I stood in the door of the transom with Lincoln's back directly in front of me. He said something about a man and his mule, and I heard the crowd laugh. Lincoln must've been telling a joke. I could see Barney's yellow scarf, and if I tilted my head, I could see his ruddy cheeks. I took a step backward. No one, not even Annabelle, was watching me. I held the papers high before tucking them into my bosom, high enough that Barney should've been able to see them. Nerves took away my memory about the hidden pocket in my dress. I'd hoped to see a congratulatory gesture from Barney – but he wasn't watching me. Instead, he was kissing a woman with dark brown hair.

For the second time that day, I felt like screaming. But I did not give in to my urge. Instead, I aimed a most unladylike gesture in Barney's direction. His eyes met mine, but his lips were still locked with those of the brown-haired hussy. I saw his eyes widen.

Just at that moment, the train lurched underneath my feet. I fell on my behind with my petticoats flying toward the ceiling. My first thought was that I was being punished for my loss of control. But then I realized that the men in front of me were struggling to keep their balance; they weren't paying me no mind. The train was moving!

I scrambled to my feet, and glanced toward my bodice to assure myself that the papers were securely hidden. I could see Hiram's mouth form an O of surprise as the train pulled away from him and the rest of the crowd. I ran to the middle car and picked up the water pitcher, saving a spill of icy water.

The train picked up speed. Lincoln came back into the middle car, shaking his head. "I guess the engineer has his own timetable. And I was just getting started with my story." He laughed and his male companions laughed with him.

Lincoln glanced in my direction, then turned toward

Annabelle. "Well, ladies, have a seat." He gestured toward a small settee across the car. "Looks like you're headed to Lebanon."

I tried to smile at Annabelle, but felt shaky. "Don't worry," she said. "I'm sure we'll get home before too long. If my husband doesn't come to fetch us, I'll find the Lebanon pastor. He'll help, I'm sure."

I tried to look like I felt reassured. Truth was, getting back to Thorntown did not worry me at that moment.

"Lookee there!" One of Lincoln's companions gestured toward the rear of the train. "Your joke must've been a good one!"

I leaned forward from my seat on the settee. People on horseback were galloping behind us, following the train.

"I guess they want to hear the end of the story. They're following us to Lebanon!" One of Lincoln's companions announced.

"The story really wasn't that good." Lincoln chuckled.

Sweat broke out under my arms. Although Barney had been seated in his buggy with horses that weren't too speedy, I knew he'd be on his way. He would manage to borrow a horse, maybe Hiram's. He'd want to find out what I was up to, especially since I saw him kiss that hussy.

I took a deep breath and approached the man who looked the most official.

"Excuse me, sir. Are you a guard? Are you guarding the President?"

His laughing expression changed to serious just that quick. "Yes, Ma'am, I guess I'd say that was true."

I tried to swallow, but my mouth was too dry. "I reckon I've got some things to tell you."

He held my gaze. "Let's move forward." He tilted his head toward the car just behind the engine. He gestured to one of the other men to accompany him. The pastry-eater was left behind with the future president and Annabelle.

I felt Annabelle's eyes on me as I moved toward the other car. The man gestured for me to sit on one of the plain wooden benches. "Now young lady, you say you have something to tell me?" He leaned forward, his forehead only a foot away from mine.

In the few seconds it took me to move forward in the train, I'd decided to tell him all I knew; even the mention of the word "assassination." I figured my impression of Lincoln was right; he was an honest, and a very tired man. Barney was a scoundrel; he'd revealed his true self right in front of me. So I told my story. The guard listened without blinking.

When I'd finished, he sat back and kind of pursed his lips. "Well, I thank you. We'll take your information under serious consideration. Is there anything else you'd like to tell us?"

"Yessir." I took a deep breath. "I need to ask you to protect me. My gentleman friend will be following this train, although it may take him a little longer than some to arrive. But he'll be here, looking for me, and I want you to tell him that I'm not here."

"So, you'll get off in Lebanon?" He'd raised an eyebrow at me.

"No. I'd rather stay on the train for a while, if I you'll let me. But I want you to tell anyone in Lebanon who asks that you sent me off the train. Say I got hurt when the train lurched, and you sent me with someone to find a doctor." I know I was being very bold, but I was scared. I wasn't sure how Barney, Hiram, and Jeremiah would deal with me. Of course, I could pretend to continue in the scheme if I went back to Thorntown, but that would only last so long.

The man nodded. "Sounds reasonable. Why don't you go sit with your friend?"

I nodded back at him and went to sit next to Annabelle. The man called for Lincoln and the pastry eater to join him. Annabelle had the most solemn expression as I sat near her. "Are you all right?" she wanted to know.

"I am. But I need to stay on the train at Lebanon and beyond. And no one is to know." I turned to face her. "Understand? This is one time when you have to lie." She had me a little worried, being a church lady and all.

She nodded with a solemn expression. "I understand."

I stood to look at the back of the train. The number of men on horseback was growing, some were much closer to the train than others. I thought I could see a yellow scarf flying in the breeze on the rider of a horse toward the back of the pack. I started to shiver.

The trip to Lebanon seemed to be a short one. The horseback riders began to close the gap as the train slowed, preparing to stop at the station. I definitely saw a yellow scarf in the middle of the pack. I wondered if Barney had borrowed Hiram's horse.

The crowd at Lebanon appeared to be a little larger than the one at Thorntown. Buggies lined the area near the station. When the train crawled to a complete stop, a couple of women entered the train, accompanied by Lebanon's mayor. I went to the front car and hid behind the coal scuttle. I saw the taller of the two ladies present Lincoln with a picnic basket. They both curtsied. If I hadn't been so scared, I would've laughed.

One of the guards took the basket – I'm sure he would go through everything in it. Then he turned to the Lebanon mayor. "This young lady," he pointed at Annabelle, "was stranded on the train when the engineer started us early at Thorntown. We'd like to entrust her to you, make sure she gets home."

The mayor bowed his head ever so slightly. "Of course." He took Annabelle's elbow. "Come with me, young lady. After the presidential train leaves, we'll see that you get home." I could see Annabelle throw a sorrowful look in my general direction.

After Annabelle stood on the platform, the mayor led Lincoln to the rear of the train, just as Hiram had back in Thorntown. Once again, a cheer went up. Lincoln said a few things about the country, but then he finished his joke – after beginning it again for those who hadn't heard the first part. I stood up, but remained in the front of the train. Suddenly, I caught a glimpse of yellow at the window of the middle car. I ducked down again. I could hear Barney's muted voice, and then the voice of the superior guard who'd heard me out.

"She was injured," I heard him say. "As soon as we arrived at this station, we found someone to get her to a doctor."

"Which doctor?" Barney wanted to know.

"I'm sure I don't know." The guard was as cool as a cucumber. "But I'm sure the locals will get her to capable hands." I heard footsteps then, and I thought Barney must've got off the train. But I stayed in my place until Lincoln ended his speech and the train started to move again. Lincoln waved from the transom, but the train was pulling away from the station. My back, knees and shoulders were stiff. I stood and stretched and raised my hands overhead, looking past Lincoln at the crowd. I saw a flash of yellow at the edge of the platform. It was Barney's scarf, but his eyes were scanning the crowd, thank the Lord. I froze as I saw him try to pick his way through the crowd toward the rear of the train. Lucky for me, the crowd was thick and the train picked up speed quickly.

The guard I'd spoken with followed my gaze. "Mrs. Lincoln will join the train at Indianapolis," he said gently. "She'll need help with the Lincoln boys. They're an active pair!"

I sighed with relief. "I'm the oldest of seven, with four younger brothers, well experienced with active boys."

The guard shook his head. "Well, that's a load off my mind. I was wondering how we'd fair with those young ones on board." Then he explained how the train would pick up additional cars in Indianapolis.

So, here I am sitting on the same train as the future president, heading into Indianapolis. Looks like I can head all the way to Washington, if I want. Sometime soon, I'll get word back to Pa, and tell him about the ten dollar gold piece. I'll send him more money when I can.

I feel the papers rustling in my bosom. I'll get them back to Lincoln sometime soon.

He does seem to be a kind man.

AUTHOR'S NOTE

Like many moviegoers, I became interested in Abraham Lincoln after experiencing Stephen Spielberg's 2012 film. The complexity of Lincoln as a man and the times in which he lived intrigued me. As a direct result of seeing the movie, I made a trip to the Springfield Lincoln Museum and read multiple books on the 16th president, including *The Lincolns: Portrait of a Marriage* by Daniel Mark Epstein, and Daniel Stashower's *The Hour of Peril*. The accounts of Lincoln's 1861 whistlestop trip to the White House captured my interest. The journey must have been grueling, particularly in the winter months. I was further intrigued to note that Thorntown, Indiana, was one of the earlier stops on the route. I settled on Thorntown as the site of my story.

I began research into the actual historic event of the presidential train's arrival in Thorntown. The sudden, unexpected departure of the Lincoln train from the Thorntown station (and the interruption of Lincoln's joke as a result) is described in several accounts and fit well with my developing tale.

The Thorntown Three captures some of the early intrigue prior to Lincoln's first inauguration. The President-elect knew he faced the possibility of assassination and publicly addressed this threat before leaving Springfield on his journey by rail to the White House. Fortunately, he survived to take the oath of office (twice) and guide the nation toward restoration of the Union.

C. L. Shore

Only a Grain of Truth
Elaine L. Orr

The silence woke her. Betsy Cochran turned underneath the warm quilt and looked toward the cabin wall. On the other side of it was the small grist mill her family operated. The mill wheel didn't turn at night, but nothing had ever stopped the fast-running creek. Until now.

She looked toward her husband, sleeping soundly beside her. Since John was back from the war, he was hard of hearing. Was that in 1813? They didn't marry until 1819, but their families farmed near each other before that. Betsy was so tired that she couldn't really mark time the way she used to. She marked it by the seasons, and the mill wheel on Doan's Creek needed to turn a lot in July.

Careful not to wake her exhausted husband, Betsy moved across the feather mattress and eased out of the bed. She shivered. The wooden floor was as cold as a stone sitting on the bottom of the creek.

The cabin had no windows, but there was a large space between two of the logs that let her look toward the mill and creek. Quietly she pulled out the dried mud and twigs that kept the space invisible to anyone outside. And kept it warmer inside.

Betsy looked through the small opening and gasped. Instead of the mill sitting across the creek with running water between the cabin and the mill, there was a muddy creek bed with large puddles in places where the water had been deeper. She straightened and automatically reached for the mud she had removed from the wall. It crumbled in her hand. She would have to ask one of the younger children to bring in fresh mud. *Before that dries up.*

"Ma? What wakened you?"

She turned to look up at her oldest son, who peered down from the children's sleeping loft. Howsan usually looked older than his twelve years. Now, with his hair uncombed and drowsy expression, he looked more like his nine-year old brother Sidney.

Betsy whispered. "The water stopped."

Howsan cocked his head as if listening, and a look of panic crossed his face. "That cannot be." He crawled to the ladder and swung first one leg, then the other onto its rungs and was quickly beside her.

Betsy hadn't realized that her hand was on her stomach, or the next Cochran baby, who was due by mid-summer. The baby's rapid movement matched her nervous heartbeat. *Lord if thou art merciful, let this child be born in your good graces, but not until we find the water.*

Howsan guided Betsy to the rocking chair beside the now-cold fire. She hoped some of the embers buried in the metal pot at the back of the fireplace would be enough to start the fire for morning. Then her mind jerked back to her son and the creek.

"What would make it stop?" she whispered.

Howsan glanced toward the curtain that surrounded his parents' bed in the corner of the room. "Elsey heard talk. I didn't believe him." He stooped so that he faced his Mother. "Some of the men in the township think Pa raised the milling price too high. They don't understand the law sets it."

Betsy stared at him in confusion. She had heard the whispered complaints when she carried cold biscuits to a family camped on the creek bank while they waited for the grist mill to turn their corn into meal. "But only God could stop the water."

Howsan's expression was grim. "And beavers. And anyone else who would build a dam further up the crick."

She gripped the edge of the rocking chair and tried not to show her fear. "Dams can be torn down."

"If they are on your land." Howsan stood. "It is almost the dawn. I'll wake Elsey and we'll steal a look up yonder."

Betsy sat as if nailed to her rocker. There was no point in disturbing her sleeping husband. One of the paddles on the large wheel had cracked two days ago, and he and Howsan and John's brother James had made a replacement. That meant they were behind in milling, and families that had planned to camp for one day while they waited for their bushels of grain would be there for two or three days. As was his custom, if there was a delay John would generally take less payment than his one-eighth share of the ground meal. That usually made people forget the extra day or two of sleeping on the ground.

But if someone had dammed the creek upstream, someone was angry about more than delayed milling.

Howsan and a sleepy but excited Elsey were tying their worn shoes. She took two boiled eggs from a bowl on the table near the fireplace and handed one to each. "God be with you."

The two boys mumbled the same to her, and Howsan put his hand on her shoulder for a moment as they walked through the door. "Be at ease, Mother. We will take down any dam."

After more minutes of staring into the cold hearth, Betsy stood and then stooped in front of it. Warmth near the back of the hearth told her that enough embers had survived the night for her to start the day's fire.

She glanced behind her. Starting the fire was a job for her sons, and John would be irritated if he saw her. She would explain where the two oldest boys were, but seeing his pregnant wife building a fire would only increase her husband's frustration. That and the fact that the boys might not be back by the time John wanted to begin work. It was another few minutes before Betsy remembered there could be no work until the creek ran again.

* * *

Betsy stood in front of the cabin and watched John reassuring farmers that the mill would soon be operating. People who had already waited an extra day were especially unhappy.

A guttural peep near her foot made her look down. She smiled at the large hen, the best of their laying brood. "You have grain," Betsy said, softly. Two more hens were making their way from their perches in a lean-to next to the cabin. "Shoo." They squawked and moved away, pecking the ground in fast cadence.

At the sound of an approaching horse she turned, and again smiled. Her brother, John Francis Seaton, took in the silent mill across the creek and John Cochran standing just outside it. He moved the reins a bit to guide his horse toward Betsy.

He frowned as he dismounted. "A new dam up stream?"

Betsy nodded. "Howsan and Elsey have gone to find it. They left before first li..."

"They should have come to me!" Seeing Betsy's alarm, he adopted a calmer tone. "They are strong boys, but it may be a man's work."

That's not what concerns him, I can tell.

Betsy nodded and her brother smiled. "Do not think of it. I'll help your good husband calm the others."

She glanced at the fire where a kettle of corn meal mush bubbled. She would take a large bowl of it and a ladle to the several families and offer them some. How often she had heard her Mother, Rebecca, say that no woman in the more genteel Virginia countryside would greet others so readily when she was with child. Things were very different in Greene County, Indiana, and Betsy would not have it any other way.

Betsy had just returned to the cabin to get more of the warm corn meal mush when a new sound added to the songs of birds and chatter of several nearby children. Water!

A cheer rose from the twenty or so campers and Betsy saw her brother clap her husband on the shoulder. When the boys returned, life could resume its normal pace.

* * *

But that was not to be. By early afternoon, a weary Howsan and Elsey walked down the road that wagons traveled to get to the mill. Betsy had expected to see them walking on the narrow path along the creek bank. It took her a few seconds to understand that the brothers were not simply walking arm in arm. Howsan supported Elsey. The ten-year-old had dried blood on his forehead and seemed to be limping.

At her cry, John Francis turned and ran toward his nephews. Betsy knew she could not run, knew that the best thing for her to do was to wet a cloth in the hot water that simmered on the hearth and prepare to clean her son's wound.

John Francis followed her into the cabin, carrying Elsey. "Be not alarmed. He is tired. Your boys have done men's work today." He set Elsey in Betsy's rocker, and she stooped in front of her boy.

"I'm fine, Ma. I fell on the creek bank and hit a stone." He leaned back to rest his head as she dabbed at his cut.

"Do you think your Mother is simple?" she asked.

Howsan looked at her and gave a brief smile. "He just needs some of your good mush, Mother." He walked to the hearth and took a bowl from the shelf above it.

"Where was the water dammed?" It had taken John Cochran a minute to get from the mill, across the logs that were his bridge across the creek, and through the congratulating crowd to the cabin.

Howsan looked at his Father. "Almost a mile to the north. Not near a cabin, or even a plowed field."

"They tried to put it far from a cabin or lean to. That way no one will have to say they placed it on their land." John Cochran's voice was bitter.

"It was making a right nice pond," Elsey said.

"It was not a strong dam. The water would have soon broken through," Howsan said. "It was supposed to frighten us, I think, not dam the creek for a long time."

As she cleaned her son's face, Betsy was frightened. People in Taylor Township and nearby were usually helpful, even friendly. But some were angry when the Cochran family bought the old mill. John and his brothers had worked hard to save the money and make repairs to the large mill wheel. They had every right to buy it.

But the Cochrans had come to Greene County from Ohio only a few years ago. There were those who thought someone who had been in Greene County longer should have bought the mill. The two people who spoke of this most often were Thomas and Andrew Darrow. They had a chance to buy it, Betsy reasoned. If they spent more time in their fields or hunting and less time drinking spirits, perhaps they could have bought it.

Replenished by bread and corn meal mush, the two brothers crossed the short distance to the mill with their father and uncle.

Betsy had wanted Elsey to sit for a longer spell, but she knew they wanted her to think all was as usual. If she hadn't spent years with the harsh winters and dry summers, it might be easier to fool Betsy Cochran, daughter of Francis and Rebecca Seaton. But she had been through those times, and she was no fool.

* * *

The summer of 1833 was hotter than the last two years, but there was ample rain. This boded well for crops and that was good for the mill. Betsy Cochran was pleased about that, but still found the heat made it hard to care for her family. It only made her more tired, and she felt older than her forty-six years.

The sound of someone near the cabin caused Betsy to turn. A thin-faced young man stood there, looking toward the mill. He was taller than her husband or Howsan, but she thought him no more than eighteen.

"My husband is at the mill, if you are looking for him."

Though he had seen Betsy, he still seemed startled. Black eyes held her gaze and then looked away. "No, I have no grain today."

Although she was alone with a man she did not know, Betsy felt no discomfort. "What brings you?"

"I thought I would speak to your sons."

This amused Betsy. People did not come calling to find Howsan or Elsey, certainly not the younger boys. "You are welcome to cross the creek to the mill."

"Perhaps another day." He left, saying nothing else. Betsy stared after him for a moment and then walked back into the cabin. She had many things to occupy her thoughts. This man-boy was not her concern.

She had not been able to carry water from the creek since early July. Betsy could cook, but the baby she was carrying was not sitting well. By late afternoon, drawing a deep breath was a harsh chore. And she was really too far along with child to be outside much of the day. If families were camping by the bank, men looked at their wives or the ground when she walked near them.

She leaned back in her rocker. If this child did not come soon the caned seat would give way, and it would be hard to repair. The sound of the creek gave her peace, but the constant grinding of the large mill stones was wearing on her.

Not that she could tell this to anyone. Her parents' graves were in nearby Knox County. Her younger sister Rebecca and her family had stayed in Knox County when Betsy and John moved to Greene. Betsy smiled, eyes closed. Her father had wanted a daughter named after his wife, but Rebecca Gregg Seaton had thought it would be prideful. Twelve years after Betsy was born her Father had his way, and the second Rebecca, as Betsy thought of her, was born in 1799. Betsy had written to her about ten days ago, but it was likely too soon to expect good cheer from her sister.

She must have slept for a bit, because shadows in front of the cabin spoke of late afternoon when Betsy next opened her eyes. She should have the fish her brother brought that morning on the fire by now. She stood, but the pain from her abdomen forced her to sit.

Finally. This baby will come. If only it could be a girl. Betsy had prayed daily for a daughter. She loved her husband and sons, but she wanted a little girl to rock and to make pretty clothes for. She tried again to rise, and sat down heavily. The boys could cook the fish.

She called out. "Sidney!" The eight year old had been just outside the cabin door awhile ago. His job was to sweep the mill floor several times a day. Betsy thought he must have gone back to the mill, but then he called from the doorway.

"Ma?" When Betsy did not stand, he walked to her. "Should I get Pa?"

Betsy could hear the worry in his tone. "No, son. But you can put the fish in the frying pan, on the embers."

He hesitated. Usually he did her bidding right away. John must have told his sons to come to the mill for him at the first sign of a new baby. Not that Sidney probably knew the signs, but he knew something was different.

"I'm fine. I think you may have a new brother or sister by morn."

His smile was almost radiant. "Can we have a sister?"

Betsy laughed, and then tried to hide a grimace. "We pray for a healthy child."

* * *

"You should sleep," Betsy told her husband. "We've done this. It's always the same with our children. They seem to take a nap midway through birthing." For the past several hours Betsy would lie down, and then she would stand. Now they were sitting on the edge of their bed.

"You need to walk, I know. You will call me when you need anything." He stressed the last word.

"Yes. It's…easier to be alone for awhile."

John kissed his wife's forehead. "My brave beauty." He always used a low tone for endearment.

Betsy wished he would let the boys hear him speak to her so. Not always, but sometimes. How were they to learn what to say to their wives?

"John."

He faced her as he stood in front of Betsy so she could lean on him to get up from the bed. "Did Elsey really get that cut on a rock? The day the creek was dammed?"

"Why do you think on that now?" He was half puzzled, half amused.

"No one harms our boys."

He nodded. "I think the anger has burned itself out. We weigh the grain fairly."

Betsy nodded. "I may walk outside a bit. No one is camping tonight."

She stood in the night air just outside the cabin door. Finally, a chance to breathe cooler air. Her eyes traveled to the very small apple tree that was directly in front of the cabin. Her sister had made a cutting from one of her trees and insisted on planting it herself, with the help of Howsan and Elsey. By the time this new child could chew, there could be apples on that tree.

By tomorrow the heavy child beneath her heart would be in the world. *God willing.* And she could breathe easily all the day.

Betsy wandered to the edge of the creek. She had hoped for the company of another woman when she gave birth, but the absence of campers meant she did not get that wish. She could ask Elizabeth Overman or one of the other young women on nearby farms. But they had so many chores this time of year. And Betsy had done this before.

A crackling sound drew Betsy's attention to the barn-like mill building. *What is that light?* She moved a few feet closer to the edge of the creek and peered at the mill more closely.

"Fire! Buckets! Fire!" She hadn't thought. Instinct drove the words, and she heard the pounding of feet behind her. "The mill!"

But she needn't have told John, Howsan, Elsey and Sidney. They ran past her, Howsan carrying the two buckets the family used for its water. Buckets to fight fires were outside the mill, in several places.

"Ma?" At her skirt was her baby, her boy about to become a big brother. Three-year old John Alexander Cochran, named after his Father, looked at her intently.

"It will be all right. Father and the boys will make it all right." That was not how she felt, but it was comforting to have someone to reassure.

The smell of burning wood traveled to her and she watched her husband and sons as they formed a bucket brigade and began dousing the fire. Sound carried far at night, and her brother and one of the Overman men were there within minutes. Even John's brother James, farming more than a mile away, arrived in time to help.

"Faster!" Betsy was sure that was her husband's voice. The fire had not reached the top of the tall, steep roof. *Please God, let it not spread.*

There was a tug on her shirt and she looked at her small son. "Fire," he said. He tugged again, and Betsy he knew he wanted her to pick him up. Tears stung her eyes. She could not even stoop to comfort him.

"Mama can't raise you now. You can climb on my lap when I next sit in the rocker." *Why did I say that? I have no lap now.* Her youngest, for now, gave her a solemn look and then turned his gaze to the men at the mill.

Betsy realized that she no longer heard the crackle of burning wood. There was only smoke, and the men were not drawing water from the creek as fast as they had been. She closed her eyes in a prayer of thanks.

"I should be at the hearth," she said. As she turned to walk into the cabin to heat mush for the men, she saw the thin young man standing back from the creek. Betsy assumed he had arrived because of the fire. "They will likely need more help."

He seemed surprised to see her. "I will tend to my horse and return."

Horse? She had not heard one arrive for several minutes. Betsy turned to see where he had stowed his horse, but he must have walked along a line of trees, because she could not make him out.

She would have to ask John or Howsan who the young man could be. She turned to walk the few steps into the cabin, and then the pain came in a great rush.

* * *

An hour later, Betsy was lying on the bed, her breathing shallow. She had barely made it there before her legs gave way. When John, face blackened with soot, had come to see that she was all right, she had waved him away. "You need to be outside."

Voices, some angry, talked outside the cabin door. Words like *deliberate* and *who would do this?* came through to her. Every now and then she heard her husband's soothing tone.

Howsan's voice held rancor. "It was the Darrow brothers. You know it, Father."

It sounded like James Cochran spoke next. "I've talked to them. Their anger is spent."

The voices of the men became a buzz in her head. She needed to tell them about the thin young man. But that would have to wait. Betsy closed her eyes and clinched her jaw as pain swam through her. *This baby needs to hurry.*

She became aware of someone beside her and opened her eyes. Howsan looked frightened. "Ma? Shall I get Father?"

"No. He needs to check the mill and talk to the other farmers." She closed her eyes again. "Is Elizabeth Overman out there?" Elizabeth was twelve years younger than Betsy and had never married. Even though she had never given birth, she would know what to do. Every Mother on the frontier taught her daughters how to deliver a baby.

Betsy didn't hear Howsan leave, but she heard the rustle of a skirt as Elizabeth came into the cabin. She looked at Betsy and turned to shut the door. "Is it almost time?"

"Yes. The water is on the fire."

"And I see the ladle and cloth," Elizabeth said.

Betsy was aware only of the pain for almost a minute. When she opened her eyes, she saw that Elizabeth had pulled a stool that usually sat by the hearth to a place near the bed.

"Hold my hand, please," Betsy said. She smiled at Elizabeth. "I will take care when I squeeze."

Softly Elizabeth began to say the Lord's prayer. "Our Father, who art in heaven..." When she finished, she asked, "Where is your Bible?"

"In the small chest, near the hooks with our clothes."

If Elizabeth thought it an odd place to keep a Bible, she did not say so. Instead, she let go of Betsy's hand and stood to retrieve the scripture, talking as she went to get it. "We will want to note when your baby arrives. Have you thought of a name?"

Betsy was suddenly engulfed in more pain than she remembered having with any birth. *Something is very wrong.*

"Betsy?" Elizabeth's voice sounded far away. Then Betsy became aware of a cool cloth that was on her forehead, and it was her husband's voice she heard.

"My brave beauty," he said.

Betsy heard fear in his voice. She knew he wanted to comfort her, but his fear became hers. She wanted to distract herself from the pain. "Was there much damage?"

"The fire was at the back side of the mill. If it had started near the mill wheel the damage might have stopped the milling for a week or more. And that only if the rest of the structure remained." He smiled at her as he turned the cloth so it was again cool on her forehead. "If you had not been outside we might have lost the mill. Instead, only one corner was badly damaged. The stones can still grind."

"Pray with me," Betsy said.

* * *

His mother was well-liked, so many close neighbors stood near the hole in the ground that was to be her final resting place. He could not bear to look at the small box that now contained her. Howsan held his newborn brother. He wanted to throw baby William into the grave. Their Mother would be alive if not for this child!

Howsan felt a hand on his arm and looked into the face of

Elizabeth Overman. It was she who had told him and his brothers that their Mother had died. Their Father had sat by his wife's side, still holding her hand, for a long time.

"Let me hold him. Your arms must be tired." Elizabeth's expression was kindly.

Howsan wanted to vent his gall at Elizabeth Overman. She lived. His Mother did not. But he said nothing and tried to appear pleasant as he passed baby William to her.

An arriving wagon drew Howsan's attention, and he went to help the owner lash its horses to a post that was used to tie wagons bringing grain. Then Howsan's eyes traveled to the small group of trees on the edge of the clearing. Two men were arguing with someone not much older than Howsan.

The older men were dressed more shabbily than others who had come to honor Betsy Cochran. Not that anyone had the kind of clothes his Mother had told him people wore back East. But these men had the stain of the drink on their shirts and their hair was overly long. Howsan could not remember why he knew them. The younger man had a thin, harsh face, and Howsan did not recognize him.

The voice of his Mother's brother reached him, calling mourners to prayer for Betsy Cochran. Howsan barely heard the Bible verse that his uncle read. There would be no preacher this way for probably weeks. When the man next came they would pray again.

John Francis Seaton's voice was hoarse as he closed the Bible and recited the last verse from memory. "The Lord himself goes before you and will be with you; he will never leave you nor forsake you. Do not be afraid; do not be discouraged."

We are forsaken, Howsan thought.

Elsey sobbed and their Father knelt in front of him. Howsan could not hear the words his Father offered. Instead he looked at his uncle, who was now holding his three-year old brother. Young John Alexander was not sure what was happening, but he sensed it was not good and placed his head on his uncle's shoulder.

Neighbor women had brought food and they spread it on a blanket near the creek. Elizabeth Overman had told him she would teach him how to cook corn meal so it did not burn.

Howsan looked across the creek to the mill. If there had been no fire, his Mother would not have been so distressed. She would not have died. He was certain of this.

Howsan's gaze fell on the two shabbily dressed men. He remembered their names. They were brothers, Thomas and Andrew Darrow. They stood apart from the others, and seemed to bear as much grief as Betsy Cochran's sons. A memory stirred. *They wanted to buy the mill when Pa bought it.*

Could these men have started the fire? But why? If the mill burned there would be nothing for them to buy, and it would be a long trek to Fellows Mill. Did the Darrow brothers have such hate that they would destroy the means to sell their own grain?

John Cochran stood next to his son and spoke in a quiet tone. "Come away."

"They wanted the mill," Howsan said, matching his Father's low voice.

"We will talk of this later," his Father said.

Reluctantly Howsan turned toward the blanket with food. He had thought yesterday's wind bore the smell of pig being cooked, and indeed there was much meat. It was a luxury, a sign of respect for his parents. For his Father, he thought, with bitterness.

* * *

Howsan yawned. He or Elsey had slept in the mill every night for the past two weeks. As the nights grew shorter they used a blanket for warmth. If there had been a sense of trouble, his Mother would never have permitted them to guard the mill, would have seen it as too dangerous.

Howsan had no concern for danger. He would welcome it, welcome those who set the fire if they returned to try again. He shifted the rifle's weight from one knee to the other. It had been his Father's weapon in the 1812 war. There was little powder to be had in the cabin, but a thief or other evil man would not know this.

The snap of twigs brought Howsan to his full senses, and he listened with care. Had it been an animal it would have kept going, unconcerned about sounds. No, this was the step of a human. He stood, but then crouched and looked toward the door that led to the creek bank. Still crouched, with his rifle in both hands, he made for the door.

Whispers! Howsan was sure that was what he heard. The moon had waned, but there was enough light for him to peer into the small grove of trees beside the mill. Surely a thief or someone who wanted to burn the mill would come from those trees. They would use them for cover.

Howsan was prepared to wait until dawn, looking for the man or men who approached. But he did not have to wait. Thomas and Andrew Darrow emerged and walked toward the entrance to the mill. Each man held something large and white. Then each one set down his burden and Howsan stared in disbelief. Goats? They were walking at night with goats?

Each goat had a rope around its neck, and they tied them to nearby saplings. Howsan could tell the goats had been awakened for this trek, for they settled quickly and appeared to sleep. Howsan stood and stepped from the mill's entrance so that the Darrow brothers could see him.

"You bring goats, in the night?" he asked. He was pleased to see that he had frightened them. Let them worry about what he intended to do with his rifle. He was not aiming at them, but held it at the ready.

Thomas Darrow spoke. "We heard the baby did not thrive without its Mother."

It was not what Howsan expected. How would they have heard that young William was poorly? And why would they care? *They would care if they set the fire.*

Howsan saw no weapons with the men, so he dropped the rifle to his side. He looked at the goats and back at the Darrow brothers. Perhaps they expected thanks, so he proffered it. Then he asked, "Why do you come here with stealth? My Father will want to thank you, perhaps mill some..."

"We want nothing," Thomas said.

There were a few seconds of silence, and Andrew Darrow spoke. "Our words were with anger."

"When my Father bought the mill." Howsan said this as a statement, not a question.

Thomas looked at the ground. "The drink makes us say foolish things, talk of deeds we should not do."

"And did you...did you do some of these deeds?" Howsan asked.

40

Both men shook their heads. "But our words were taken by others. Acted on by others," Andrew said.

Howsan thought of the man at the funeral, the man with a thin face. He had not stayed for food, so Howsan had not spoken to him. "Why would someone else take your words to act in anger?"

"Because we said them," Thomas said.

"And because we owed money," Andrew said. "We said we would pay it with profits from the mill we planned to buy."

"This mill," Thomas said.

The two men turned and walked back in the direction from whence they had come.

Howsan called after them. "Who did you talk to on the burial day?"

The men did not stop, but one of them said, "He is also gone."

Howsan's eyes followed them, and then he walked to the goats and knelt next to them. They were a fine gift, one not expected from the Darrow brothers. They must have bought them from someone moving west. Animals rarely fared well on the trek, and people sometimes sold them rather than see them die.

The larger of the goats tried to bite the butt of his rifle, and he moved it out of its reach. He didn't know how to milk a goat. His uncle had a cow, he could show Howsan how to do it. He frowned. They baby did not take the cow's milk well. Betsy Overman and another woman had fashioned a leather pouch of sorts, and they put milk in it and tried to get young William to take it from a small hole at one end. Perhaps his youngest brother would take the milk of a goat.

Howsan knew he could sleep now. He thought it likely that the brothers had started the fire, despite what they said. The thin-faced man likely knew of it and was chastising the brothers on the day of the burial. Or what the Darrows said was true, and perhaps the man who was angry with them tried to burn the mill out of spite. Did his mother die for a debt that was not hers?

Howsan wanted truth, but he knew that he was probably going to accept words that were only part of the truth. If he didn't, he would seek an answer that would not come. He would grow bitter. His mother would not want this.

Howsan thought that the Darrow brothers believed that their actions had hastened Betsy Cochran's death. The brothers were ashamed, and the goats were meant to appease their pain. It would not appease Howsan's.

At the thought of his Mother, Howsan's throat tightened. His Father did not believe the shock of the fire led to his Mother's death within minutes of William's birth. He thought God had decided to call her home, and they should not question her death.

Maybe the Darrow brothers did not cause Betsy Cochran's death, but she was still gone. Her last hours were consumed with pain and worry about her boys and the mill. Two goats were not a fair trade for his Mother, but perhaps they would save his brother. In the rough life of the Indiana frontier, it would have to do.

AUTHOR'S NOTE

The names and setting of Doan's Creek Mill represent real people and a business that existed in the 1830s in Greene County, Indiana. Howsan Seaton Cochran was my great-great grandfather. Census records and local history books let me know who was in the extended family, and that for a brief time Howsan's father and a brother owned a grain mill in Doan's Creek. The rest is a combination of extrapolation and, well, fiction. I knew when Howsan's mother died, and it looked as if she died soon after giving birth, not uncommon on the frontier.

The mystery to me was why the Cochran mill lasted a fairly brief time. Mills were important, and they had to be near a power source, which often meant water. Creeks could have been as wide as a river, so flooding was a possibility. Floods are routine, so I planted the threat of sabotage. There's no way to know what happened two hundred years ago in sparsely populated Indiana. Without musings there would be no stories. I feel fortunate that there was even such scant information about my Indiana ancestors. That's all a fiction writer needs to craft a tale.

Elaine L. Orr

A Piece of Pie
Claudia Pfeiffer

Sheriff Owen Kelly leaned his tall, solid frame back in the chair, making it squeak. He looked at the man seated across from him, slumped, head down.

"Why didn't you just bury him out there instead of hangin' him from the fence, Caleb?" The sheriff's voice was calm and filled with concern. "No one would have ever found him and you'd be free."

Caleb didn't answer. He hadn't answered any of the sheriff's questions over the course of the past two hours. He'd just sat there, looking small and tired.

"You can't help yourself by sittin' there sayin' nothin'. If you talk to me, maybe I can figure out why you did this, and perhaps the charge won't be murder. Perhaps it'll be some lesser charge. But I'll never know if you don't talk with me." The sheriff leaned forward trying to see Caleb's face, but it was dropped low.

Sheriff Kelly tried for another half an hour, then had Caleb returned to the jail cell at the end of the hall. He stood to stare out the window, seeing nothing, rolling his shoulders to release the tension of frustration.

"He's not gonna break, Sheriff," deputy Roland Faris said, pushing his shock of dark hair back with disgust. "Why don't you just give up, charge him with murder and let us build the scaffoldin'. We could have him hung and the crowd sent home by day after tomorrow. The whole thing would be over an' done with an' no loss to anyone."

"That's not my way, Roland, and you know it." Owen glanced over his shoulder at the deputy. "The signs say this man may have killed his brother, but that goes deeper than killin' a stranger or an acquaintance. I wanna know why. I wanna know what made him decide to make a public display of his brother, not just kill him. There's more to this than just murder."

"Whaddaya mean he may have killed his brother? Of course he did. I told you about the bad blood between them. If not Caleb Saunders, then who else would it have been? And if he won't talk you'll never find any of that out. You're just wastin' your time."

The sheriff watched as the tall, slim deputy stomped out of the office, untied his horse from the hitching post and mounted him in a fluid motion. He headed down Main Street, yanking the head of his horse to make him toss it dramatically. The horse stepped high as Faris raked its sides with his spurs. The deputy stopped to disperse a small crowd that was gathering. Then he continued on his way, settling back into his saddle, jerking the horse's head even higher.

The sheriff returned to his chair and sat there thinking. He bent forward and rubbed his eyes then stood to pace. There was a key to this murder. Something he was missing. And he wouldn't decide a man was guilty until he could prove it to himself with certainty. Perhaps it was time to talk with his wife. She had a good, calm head on her shoulders. He heaved himself up from his desk, reaching for his Stetson. As he placed it on his head, he locked the office and strode out to the hitching post. He mounted the paint tied there and headed for home.

The broad front yard started where the barbershop ended, marked by a white wooden fence with pink and red roses climbing over it. More flowers lined the porch and flowed from flower boxes beneath the windows. He smiled at Meredith's spots of color in the dusty town. Dismounting, he tied Banjo to the hitching post in front. He closed the gate behind him, mindful to latch it to keep the loose dogs around town from entering and disturbing the flower gardens. Meredith heard his footsteps on the front porch and opened the door for him, smiling at this unexpected visit.

"Hello, darlin'. What brings you home at this hour?" she asked as she kissed him on the cheek and took his hat from him, hanging it on the rack in the corner of the entry.

"I need a cuppa coffee with my best listener," he responded with a solid kiss on her lips and a smile in his eyes.

His face became more serious as he sat at the table. Meredith brought him a cup of strong, black coffee from the pot heating on the wood stove.

"So, what's the problem, sweetie?"

"You know Caleb Saunders, from the mercantile? You've heard he's in jail right now for murderin' his brother."

"Yes. I've heard that, but it's really hard to believe. Caleb's such a gentle soul. So quiet and pleasant. I find it difficult to understand how he could do somethin' so awful as what was done to his brother." Meredith pursed her lips and sat at the table.

"I've been questionin' him for hours, and he hasn't spoken a word." The sheriff shook his head. "Not one word. His expression doesn't change. He doesn't fidget. Just sits there. Head lowered to his chest. Won't say a thing. I can't understand why he doesn't try to defend himself. Or at least explain what happened. I'm like you. I can't imagine him killin' his brother and displayin' his body in such a painful and public way." He lifted his cup and inhaled the comforting aroma then drank in long, satisfying swallows.

"Well, we all know the rumors around town." Meredith caught her husband's gaze. "About how his brother ran off with Caleb's girl. There's bound to have been bad blood between them."

"Yeah. I've been thinkin' about that. But that was quite few years back, and he's never mentioned anything about it. We didn't learn about that 'til Roland moved to town."

"You mean Deputy Roland? How would he know about Caleb's background?" Meredith looked surprised.

"Says Caleb got drunk one night and told him about it. Right soon after he moved here. Caleb hadn't been here long himself. Roland says Caleb didn't seem the type to drink, but that night he obviously had more than he could handle." He held his cup up to signal he'd like a refill. "He told Roland he was in love with Andrea Hart, but she ran off with his brother, Dawson. Supposedly Caleb didn't hear anything more for about a year. Then he heard Dawson was alone again. He tried for a few years to find Andrea and discovered that she died of syphilis from making her livin' on the streets. That's when Caleb moved here to Twin Rivers. Probably to put all that behind him."

"I can't imagine Caleb gettin' drunk with Roland. I didn't think he drank. But that's some years ago. So what's the problem now, Owen?" His wife filled his coffee cup and returned the pot to the stove.

"Well, you know all about how we found his brother, Dawson, dead in that hot sun. We arrested Caleb, but like I said, he won't say anything. Not a word. Won't defend himself. Won't even look up." He wrapped his hands around the coffee cup, feeling the heat radiating from it. "Somethin' just doesn't set right with me. I don't feel sure that Caleb killed Dawson. But if he didn't, then who did? I thought your clear mind might have some ideas for me." He blew on the scalding coffee then took a swallow.

"Caleb's always been the quiet type. Never has talked much," she responded as she sipped at her coffee. "When I've seen him at the mercantile, he's always been friendly and willin' to talk when approached, but never about himself. I hear he doesn't go out, doesn't have close friends. He's just an independent man who's satisfied with his quiet life alone. At least, so it seems." She looked over the rim of her coffee cup, her face puzzled, then shook her head and continued.

"I don't understand why he doesn't defend himself, though, unless he's guilty." She frowned. "And it's hard to see him bein' guilty of such a horrible crime. I can maybe see him killin' the brother who ruined his happy life. But to stab him over and over and hang him from a barbed wire fence, leavin' him exposed to the sun to die? That doesn't fit that quiet man, the Caleb who always treated everyone so respectful and considerate."

"So you feel somethin's wrong with this picture too?"

"Yeah, I guess. I agree that it doesn't seem like somethin' Caleb would do. Besides, why would he leave him out in the open? Why not just kill him and bury the body where no one would find it? That would seem more like somethin' a quiet man like Caleb would do than this crazy display of murder."

"Thanks, honey, for the coffee and the talk." Owen stood from the table.

Meredith followed him to the front entry. Owen kissed his wife goodbye, grabbed his Stetson and walked out to mount

Banjo. He headed the paint out into the country. Wading across the Little Butte River, he rode toward the Circle Eight ranch.

Sheriff Kelly stopped at the murder site and stared at the barbed wire fence, remembering the body hanging from it as he had seen it several days before. It was a gruesome sight. The body burned from exposure to the sun, dried blood from the belly stabbings pooled in the sand below. It had been a horrible death, slow and painful. A vengeful one. Not a death done in an impulsive act of anger. That was the part that had him stumped.

Caleb Saunders was the most unlikely person he knew to hold a grudge, especially one that would result in such a revengeful death. He could picture Caleb being hurt. Feeling angry. Maybe even killing in a moment of anger. But being vengeful? No. Especially not openly and gruesomely so. This seemed the work of a more cunning person. But there was no one else.

It had rained since the murder, and the pool of blood thinned and mixed with the dirt. The surrounding dust had settled into hardened crusts around the area. The sheriff dismounted, dropped the reins, and walked in an ever widening circle around the scene of the murder, watching the ground. He picked up a small piece of old, frayed rope, studied it for a moment and discarded it. He resumed his slow walk. His eye caught the flash of something in the dirt, and he bent to pick it up. A round piece of silver metal, about the size of a quarter, fluted on the edges. He fingered it, brushing the dirt off. Stared at it, then slipped it in his pocket. He continued his circle until he was satisfied there was nothing more to be found. He walked to Banjo and remounted. When he returned to the office, he brought Caleb out for further questioning.

"Caleb, I don't think you killed your brother, but if you don't talk to me, you'll hang for it. I have no other suspects to question. No evidence to look at except the bad blood between you and Dawson. Please at least tell me why your brother suddenly appeared in Twin Rivers. Why, after all these years, did he come to find you?"

He placed a cup of coffee in front of Caleb and sat across the desk from him. Sheriff Kelly waited for an answer or some action by the man to indicate he heard what the sheriff asked him. Short and stocky, in his early thirties with the unlined face of someone who worked inside, Caleb ran his hand through his thin, sandy hair then dropped it to his lap. Nothing more. He didn't even reach for his coffee. Just sat, head down and silent until the sheriff returned him to his cell. There he did nothing except sit on his cot and stare at the walls. His meal trays sat until the food congealed and were replaced by fresh ones. His coffee got cold. The only thing he did was drink his jugs of water.

After a week of questioning and getting no closer to finding out anything new, the town was clamoring for closure of the matter. The Circuit Judge came to town and demanded that a trial be held. Because there was no one else to accuse of the murder and Caleb Saunders refused to defend himself or speak to his defense attorney, the judge found him guilty. He sentenced Caleb to death by hanging. Still, Sheriff Kelly delayed. The mayor and deputy were pressuring the sheriff to carry out the judge's sentence, and he finally had to do something.

"Caleb, I'm sure you can hear them buildin' the gallows just as clear as I can. You're gonna hang if you don't give me some information to help me in this investigation." All afternoon and evening the sheriff had heard the hammering. It jarred his nerves.

But Caleb didn't respond or react in any way.

"Dammit, Caleb, talk to me. Say somethin'. Gimme me a clue to what happened." He waited, then stomped off when the man in the cell made no response.

Owen Kelly had to escape the hammering. But even when he rode into the country, he heard the sound in his mind. He urged Banjo to a fast gait, feeling the wind against his face, hoping to clear the noise that made fear pool inside. Finally, he returned home and sat with Meredith at supper and talked again.

"I'm sure Caleb didn't murder his brother. But I don't know how to prove it." He pushed his half-eaten meal away.

"Why don't you go back where he came from and ask questions there? You might get a different picture of Caleb. It seems so strange to picture him drinkin', but maybe you'll find out he used to be a drunk. Maybe after revealin' so much about himself he decided to quit drinkin'." She began gathering up the plates and silverware.

"Maybe so." The sheriff nodded. "Goin' back to where he

came from's a good idea. Maybe I'll have to do that."

All evening, his stomach balled up at the thought of hanging Caleb the next day, and the nagging got worse. He finally told Meredith that he was going to delay the hanging and use her suggestion of going back to Caleb's hometown. Maybe he could uncover something to help settle the questions that plagued him.

When he told Roland about the fact-finding trip, the deputy was angry that the sheriff planned to postpone the hanging in light of the verdict. Owen talked with the judge and convinced him to give him a few days to look further into the matter.

"I think there may well be a miscarriage of justice here, Judge. Let me get all the facts before we execute a man."

"That's somethin' that shoulda been done before trial, Sheriff."

"I know, your honor, but I've still got doubts. Just lemme have a few days."

"All right, Sheriff. You've got until I come back through. But you know it's hard to overturn a verdict."

When Owen insisted he was still going to delay the execution until he returned from his trip, he put Roland in charge of keeping peace while he was gone. He was sure the townsfolk would become aroused by the delay. They were already incensed by his long and tedious investigation, gathering in groups to loudly berate his actions.

"What's takin' so long, Sheriff? Hang 'im."

"Yeah, look what he did to his brother. It was inhumane. What're you stallin' for?"

"Hang 'im now, Sheriff."

They yelled at him whenever he stepped outside the office, their faces red, their fists in the air.

"You're behavin' like a fool, Sheriff." Roland Jarvis stood, hands on hips, jaw jutted out. "This town's gonna explode." He slapped his hand on the desk with a loud snap.

"Just be sure you keep order 'cause if I return and that man's been hanged, I'll be holdin' you personally responsible," the sheriff said. Roland's face flushed with anger, and he glared as the Sheriff plopped his Stetson on and walked out the door.

It took Sheriff Kelley two days of steady riding to reach Catliss, Saunders' previous home. His first talk was with Sally

Turner, a resident of the town who was familiar with Caleb and his brother, Dawson.

"Caleb was a quiet one," Sally told Owen. "He was shy. That's why I was surprised when he took up with Andrea Hart. She was quite lively. You know, liked a good time. But Caleb was in love with her."

"What happened to Miz Hart?"

"Oh, didn't ya hear yet? She ran off with Caleb's brother, Dawson. He was a big shot around town, Dawson was. Almost a complete opposite of his brother. He swaggered when he walked and always gathered people around. He worked at one of the neighborin' ranches." She paused to hold her bonnet against a brief gust of wind.

"I never seen Caleb drink but that don't mean much. I have four kids so don't have much time for gaddin' about town." She smiled and stepped away. Owen tipped his hat and continued down the street.

"Caleb was a good worker," Maynard Baldwin, the owner of the hotel advised. "All the time he worked here as manager and bookkeeper, he was a friendly, quiet, person. As far as I knew, he never drank. Or smoked."

"Did you know of his association with a woman named Andrea Hart?"

"Well, according to what I heard, he was in love with her. I saw them together at dinner a few times. Rumor has it she left town with Caleb's brother, Dawson, and that's the last I heard of either of them."

Baldwin didn't have anything more to add, and Owen walked to the local sheriff's office. Sheriff Perkins was happy to help a fellow lawman and answered all of Owen's questions without hesitation.

"I'm here about Caleb Saunders. I heard a rumor that Caleb was in love with Andrea Hart but that she left with his brother. What do you know about that?" Owen fiddled with the brim of his Stetson.

"Yeah. Caleb's gal left with his brother, Dawson. T'was the talk of the town for a while. Caleb hung around for another month then left, and your visit is the first I've heard of him since. I'm surprised to hear he's guilty of murder. It's difficult to believe that someone as quiet as Caleb would turn rogue like that. Maybe you should check into a lil' town called Los Cantos. Maybe they have more information on Caleb that would explain that."

"Can you think of anyone who woulda wanted to frame Caleb for murder? An enemy he might have?"

"I doubt Caleb had any enemies. Perhaps his brother, but no one else I can think of." Perkins rubbed the stubble on his chin. "Now I can think of several would've liked to see his brother dead. Dawson Saunders was pretty rough on a few of our townsfolk."

"Could you give me their names?"

"Well, one of them was Jake Cromer, but he moved away from here, and I've heard nothin' about him since. Then Roland Jarvis."

"My deputy? Why was Jarvis upset with Dawson Saunders? I didn't know they even knew each other."

"Oh, he claimed Saunders cheated him on some sorta business deal. I don't know any more than that. Perhaps Dawson lost a poker hand to Roland and didn't pay up." Sheriff Perkins shrugged and squinted in thought. "Then there's Curt Mantis. He and Dawson used to go 'round and 'round every time Dawson came to town. Mantis works at the livery stable. Had to put them both in the hoosegow for brief coolin' off periods a coupla times when they started brawls in the bar or just on the street." Perkins chuckled. "Mantis is small, and it was like seein' a banty fightin' a full-sized rooster when the two of them had at it. Curt always ended up bloodied and bruised, and Dawson would just lay in his cell and laugh."

"Can I still find Mantis at the livery?" Sheriff Kelly felt a tremor of excitement to be able to talk with one of the people who had a problem with Dawson Saunders.

"Yes sir. Most days but Sunday." Perkins nodded his head.

Owen thanked the sheriff and headed for the livery stable. Curt Mantis was a short, frail man with a shrunken left arm. He showed no displeasure when he heard of Dawson Saunders' death.

"He was a mean man. Just plain ornery. I figured someone would turn on him some day."

"I hear you and he had quite a few run-ins when he lived

around here." Owen watched Mantis closely and could see the disgust on his face.

"Yeah. Lotta good it did me." He held up the shrunken arm. "He always had the upper hand. I hated that man. He was cruel. Just a conceited, unpleasant person. He was rude to women. Belligerent to everybody. And abusive to the horses he rode. That really set me off. I don't like to see animals treated bad. It made me see red." Mantis slammed his right fist into the palm of his left hand.

"I'd fight with him about that. We'd go round and round and usually end up throwin' punches. He'd always get me down and laugh at me. The sheriff wouldn't charge Saunders with anything, sayin' we didn't have no say in the way he treated his own animals. That made me mad, but there wasn't much I could do about it. Dawson Saunders was just a mean man, and I'm not the least bit upset to hear of his death."

"Do you know what the beef was Jarvis had with Jake Cromer and Dawson Saunders?"

"No, but I heard they split up over somethin'. They were all friends for a while. Were drinkin' buddies. Saunders and Jarvis always rode into town together. Jarvis was abusive, too. Used to rake his horses with his spurs until they bled. It made for a high steppin', showy animal. But anyway, I just heard the three of them had a fallin' out and Cromer left town. Next Jarvis challenged Saunders to a fight, with or without guns. Saunders just laughed at him, and the next day he was gone. So was Andrea Hart, his brother's girl."

"Do you know why Cromer left the area? Or Jarvis?"

"Don't know why Cromer left. I just assumed Jarvis went to find Dawson, but no one around here heard any more about any of them after they left."

"Thanks for your help." Owen doffed his hat and mounted Banjo. He didn't think Curt Mantis could be a suspect in Dawson's death. He was too frail to have overcome someone of Dawson's size.

Owen headed out of town. Now he had a two-day ride back to Twin Rivers to think everything over. It surprised him to learn Roland Jarvis had known Dawson Saunders. And Caleb. That seemed significant and suspicious. But if Jarvis had something to do with Dawson's death, why wouldn't Caleb talk about it? It seemed he had more investigating to do. Maybe it was time to take a side trip to the little town of Los Cantos Sheriff Perkins had mentioned and ask more questions.

When Sheriff Kelly arrived back home, he was disheveled and exhausted. He was also three days later than he had originally estimated. Meredith shooed him upstairs to a hot bath while she unsaddled and took care of Banjo, rubbing down the dust-caked, sweaty horse. By the time Owen was finished with his bath and dressed in clean clothes again, his wife had a hot meal waiting for him.

"After you eat, you should sleep for a while," Meredith advised him.

He shook his head as he dove into the pot pie she set before him.

"I can't give in to sleep yet. Just keep the black coffee comin' for a while. I have a few things to do at the office before I can sleep. If everything goes as I plan, this matter will finally be settled."

"Did you find evidence that Caleb was a drunk back home?"

"Nope. He was the same person he is here. Quiet and friendly. Non-drinker. Non-smoker."

"Then you must still have questions about his murder conviction." Meredith refilled his coffee cup.

"No, I think I have all my questions answered. I have one stop to make before I go back to the jail. Then my only question will be if I can settle this mess quickly. This problem of Dawson Saunders' death."

He stood from the table, placing his napkin beside his plate. He embraced his wife and kissed her firmly.

"I wish I had time to tell you all about it, but I have to run. Thank you for always bein' ready to talk, to give me your advice and wait patiently for me. I'm afraid this will be another time of patient waitin'." He kissed her again and Meredith leaned against him for a brief moment.

He walked to the front door, grabbing his Stetson from the hat rack as he passed. He took his weapon from its holster and checked to make sure it was loaded. Sighing, he opened the front door and nodded at his wife. At the barn, he saddled Banjo and rode him down the street. After making his stop, he rode back to the sheriff's office. There was a crowd gathered on the boardwalk. Larger than the ones that were gathering before he left. They began questioning him and calling to him belligerently. He simply doffed his hat and entered the office. Roland sat with his feet up on the desk and jumped up when he saw the sheriff enter.

"Well, I wondered if you got lost out there. The town is goin' crazy about Saunders. You have to do somethin' or they'll be riotin' soon. You can see the group that's gathered outside now. It's been growin' while you've been gone." Roland pointed to the door.

"Don't worry. I plan on takin' care of things quickly from here on out," Owen replied. "The first thing I need to do is ask you to turn in your badge and place your gun on the desk."

"Do what?" Roland frowned and raised his voice.

"Turn in your badge and place your gun on the desk," Owen repeated.

"What for? What's goin' on? I take care of an unruly town in your absence and this is the thanks I get?"

"Yes. I'll explain, but first you need to do what I asked."

"The hell I will," Jarvis barked as he reached for the door. Kelly's weapon appeared in his hand immediately.

"Do as I say or I'll have to shoot. You're under arrest, and I have no choice but to use force if necessary." Kelly kept his weapon trained on Jarvis.

"Under arrest? Me? What for?"

The sheriff waved his gun at Jarvis. The deputy stared at the gun in the sheriff's hand, unfastened his holster and angrily slapped it down on the desk.

"And the badge," Owen stated as he took possession of the holstered gun.

"You have no idea what you're doing," Jarvis said, fury coloring his voice as he threw the badge down.

"Yes, I do."

Owen prodded his prisoner indicating he should walk back to the cells. Once there, Owen slammed and locked the heavy door.

"Now tell me why I'm under arrest." Jarvis demanded.

"You're under arrest for the murder of Dawson Saunders."

From the corner of his eye, Owen could see Caleb's head snap up.

"But that's ridiculous. The jury has already found his brother guilty."

"That's somethin' I'm gonna try to fix," the sheriff informed him. "I'll see to it this time that the right man is punished."

Owen saw that Caleb's face was white, his lips tense with fear. The sheriff turned and walked to his cell and unlocked the door.

"You're free to go. I have proof that Roland Jarvis killed your brother." Owen spoke kindly to the man still seated in the cell.

Caleb stared at him and began to shake his head.

"Come on out to my office and we'll discuss it." Owen turned and walked back to his desk, leaving the cell door open.

"What proof are you talkin' about, Owen?" Jarvis demanded. "Caleb's been found guilty and rightly so. What bug's eatin' you? Tell him, Caleb. Open that mouth of yours and tell the sheriff that you killed your brother, and he's makin' a big mistake arrestin' me."

The sheriff sat at his desk and pulled some papers from his drawer. As he began writing, Caleb quietly walked from his cell to stand beside the desk.

"You're makin' a mistake," he said in a very quiet voice.

"What's that, Caleb? I'm making a mistake? Why don't you take a seat, and I'll explain why Roland Jarvis is guilty of the death of your brother." Owen looked up at the man.

Caleb sat on the edge of a chair in front of the sheriff's desk.

"Please, Sheriff, don't do this. You're makin' a mistake. I killed my brother and I'm ready to hang for it. Jarvis had nothing to do with it."

"That's right," Jarvis yelled from his cell. "You tell him the truth, Caleb."

"I just came back from Catliss," Sheriff Kelly stated looking Caleb in the eye, "where I learned several interestin' things. I learned, for instance, that Roland Jarvis came from there, somethin' he never mentioned to me when I told him I was going to Catliss. I learned, too, that he left that area shortly after you did. It appears he followed you here. I believe he did that to keep pressure on you. So you would keep quiet about some things he and your brother argued about."

"Please, Sheriff, I'm begging you to drop all this. The jury proved I killed my brother. Just get on with the hanging and drop all this other stuff you think you've learned." Caleb was white as a sheet, and his hand shook as he placed it on the corner of the desk.

"I can't do that, Caleb. I'm sworn to uphold justice, and that's what I'm tryin' to do here." He watched Caleb for a moment before continuing.

"I also discovered that a bank was robbed by three men in Eubanks, about twenty miles from Catliss, and the robbers were never found." The sheriff toyed with something small and silver as he talked. "I discovered that your brother, Dawson, was suspected as being one of the robbers. It's my belief that Roland Jarvis was also one of the robbers. And Jake Cromer. I stopped in Eubanks and the descriptions of a high-stepping horse at the robbery matches the horse Roland used to ride in Catliss. One of the witnesses said the rider, whose face was covered with a bandana like the others, kept raking the horse with his spurs." Owen glanced toward Jarvis leaning against the bars of his cell.

"I've seen him do the same thing when he rides here. In addition, I have testimony from Curt Mantis that Roland repeatedly did that with the horses he rode. He also said that Dawson and Jarvis always rode together. I imagine if I place Jarvis in a room with the witnesses, they'll pick him out even with the bandana because of his tall, slim build and shock of black hair. That and his high spirited horse."

"But how are you gonna tie a bank robbery in with my brother's death?" Caleb stared at the sheriff.

"People in Catliss said there was a beef between your brother and Jarvis and Jake Cromer. They say Cromer left town, then Dawson, and Jarvis followed shortly after. The people I talked with assumed it was to look for Dawson. I think the beef is that Dawson didn't give Jarvis his share of the robbery revenues. I believe, but don't know for sure, that Dawson killed Jake Cromer so he could keep his share, too. Cromer simply disappeared so I can't prove anything." Owen leaned back in his chair before continuing.

"I think Jarvis figured he'd finally catch up to your brother by followin' you here. He probably reckoned that someday your brother would come lookin' for you, and when he did, he'd kill him and let it look like you committed the murder."

"What a bunch of hogwash." Jarvis shouted and rattled the bars of his cell.

"You're wrong, Sheriff," Caleb insisted, his voice becoming stronger. "I killed my brother. Roland Jarvis had nothing to do with it."

"Don't worry, Caleb, he can't hurt you anymore. I have him locked up, and the jury'll find him guilty. You see, I found this at the scene of the murder and it's been botherin' me ever since." He placed the silver piece he'd been toying with on the desk.

"I checked and you don't wear belts that sport these conchos, but Jarvis' holster has them all the way around the waist. When I found it, I didn't think of Jarvis because none of his are missin'. But with all the other evidence of his wrongdoings, I checked his holster out and one of his conchos is shinier than the others. I went to the saddle shop this mornin' and found out he had one replaced around the date of your brother's murder. I believe this one will fit the spot of the one that was missin'. I think when I present the evidence of his involvement in the robbery and the evidence of this concho bein' at the scene of the murder, the jury will find him guilty. Then he'll be the one hung on the gallows, not you."

Caleb started to speak again, but the sheriff held up his hand. He stood and walked to the window and looked out for a moment then turned to look at Caleb.

"I also took a side trip to Los Cantos." Caleb's pale face turned bright red, and the sheriff continued to stare at him. "Once Roland's found guilty, he can't hurt you anymore. It won't matter that you know about his involvement in the robbery. He won't be able to hold that over you." The sheriff paused, watching Caleb closely. "And he can't hurt Mandy either. She's safe now."

"Mandy?" Caleb started to stand but sat again, trembling all over, his face growing redder. "What do you know about Mandy?"

"In Los Cantos I found a young girl named Amanda Hart, Mandy. She's the daughter of Andrea Hart and is either your daughter or that of your brother. But she's been raised by her mother's parents with help from you since her birth." Owen walked back to the desk and looked with compassion on Caleb.

"Her grandmother died three weeks ago, and her grandfather is unable to take care of her alone. I believe that's what your brother came to tell you."

Caleb raised his hands to his face, and his shoulders began to shake. The sheriff put his hand on his shoulder.

"Caleb, she has no one but you left to care for her. She'll be arrivin' by stage in two weeks. That should give you time to prepare a place for the two of you. If I've got the situation all wrong and you're not up to carin' for this young lady, let me know and my wife and I will make arrangements for her."

"Don't listen to him, Caleb. You can't be assured of her safety. Especially with her grandmother gone." Jarvis' voice was filled with venom.

"And I say, don't listen to him, Caleb." The sheriff's voice was soft. "He's the one who's been threatenin' you with harm to Mandy. He'll be found guilty, and soon won't be a problem to you or your daughter, 'cause she'll be completely yours when she comes here."

Owen sat. He stopped to take a gulp of his coffee and to give Caleb time to digest all he'd told him. Then he faced him again and spoke with a smile on his face.

"Until I have a chance to explain all this to that crowd outside, perhaps you should stay here. They're liable to string you up until they know the truth of the matter. The judge is due here in two days." Owen shrugged. "I believe I can have a good case ready against Roland Jarvis by then. You can stay in my fine hotel here for protection until Jarvis is proven guilty, or you can stay with me and my wife if you prefer."

Caleb lifted his head and wiped at his face with both hands. He started to speak but had to stop and clear his throat. Then he lifted his head, his face returning to a normal color.

"I believe I'll stay in your hotel here, Sheriff, until this matter is over. And thank you for all you've done to prove me innocent. And for bringing Mandy to me."

"I felt you were a fool not to speak before, Caleb, but when I found Mandy I understood that you were protectin' her. You're a good man. A strong man. Now, is there anything more I can do for you at this time?" The sheriff stood and placed his hand on Caleb's shoulder.

"Yes, Sheriff, just one more thing. I'm feeling pretty hungry. Could I have a sandwich and a cup of coffee?"

"Caleb," Sheriff Kelly said as he laughed, "you can have the biggest steak they have from the café and all the coffee you can drink. I'll even toss in a piece of pie."

AUTHOR'S NOTE

I'm a writer of long fiction. Mystery, romance and romantic suspense novels. In the revision phase of my writing, my most difficult task is reducing the number of words. Ridding the manuscript of all the excess verbiage. Reining in my desire to ramble. So writing a short story was an immense challenge, one that fascinated me and frightened me all at the same time. *A Piece of Pie* is the result of that challenge.

I was surprised when I started to write it that my characters turned out to be situated in the Old West. But perhaps I shouldn't be surprised. I was probably inspired by my stepfather, Jack Schaefer. He was a western writer. Author of *Shane* and *Monte Walsh* and many other novels and short story collections, all set in the West and in the past. I remember him often sharing his writing with my mother and sisters and me by enthusiastically reading to us portions of what he had written. Those are great memories and a wonderful legacy.

My mother was also an author. She wrote and published two plays. One was staged in various venues, from the drama department at Yale University to the opera theater in Santa Fe, New Mexico.

With inspiration from both parents, I guess it was inevitable that I would write. Today, I am addicted. I can't not write. That's an awkward sentence, but so true. A day without writing is empty and unfulfilling for me. I'm glad I faced the challenge of writing this short story, as every challenge teaches a new lesson.

Claudia Pfeiffer

The Circle Effect
Diana Catt

My father's admiration for art influenced my life to no small extent. Just so, his fervor plunged me into an ethical dilemma as a young man that I wrestle with to this day. The tale of the events that transpired is both terrifying and regrettable.

The affair began over twenty years ago, in 1887. Indiana's Legislature handily approved the money for the greatest monument in the state, and the task to hire the architect proceeded at a fevered pitch. The good citizens of Indianapolis were eager to witness a noteworthy use of our city's central circle of land and loyally followed each step in the proceedings of the Monument Commission's contest for designs. Cheers arose from the crowd when they unveiled Bruno Schmitz's winning model.

As a mere child, I was taken periodically to the circle, now commonly called 'Monument Circle,' to follow the progress.

"There will be amazing fountains continually filling clear pools on each side," my father explained as we marveled near the edge of the thirty-foot hole dug for the foundation.

My young mind couldn't begin to imagine the engineering involved in such a project, but I could anticipate the effect.

Over the next ten years, the shaft slowly expanded, stage by stage, until the Indiana State Soldiers and Sailors Monument reached its glory of 246 feet. I simultaneously grew in height and maturity during this time. I'd reached my fifteenth year when Schmitz prepared his supporters for the arrival of his artist, sculptor Rudolf Schwarz, who would adorn the monument with intricate groupings reflecting moments of war and peace. My father and his friends found it amusing to provide the philanthropic support to enable Schmitz's vision to become reality. They recognized the sculptor would need a studio near the construction site and were successful in procuring a suitable lot. Because of my father's influence and my able-bodied enthusiasm, I was allowed to assist in modifying the artist's studio to meet his specifications.

We finished preparations for the studio by early December, but we weren't prepared for the man, Rudolf Schwarz. His Bohemian appearance and lifestyle fascinated me, and I volunteered to serve in any capacity, just to experience this oddity first hand. He scrutinized my face and physique while listening to my offer to work before and after school and on my days off.

"Ach, you are the perfect model," he said. "I pay you if I have money, no?"

I laughed at his cavalier attitude. I knew the money came from my father and his friends, but Schwarz didn't seem to concern himself with that level of detail. From the first day, he concentrated on the sculpture, and paid no heed to the condition of his workshop, his appearance, or his diet. As long as he had clay to model, stone to carve, and enough money for liquor at the end of the day, he remained in good spirits.

My own aspirations were to study architecture, and I anticipated the chance to examine sketches, plans, diagrams. But, no. This enigma went directly from mental image to clay model. Schwarz worked with amazing concentration and speed, ignorant of the detrital trail he left behind. Each evening before I left, I picked through the litter - metal scraps or wires, lumps of discarded clay, broken plaster casts and other rubbish in order to locate, clean, and organize his tools. He didn't seem to notice. In fact, he frequently appeared in the morning wearing the same clay-smeared clothes from the previous day, often with gypsum particles still imbedded in his black beard!

My father and his friends enjoyed hearing these descriptions.

"What a character," my father said.

"Single-minded," added his artist friend, Mr. Samuel Morgan. "The best artists often are."

"Very much so," I added. "He usually works straight through meal time without a break. I'd waste away if I tried that." The gentlemen nodded all around. "And after he's done for the day, he heads straight to Germania House for the evening." My father raised an eyebrow. "I followed him once or twice." I studied my shoes while they laughed at my discomfort. I'd heard what went on in a saloon.

Mr. Horace Greenly, my father's lawyer friend, cleared his throat before commenting. "Schwartz's already a frail fellow. Least we can do is make sure he eats one good meal a day."

They decided to supply a cook of sorts until Mrs. Schwarz could arrive from Germany to join her eccentric artist husband, and also a handyman to do a more thorough cleaning a couple times a week.

Mrs. Mae Cooper, whose father had been a well-respected artist in the Indianapolis area, agreed to prepare food. Every day she brought lunch and dinner for Schwarz, and for me if I was there. Her daughter, Amelia, often accompanied her. I recognized Amelia from the class two years behind me. Schwarz immediately enlisted Amelia to be his female model in his 'Peace' display that would be on the west face of the monument. I modeled for the boy in the same grouping.

They also hired an elderly gentleman, Mr. Singleton, a disabled Civil War veteran, to help with the maintenance one or two evenings a week. He performed a similar function at the Capitol building during the week days. I would often stay and help Mr. Singleton because I'm able-bodied and I enjoyed hearing the old fellow recount his war experiences.

"How'd you earn that scar?" I asked him, after only knowing him a few hours.

"Bayonet, boy. Hand to hand combat. Damn Reb had thirty pounds on me and a powerful swing. Last thing I ever saw with this eye was that blasted blade slicing down." He slashed downward with his arm, and then fingered the raised pink mark that disfigured the left side of his face.

Mr. Singleton continued to regale me with his escapades and so many point-of-death moments that I wondered how one man could have lived through that much evil without becoming permanently soured on life.

One morning, only a few weeks after I met Mr. Singleton, evil caught up with the old soldier.

I opened up the workshop as usual, but found a box of old

metal scraps that Mr. Singleton failed to deposit on the trash pile in the alley behind the workshop. I carried the box out back and that's where I found the old man, dead atop a pile of blood-soaked rubbish – a mysterious symbol painted on his forehead and a slice across his throat that would never produce a scar.

The studio didn't have a telephone, so I raced my bicycle through the streets of Indianapolis to our home on North Meridian Street in time to catch my father at breakfast.

"He's dead, Father. Someone killed him." I was panting and trembling and could barely get the words out.

My father rose from his chair. "Who? Schwarz?"

I shook my head. "The old man. Mr. Singleton. He's in the alley. There's blood everywhere."

He immediately telephoned the police, then his physician, and finally, his lawyer friend, Mr. Greenly. My father's influence reached marvelous lengths; I received an excused absence from school for the day, and the poor gentleman's body was photographed and removed from the site before Schwarz arrived to begin work.

Later the same morning, the police questioned me about Singleton's activities at the studio and whether he'd had any visitors. I explained what little I knew. They also questioned Schwarz but he barely recognized the victim's name and knew none of his history. By early afternoon, we'd returned to business as usual. Amelia joined us after school for another modeling session. She and I whispered about the Singleton horror as we stood side by side in our Civil War-era costumes, speculating on whether the reported animosity at the Capitol building had followed Singleton and spilled over into our back alley during the night.

That evening, after Schwarz finished for the day, I swept the rooms. A folded piece of paper in the debris pile caught my eye. Thinking it might be an important receipt, I picked it up for closer scrutiny.

I stared, uncomprehending, at a sketch of a younger Mr. Singleton. The disfiguring scar through his left eye distinguished him, but he wore a Rebel uniform and brandished a whip on an emaciated Union prisoner. An arrow pointing to the prisoner was labeled 'me'. The drawing was signed George Hawking.

What type of slander was this? Who would dishonor the murdered old man in such an evil way? The same triangle symbol I saw earlier in the morning on the dead man's forehead flew at me from the lower corner of the page. It was encircled by the twisted image of a copperhead snake.

Without the powerful emotions that had forced me to flee to my father that same morning, I had the presence of mind to study the symbol on the paper. I'd never seen anything like the triangle with the internal 3, 5 and 7 at the angles and the letters KGC in the center. Whatever the secret to this code, someone had decorated Mr. Singleton's forehead with it, which made this piece of paper an important clue. I refolded it and stuffed it deep into my pocket, intending to show my father.

I finished my chores by sweeping the debris into a box and carrying it to the alley out back. I felt a chill when I recalled the gruesome sight of Mr. Singleton's body lying across this very rubbish pile. Did a man's spirit linger at the site of his death? Did the killer linger at the site of his atrocity? I tried to shake these thoughts from my mind and hurried to throw the trash onto the mound. A movement from the back of the bin sent my heart into my throat. It was only a rat. I pretended to lunge toward it and the rodent scurried deeper into the muck.

Moments later, with my hand still shaking slightly, I locked up for the night. As I pointed my bicycle toward home, I heard the unmistakable clicking of footsteps approaching from the south. Human footsteps. As far as I knew, the murderer was still at large. Would he dare return to the scene? I hid myself and my bike in the impenetrable shadow of the thick shrubs beside the studio. As the footsteps neared, I quietly pushed deeper into the darkness. Had Singleton heard his murderer's approach? I tried not to breathe lest I meet the same fate.

When the threat eventually appeared at the door, I momentarily felt relief. It was only Mrs. Cooper. She must be coming back to pick up those dirty dishes from today's dinner. I didn't wish for her to see me cowering in the bushes so I remained silent. But before she entered the building I heard more footsteps coming from the other direction. She heard them too and paused with her key in the lock. I could see her face from my hiding spot, and she looked anxious but not afraid. Indeed, she greeted the newcomers in a manner suggesting this was not a random meeting.

"Thank you for coming," she said in a whisper. "Sam, were you followed?"

Followed? What sort of clandestine meeting was this? I could make out the silhouettes of three men, but couldn't see their faces from my position.

"Greetings, Mae," the taller man said. "No one saw us."

With shock, I recognized the voice of my father's artist friend, Samuel Morgan. My curiosity kept me hidden, watchful. I stared into the darkness at the backs of other two men. One displayed a short, round stature unmistakably that of Mr. Horace Greenly, my father's lawyer. And wherever Mr. Morgan and Mr. Greenly were, there, as expected, was my father, the third man in this strange group.

Mrs. Cooper opened the door, entered and turned on the lamp in the corner of the room. The men followed her in. The door didn't latch behind them and I crept closer to peer inside. Mrs. Cooper was leading the men to the dressing area. I took the opportunity to slip inside and hide behind the massive sculpture in the center of the studio floor.

"She admitted to bringing the drawing with her today," Mrs. Cooper said. "She must have dropped it in here when she was getting into her costume."

"Why did she even bring it?" Mr. Morgan asked, irritation evident in his voice. "You said she'd never met the Copperhead."

"She only wanted to show Schwarz her grandpa's uniform. His regiment had a unique patch. She thought it would look good on the sculpture."

"It would, too," my father said softly. "George deserves recognition in a memorial. Her heart's in the right place."

"So's yours," Mrs. Cooper said. "But you risked too much. If anyone finds Dad's drawing and puts it together..."

"I'd do it again," Morgan said. "Even if someone finds the picture, they can't tie anything to me. It'll just serve to tell the world what a traitor the old man was. Maybe we should hope it *is* found and makes the front page of the *Sentinel*. 'Knight of the Golden Circle in Our Midst' or 'Beloved Artist Suffered as POW at Hands of War Criminal.' Great headlines, you must admit."

"Don't be insane, man," Mr. Greenly said. "Amelia knows you and I were at Mae's and saw the drawing. It would spell our ruin. It's enough to know the deed is done."

"Be still, you old fools, and keep looking," Mrs. Cooper said. "I don't want to regret I told you I'd found the traitor. My father loved all three of you. He won't rest any easier if you hang."

I sucked in my breath. Surely I hadn't heard her correctly. Fear of a different sort caused a cold sweat to form on my torso.

"No one's going to hang, Mae," Morgan said. "Quit worrying. We still turn a blind eye to vigilante killings here in Indiana. I know for a fact the police will understand the clue I put on the bastard's forehead. Once they confirm it applies to this traitor, they won't look any further. Guaranteed."

"That's true, Mae," Mr. Greenly said. "After all, this monument is for remembering those who died, and we sure can't forget George. We made a vow."

They were quiet for a moment, allowing me to process their conversation. So, the KGC in the symbol meant Knights of the Golden Circle. I'd read about them in the paper. They were a much decried cult supporting a second Civil War and the return of slavery. And I knew the expression 'Copperhead' referred to Southern sympathizers from Indiana and other Northern states. I eased the piece of paper out of my pocket and studied the face of young Mr. Singleton. I remembered his wild, unbelievable accounts of his war adventures. He'd been nice enough to me. But this concerned my own father. He and his friends couldn't be wrong about something this serious, could they? I knew who I had to protect. I slid the piece of paper with the drawing on it around to the opposite side of the statue and waited in hiding.

After a few minutes Mrs. Cooper said, "Oh, praise the Lord, that must be it," and I heard four sets of footsteps rush to the sculpture. I heard the paper rustle as it was passed from hand to hand.

"Sleep well tonight, Mae," Mr. Greenly said after a moment. I heard some backs being slapped, the light went out, and they all left by the front door.

I sat for a while in the darkness, stunned by what I'd learned and wondered what I should do next. It didn't seem like I could do much since I'd relinquished the picture.

The next morning, I asked my father about the meaning of the symbol I'd seen on the dead man's head. He confirmed the police were looking into the KGC and Copperhead angles, and said it probably meant the man wasn't who he pretended to be. He studied me for a moment then said, "I wish you hadn't been the one to find the body, son."

I wholeheartedly agreed. And silently wished I hadn't been the one to find the drawing.

* * *

Five years later, Mr. Greenly waited in the back of the church to escort my lovely Amelia down the aisle at our wedding ceremony. My father and I stood side by side in the alcove by the altar, and I worked up my courage to ask him about Amelia's grandfather, his old artist friend.

"Ah, George has been on my mind today. I wish he could be here." He straightened his tie and studied the top of my head.

"We were a tight circle of friends, George, Samuel, Horace and I. Enlisted together and made a pact to watch over each other's families if we didn't make it back." He let out a deep breath. "The Rebs captured George and he died in that hell hole, Andersonville, at the hands of a butcher, shortly before the war's end." My father squared his shoulders. "Our own war ended sometime later."

I remembered the drawing on the piece of paper I'd found in the artist's studio and understood which event ended the war for my father and his veteran friends.

He smiled at me and his dark eyes met mine. "We kept our vow and watched over George's wife and little Mae. Now you're going to watch over Amelia."

He pulled me into an embrace. "You don't know how happy that makes me, son."

After the ceremony, the wedding party met at Monument Circle for a photograph in front of the 'Peace' sculpture and fountain. I could see Amelia's grandfather's regiment patch on one of the returning soldiers. I could see my likeness in the boy and Amelia's in the girl. I wasn't alone in appreciating these features, and I suddenly understood that for my father, Mr. Greenly, and Mr. Moore, this monument and this wedding confirmed that justice for George Hawking and his family had been achieved.

The circle was complete.

AUTHOR'S NOTE

The Circle Effect was inspired by the picturesque Soldiers and Sailors Monument on the Circle in Indianapolis. To learn the history of the structure, I searched the Internet, visited the museum beneath the monument and took the elevator to the top for the fantastic view. I examined the statues and designs that decorate the monument. I studied newspaper accounts describing the design competition won by Bruno Schmitz and an eyewitness description of the artist, Rudolf Schwarz. The Civil War sympathizers of the time were real, but the crime described in *The Circle Effect* was a product of my imagination.

Diana Catt

The Third Deadly Sin
S. Ashley Couts

The explosive discovery of natural gas on farmer Ezekiel Clampitt's land in 1887 changed everything in Hamilton County. A new industry was born. The local economy blossomed. The Ball Brothers opened a bottle and jar company in Muncie. Indiana Glass and Arcadia Glass were pumping new life into the rural economy. Rough and tumble workmen – Portuguese, Italian, Turk, Greek – suddenly poured into the sweet Quaker village of Little Hope. It quickly morphed into something akin to an Old West boomtown. Perhaps what happened next had to do with liquor. The village, that once had only one bar – more a café and soda place than anything else – a suddenly had twelve neighbors. Full-out saloons, and not all of them sedate like the mahogany paneled Monon Depot Club, crowded into one block. Most were places to get soused and brawl, knock-down, drag-out joints with shady ladies at the door.

Given the reckless atmosphere, the town sorely needed a savior.

* * *

Snake Eyes Jackson leaves a dollop of spit on the ground below the Flambeau at Main and Cross streets. He hoists his dusty, rumpled pinstripe trousers then adjusts his derby hat. The shadow of the big Roman cross perched atop Holy Name Church falls across his face then elongates, forming something like a dagger, at his feet.

"Rich bead bangers with their rosaries. Sin all week long. Bleed to the priest and it's forgiven. Some racket," he mutters.

By no accident, he's floated in on the wave of drifters, grifters, gamers and rowdies wearing the story that he's a rectified sinner, born-again fornicator and cheat come to spread his own unique brand of fire and brimstone salvation over this Sodom and Gomorrah. Like any convincer, he possesses the magical ability to glimmer a susceptible crowd; his weapons a tattered Bible, gift for gab and a six-shooter.

Sober, he's a dead-on shot.

The revival tent is over by the Monon track and each night the place is filled with sinners, believers, the gullible and anyone who just straggles in.

Just across the way, the train has chugged into place, hooted its signal and burped a gulp of smoke. Among the black, brown and cream flurry of disembarking movement is a band of slick confidence men. These are the type who flash a gold-toothed smile, spin a likable tale and shake a gentleman's hand while robbing him blind.

Their games aren't exactly new. Carnies know them, as do pickpockets, railroad grifters, hobos and card shufflers. But this is something bigger – more organized. They're promoting "The Big Store," organized by a dude named Slick Wilson, affiliated with master con Ben Marks out of Council Bluffs, Iowa. Wilson is about to launch a smoke and mirrors charade, involving a cast of players. The crux of it involves a purported prizefighter, Ivanovich, the Terrible, and his bored, extravagantly rich benefactor, Gordon J. Snodgrass III. They are arriving now in a private Pullman car and the marching band has struck up a rousing welcome.

According to advance posters, the fighter will be pitted against anyone bold enough to give it a try. To stir the pot, a huge gold safe filled with cash is off-loaded under guard and rolled into position. When the crowd scrambling toward it is thwarted by two huge bodyguards, someone calls out, "Look at that tiny glass window. How do we know that thing is all the way filled with cash money?"

"Fool," says one of the bodyguards. "It's plumb full to the top."

Just then, applause clatters because the prize fighter's slick pompadour has appeared. It gleams in the sun. His fierce, dark handlebar mustache barely moves as he pumps a beefy arm. Right behind him, ignoring applause and the crowd, is Snodgrass. Whispers through the crowd have it that he made his big buck as a railroad and utilities heir. In an affected aristocratic tone, he gives orders to the Negro porter who then hoists expensive-looking bags onto a cart. The band ends a rousing rendition of "Hello Ma Baby, Hello Ma Honey" as the entourage heads toward the hotel.

Watching from behind his newspaper on the hotel porch, Wilson observes Snodgrass. Slender. Elegant and dapper in monocle and black morning coat, he uses a cane, a well-placed prop. It's ornate and hand-carved from some exotic place he's never seen.

The organizer checks his watch. Timing is crucial.

On cue the band begins playing the "Star Spangled Banner" and the fighter takes his place on stage beneath the red, white and blue buntings. He preens, bowing and pumping his massive arm to the hoots and hollers from the appreciative crowd. Behind him an announcer booms out, "Anyone willing, able or foolish enough to take on this decorated, undefeated Bulgarian, line up, sign up." He says nothing about the gold chest but tells them the betting booth will open as soon they have a viable opponent.

A scramble of dust and footsteps follows as skinny, flabby, puny and some just plain fat boys hustle, push, and claw their way to sign up, hoping to take "a lick at that greasy-haired goon."

Above them, those patriotic buntings flutter, caught by the same breeze that puffs and sucks at the tattered canvas revival tent where Snake Eyes Jackson is just now belting out his vitriolic message.

He points a crooked finger, railing against any man stupid enough to use his fists, gamble, carouse with impure women or seek ungodly riches. His voice climbs octave-by-octave as he flaps his arms, pounces, dances, shouts and stomps. Lips curled, he debunks filthy lucre and brands that millionaire a "fancy Dan." The sermon spirals to a pistol-waving climax and ends with a hard slap of his tattered Bible that scatters black bits of binding. Twelve sobbing, repentant sinners throw themselves at his feet begging mercy. Eyeing the offering plate and that pretty lass with tear-filled eyes, he makes quick work of it.

Next morning, twenty contenders wearing droopy long johns, striped bathing suits or sashed tights, clutch entry forms. One-by-one they audition, some clowning, others showboating or flexing. In the end, Leroy Haskell, a scrawny town kid, is selected. If it didn't look like a fair fight, it promised to be great entertainment. When the wager booth window slid open, from all appearances, no one was betting on stringbean Haskell.

* * *

Across the street, Mazy Dahlia, her eyes squeezed shut, perches on a purple, tufted hassock. Hours before, swept up in the emotion of the revival, she'd followed the preacher man home, confessing all the way. In that vulnerable moment, he'd caressed her and wept with her, begging for her soul. Then, with the soft glow of the flambeau outside transforming him into something more handsome than he was, he told her he had magical powers that rivaled the master himself. Using the parable of the fish and loaves to illustrate, he prodded her to tuck one hundred dollars inside her shoe. She balked. It was her entire savings. But he'd chastened her, chiding her as a fool and a disbeliever. But through God and, of course, an act of faith, she could prove her worth. He told her to shut her eyes.

"Just keep those pretty peepers shut all night. By morning, this money will be more. Maybe double. You will see."

Then, the good preacher showed her how to be delightfully naughty, giggling, teasing and the rest of it—and all through that she didn't peek.

When the pink light of morning tinged her eyelids, she remained still, anticipating the miracle. She heard the swish of his leather belt, the brass buckle clink, the soft thud of his gun hitting his thigh. He cleared his throat, coughed, and she heard the crisp shuffle of paper followed by the click of boot steps, then finally the creak and snap of the door.

Five minutes passed before she dared open her eyes, then she dove forward tearing at the string laces. Her fingertips touched paper's edge. She pinched it between finger and thumb carefully, unthreading a fold of white tissue. Probing further, she found more, a tight wad of it in the toe. Tissue paper, nothing more.

Flustered she stuck her fingers inside again, pulled both shoes open and used her fingers to explore inside.

Surely this is a mistake. A joke, a lesson? Is he punishing me to make a point about sin and greed? He is right. I'm a bad girl. And a foolish one, for sure.

Sauntering down the wooden sidewalk, Snake Eyes pats the bank note inside his pocket. He has pulled off this little caper, called "the tish," a hundred times, stealing cash from pretty girls with liquid, trusting eyes. It is almost too easy, but he still basks in the thrill. They never tell but if they would, he has a ready answer.

"You accuse a man of the cloth. My dear, what vile devil has seized your soul?" Then, of course, he'd beg to pray the devil away in private.

His boot heels click in tune to his whistle.

"Morning Reverend." Two ladies catch his self-satisfied smile.

He tips his hat, then twists to catch their backsides, imagining them without skirts.

* * *

Later, in the Blue Bottle Saloon, he is extravagantly loud and flashes the ill-gotten money.

"Come join me, my pretties," Snake Eyes chortles, pulling two zaftig bar girls into his arms.

They giggle and snort, snuggling happily into his rough embrace, for they are trained to entertain drunks and miscreants.

"Come help me spend this," he boasts, gently touching the pert nose of the blonde.

In the shadows, two confidence men, Pretty Boy Greghoff and Dog Face Joe, nudge each other, having picked a 'mark.' Now, Dog Face will go about reeling him in.

Pretty Boy gives Dog Face a sly wink, the two men part ways.

Dog Face is a little, squat man whose name describes his face but not his finesse. He slides onto the bar stool beside Snake Eyes, nods in friendly greeting and counts off a few seconds before he touches the preacher's arm.

"I'm traveling with that outfit that has the gold safe with all the money. I wager you've seen it?" he says.

Snake Eyes tucks his money with an unwelcoming scowl. "Yep, I seen it. So what?"

"My good man, allow me to introduce myself. The name is Joe but they call me Dog Face. I am a stranger in a strange town." He offers a hand. "May I grace you with libation? I wager you prefer hard liquor." His hand is up calling for the barkeep.

"I pray you witnessed the commotion, seen the posters around town," Dog Face continues.

The preacher raises an eyebrow. "You have to forgive my skeptical nature, but I've been privy to many a scam. I doubt that box is truly filled with cash money."

"Oh, I assure you. It's real. You can clearly see it through the glass window. The fight will be a tough one. The man is undefeated. He clobbered George Godfrey. Jimmy Carroll, out in no time. Sparrow Golden got barely a nip at him, then went down."

Snake Eyes returns a glance at the poster and lets out a low whistle. "He took out all those champs?" Snake had bet on Godfrey once and lost. If ever he had a chance to ante-up on an inside deal, he'd be a happy man.

Dog Face Joe picks up his drink and pauses for a moment to observe the movement of the other man's Adam's apple as he swallows. "It's just too bad the rich man that owns this show is such a louse."

"A louse, you say? How so?"

Dog Face glances around, then lowers his voice. "Between you, me and the fence post, Moneybags Snodgrass is not all he seems to be. Not at all a fine upstanding citizen, such as yourself, an esteemed reverend."

Snake Eyes stares at the man with the unfortunate nickname. The poor fellow actually did look like a droop-jowl mutt. Snake Eyes always marks a friendly, talkative man as easy prey, the type who shows his poker hand or blurts out secrets. A guy like that, gullible and overly convivial, and with an inside connection to the fight promoter and the fighter himself might be of use.

"Between you and me, that fellow got rich by sinister means," Dog Face says, adding, "Believe me, he has money to burn. You saw it. The box filled with money."

The preacher's eyes glisten in the interior gaslight and Dog Face picks up the scent of avarice. "Imagine day after day, seeing bundles of money, touching it, holding it but taking home a pittance." He lifts a threadbare cuff to demonstrate.

Snake turns toward the noise coming from outside of the window. A scuffle has broken out between the guards and spectators trying to see inside the gold filled box.

"Bundles of money." Snake Eyes' lips spread in a gleeful grin.

"Posh, that box is just a small thing. The real money is what that fight will bring in."

"I can see that we are two of a feather, my man," Snake Eyes says, tipping his drink.

"That was a powerful fine sermon you brought last night. If you don't mind my saying, your words touched me deep." His fist goes to his heart.

"You heard my message then? That is something." He smiles, impressed that a traveler – a stranger like this man – would do such a thing.

A burst of laughter again catches Snake Eyes' attention. His eyes stray to the corner where an unladylike display of flouncing skirts are teasing workmen. "Sinful women," Dog Face scowls. "I see you as a better man, above all that." He hushes and takes a look around before adding in a whisper, "I see you as a man I'd trust with a confidence."

Snake Eyes straightens, lifts his hat and dusts it off before setting it on the bar again. "Yes, a man of my ilk is a blessing in this Godless place. I'm sure you understand my role here. I simply befriend these lost women and minister to them, God bless their sinful souls," he bows his head.

"Amen, Brother." Dog Face waits a beat before asking, "Do you believe in fate?" He doesn't wait for an answer. "I do. I wager it's no accident we have crossed paths."

"How so?" Snake's green eyes narrow.

Dog Face's brow furrows in worry. "I am torn about telling you this. I have confidential knowledge of a plot regarding the fight, and I need advice." He nods toward the poster. Ivan the

Terrible stares back. Snake Eyes leans forward fully engaged. Dog Face shuffles his feet, appearing uncertain. "No, perhaps I should not say. I dare not unburden myself to a complete stranger, no matter your position with the Almighty." His eyes roll upward as he continues, "Believe me, I could use His help because my heart is heavy." He pauses again as if considering his next move. "If I confide in you, I'll surely risk my job with Mr. Snodgrass."

"And exactly what is your job? You polish that rich man's gold vest chains, carry his valise, shine that ivory-tipped cane or something? Sounds like a real Nancy man's job."

"You'd think that," Dog Face answers, ignoring the sneer. "Folks absolutely wait on him, hand and foot. He parades like a dandy ordering everyone to do his bidding. Tell you the truth, he's a selfish man, a penny-pincher and a cheat. He owes us all weeks of back pay. I know you, a man of God, would not treat employees as servants lacking any compensation. It's criminal. We are helpless, just helpless." He flaps his hands in despair.

"And the money in the safe is just a drop in the bucket, you say?" the reverend says.

Dog's eyes go to him. "Of course," he chuckles. "Imagine a man so powerful and rich that money is his play-toy. He treats the fighter the same way." Dog Face's fingers jab toward the poster of Ivanovich again. "A decorated prize fighter like that. I don't blame him wanting to quit. The star of the show and owed months of back pay. Without him, it all falls apart."

"Truly, I'm surprised he hasn't walked off long ago."

"I have told Snodgrass my concern. The man gets pummeled night after night, but he refuses to walk away without his money. I see his point." Dog Face lifts his bottle, takes a long swig, clears his throat and brushes his mouth with a sleeve. "You do realize how much that fight will bring in? Thousands. Wealthy Mr. Snodgrass reaps his share, and his pile gets bigger with each fight, no matter the outcome." Dog Face grasps Snake Eyes' wrist. "What would you do with a cut of that money? We should all get a cut if you ask me." He lets the idea simmer.

Snake Eyes rubs his chin. "No doubt the foreigner will win."

"The skinny ones are scrappy, but I'd bet on the champ."

"We are doomed, aren't we?"

Dog drops his head into his folded arms. After a moment of despair, he looks up again. "I am just at a loss, Reverend. Please advise me. What would you do?"

"It is a difficult proposition."

"Please, I beg the advice of a wiser man. If I had money, I'd sure pay for it." Dog Face lets the words germinate in heavy silence as the other man ponders the situation.

Finally, Snake Eyes speaks. "If the line of fools laying out money is any predictor, the farm boy will take a beating or turn tail and run. He will go home penniless for sure. But given your influence with Ivanovich, who is fed up and wants to quit, maybe there is a way for everyone to win." He rubs the butt handle of his holstered six-shooter, happy to be included in something so big.

* * *

"Welcome to the angry employees of a Smug Cad's Club," Slick Wilson says, pouring brandy from a crystal carafe. "Don't worry. We snitched it from the boss. He owes us." He smiles at Snake Eyes and passes him a box of cigars.

The preacher settles back, enjoying his newfound position of favor. Blowing out a smoke ring, he listens, pleased to be included.

The men paint the picture of Snodgrass as a rich creep living a posh life, while he refuses to pay his employees, including his fighter, who's owed months of wages. They should quit, they say, but they'd need money to get away.

"No good."

"No good?" Snake Eyes feels the liquor take hold. "Yes. Quit."

Pretty Boy regards him patiently as if seriously considering the option but Wilson speaks up. "Walk out on a big purse like that? Leave all that money on the table?" Dog Face scowls at Pretty Boy, who hopelessly shakes his head. "Is there any hope that kid can take our man in a fair fight? Is anyone betting on the local boy at all?" Wilson pours Snake Eyes another drink. The air is heavy with smoke and doom.

"But an unfair fight?" Snake Eyes offers. "What about that?"

A dismal silence falls over the room.

"Ivanovich the Terrible, take a dive?" Wilson asks, horrified. "Mar his reputation, jeopardize his title?"

Snake Eyes hangs his head but eventually Dog Face speaks up. "Perhaps the good pastor has a point. Perhaps there really is no other way? I suppose we could ask Ivanovich."

"I don't like it," Wilson says, stamping out his cigar.

* * *

Dog Face speaks quietly, although they draw no attention. Everyone else in the square focuses on the tall flambeau, which dances like a woman in a blue gown. Pretty Boy slumps on the park bench, arms locked behind his head, eyes on the flame, as if peering into the dismal future. Snake Eyes, still hung-over and rumpled, watches pigeons as they circled then land nearby.

Dog Face begins by smacking Snake Eyes on the back. "No questions asked." He nods toward his companions. It's clear they trust him in this private matter.

The preacher nods, happy to be included.

They have news. Ivanovich has reluctantly agreed to take a dive. "In the tenth," Dog says, adding that it should duly embarrass Money Bags Snodgrass.

"To tell the truth, I think this is too risky," Pretty Boy interrupts. "So he takes a dive. How does that benefit us? All that money and he walks while we all get fired and have to go on the lam. Preacher, I know you stand for what is right and good. But we are hard workers who have earned an honest wage. Should that be sacrificed to prove a man a thieving scalawag?"

Snake Eyes taps his foot for moment. *Of course.* His grin is broad. These fools have just given him the lucky ticket. "I've done my fair share of gambling," he says. "This is a golden opportunity for all of us. We simply pool our money and put it on the green kid to lose."

"Great idea but we can't bet. We're employees," Dog Face says.

Snake Eyes' answer is quick and enthusiastic. "I'll do it. I can place the bets."

Pretty Boy, his face twisted in concern, says, "I don't know. Too risky."

Snake's stomach twists into a knot. He glances toward Wilson, who is scratching his head and appears skeptical. "We'd need assurance of some sort, I suppose. There would be a lot at stake."

A question hangs in the air which the preacher answers. "I have collateral. You won't have to go on faith alone. "

"Collateral," Slick Wilson repeats, watching a pigeon peck the ground. "Reimbursable, of course, upon winning. Plus much more. No real risk. None at all."

Then playing devil's advocate, Pretty Boy leans toward the disheveled preacher. "I truly hate to cast aspersions, but I doubt you've proper funds to stake. I think we should find someone else."

"No, no. I have money. I can do it," Snake Eyes pleads.

He's bilked dozens of parishioners and more. He has lifted gold watches off funeral corpses, robbed farmhouses and snitched items from merchants. A safe deposit box filled with stolen loot and hidden in his boarding house stands witness to his crimes.

Snake Eyes leads them to his room, opening the box and eagerly showing off diamond necklaces, topaz rings, a bag filled with antique coins and a stack of currency pilfered from a Cincinnati widow.

Dog Face, watching over his shoulder, gives a disappointed headshake and nods toward the six-shooter. "This is going to be a huge purse," he says as his partner slips Snake Eyes' prized gold watch into his breast pocket. Dog Face takes the six-shooter. "You'll get this back. You'll get it all back."

* * *

Shafts of amber dust particles dance inside the fight tent. The smell of sweat and dust clog the air. Betting is furious. Eight cashiers can barely handle the last minute action.

Snake Eyes imagines changing places with Snodgrass – wearing a silk top hat, owning a pipeline and stocks in natural gas and coal. He'd hire a boat to Bangkok or Havana, buy a tropical island and dally his days away with expensive liquor, women and pleasure.

A sea of derby hats, dusty boaters, silk top hats and shiny baldheads fill the arena. Above them, in the ring, the hometown boy, Leroy Haskell, wears red, flannel long johns and is prancing a silly dance punching air. In the opposite corner, Dog Face Joe is huddled with the large, exotic-looking Ivanovich. Snake Eyes' fingers clutch an empty satchel. He knows it will soon be filled with more money than he can imagine – and he can imagine a lot.

The air is filled with catcalls and feels thick and hostile. It won't be quick but Snake Eyes hopes for a good show. He watches Haskell, his bare fists pale and vulnerable, his feet quick on long skinny legs. He knows Ivanovich might get caught up in the moment and injure the boy. An accidental knockout and everything would be blown.

By the eighth round, Snake Eyes wonders if he got it wrong. Ivanovich is going after Haskell with a vengeance. Standing, the crowd shouts for blood. He edges closer to the ring and finds himself next to a man wearing a Safari helmet, high leather boots and a linen sporting jacket.

It is Gordon J. Snodgrass himself.

"It doesn't seem like a fair fight. Your man is pummeling that lad," Snake Eyes says, his words nearly lost in the roar as Ivanovich goes into overdrive. Blood spurts from Haskell's mouth and the bell dings.

"Ahem. But isn't that the fun of the sport, ole chap? The blood? They all come to see the blood don't they?" Snodgrass answers and moves away.

In the ninth round, Haskell finds his footing and goes for a chokehold. The champ brushes him off with a cut to the chin. Suddenly, Ivanovich is on fire but the kid retaliates, hammering the Bulgarian. Dazed, Ivanovich falls back, briefly rallies, then takes a hit to the eye and another in the gut. The crowd goes wild. His eye swollen, the large man staggers, disoriented. Nevertheless, he gives a good show fending off the smaller man. Ivanovich has power and bulk but Haskell is like a mosquito that won't quit. The battle goes into the tenth round and, despite the odds, Leroy Haskell – right eye swollen, lip bleeding, bare fists raw – wins the fight.

* * *

Snake Eyes grabs Dog Face by the shoulder, swinging him around. "Lord Almighty," he screams. "We won. We won. Let's go cash in!"

Dog Face quickly shushes him.

"Take the satchel to that cashier at the end. He knows what to do. Whatever you do, don't say anything to anyone else. He will take the case into a private room to fill with the loot. It is a sizable sum so don't open it in public. You will be tempted but don't look until we meet. Do not speak to anyone. Wait for us. We will come as soon as possible to divvy it up." He slaps the preacher on the back. "You will be rich soon, my good man."

"I feel naked without my pistol and my watch," Snake Eyes laughs.

"Don't worry. You will get your gun back. I have no use for a weapon. In fact all of your collateral will be returned. Look into my eyes. An honest man can recognize another. I'll see you soon."

* * *

The train whistles off in the distance, but the street below seems strangely empty.

Snake Eyes laughs thinking of his good luck. It's fate: A chance meeting, two strangers crossing paths in a random bar. Events that led to a case filled with bundles of money. Feeling the weight of it, Snake Eyes itches to actually touch it. But he is a man of his word. He likes his partners in this endeavor. They are jovial men. But he doesn't trust friendly men as much as he trusts cash money. Walking toward the boarding house, it occurs to him that he could run with the loot, leaving them in a lurch.

* * *

Perhaps the Constable caught up with them.

A shiver courses through Snake Eyes' body as the wind tugs at his trousers. A few bars are open, but the gold safe, barricades, even the fight posters have vanished. The only sound is the flapping of canvas and his tattered revival tent, with its hand-written sign, "Repent Sinner."

Snake Eyes feels hopeless. The Dog Face fellow had a pathetic face but, under all of that, he seemed a sincere lad – simply pulling off a money scam. Snake Eyes knows the type. Perhaps the fellow will be kind enough to return the watch.

He looks for anything to pry the lock, finding only a bob hairpin. A strand threaded through reveals that it belonged to that blue-eyed girl, his victim just before he met Dog Face. The sweet, spicy scent of her washes over him, bringing a full-blown memory of porcelain skin, trusting blue eyes, flower lips and that night of tearful confessions.

The spindly pin twists in the lock, finally bending under duress and nearly breaking in half. Then the case suddenly pops open.

Tissues inside. He plows through them knowing there is more, something heavier. His back aches from the weight of the case, his wrists remembering it, heavy in his arms. His loot, the collateral must be inside.

"Yes." He sees brown leather. His holster?

"No." It is just the toe of a leather shoe.

Frantic now he tears at the tissue but there's no money, no collateral. The case is filled with old shoes.

In the sad, dejected quiet that follows, he hears something — perhaps the huff of the next train or the hiss of the flambeau or just the wind against the window, or his mother's voice — but he hears *something* whispered.

"Do unto others as they do unto you."

He scratches his head and opens his Bible to look it up.

AUTHOR'S NOTE

This story was the culmination of several ideas that came together after reading a book I'd picked up at a small town book sale. The book was a fascinating history of the con game and it blew some of the secrets right out of the water.

Reading it, I imagined a place ripe for a con like that. Hamilton County, Indiana, right after the discovery of natural gas, was the perfect setting. Then came to mind Dirty Helen, a notorious madam I'd written about in a three-part story based on interviews with her son and from her book. (In fact, in Noblesville today, one can buy a beer named Dirty Helen.) She'd remembered the transformation of her little town from Quaker village to a teeming town filled with bars and recalled the street fights and all of those men—brawny workers from Cincinnati and other towns who had come to work in the glass factories. She'd met and married one, left him, put on her red hat and danced right out of town to walk on the wild side.

I love the idea of strangers crossing paths and of that meeting changing the course of their lives. But also I love the idea of people getting their just due.

Truthfully, I never meant my story to be a moral play but it took on a voice of its own. I guess in the end, I drew a bit on my own history with fervent ministers but it was all fiction. I admit, I do enjoy the idea of the con and that is why I picked up the book in the first place. I think, however, this fascination is not born out of wanting to get one over on someone so much as to be 'in on the know.' I guess, ultimately, that is probably what got Snake Eyes into trouble, wouldn't you say?

S. Ashley Couts

A Harrowing Death
Sarah Glenn and Gwen Mayo

"Oh, look, there's the Arts Building," Teddy said, wandering away from them in the crowd. Cornelia took her elbow and drew her back.

"Arts are for after we meet Uncle's protégé, dear." The pair trailed Percival Pettijohn, professor emeritus of the Agricultural and Mechanical College of Kentucky, which was now part of the new University of Kentucky. Despite his age and need for a cane, the barrel-chested man set a brisk pace.

"It'll be good to see Ryan again," the professor said. "I can't wait to learn what new equipment he's designed. Look, there's the banner for Browder Farm Equipment. I can hardly wait to examine..."

Teddy stopped him mid-sentence and pointed her finger. "Is that your friend lying under that big machine?"

"Oh, good Lord," Percival Pettijohn said, as he spotted the man lying face down in the grass. "Ryan." He lurched forward, but Cornelia stopped him.

"Let me, Uncle. He may still be alive."

She rushed to the disc harrow and knelt beside the body. A cursory glance told her he was not, in fact, alive. One heavy steel disc, new and sharp, rested deep in his torso. From its location, Cornelia was certain the blade had hit at least one vital organ, not that it mattered. The first disc was buried in his neck, nearly decapitating him. At least death was rapid and nearly painless.

Behind her, Professor Pettijohn bellowed for help. The gates had opened moments ago, so the Fairgrounds weren't full yet, which was fortunate. Cornelia was certain the hosts of the Indiana State Fair hadn't intended this to be the opening exhibit.

One of the physicians from the Better Baby contest pushed through the crowd that had quickly gathered after the shouting started. He stopped short of the body and shook his head.

"There's nothing to be done but call the authorities," he said. "He has a near-complete laryngeal transection."

* * *

"An accident?" the professor fumed over the investigating officer's pronouncement. "How could they think it was an accident? Ryan would never be so careless with his farm equipment."

"Uncle, let the police do their job," Cornelia said, ushering him further away from the cluster of officers. "They are only speculating. The medical examiner hasn't even arrived yet."

"Accident, indeed," Professor Pettijohn grumbled. "Any fool can see the safety bar is off. This was murder. Do they think an engineer would turn his back on a heavy machine that wasn't secured?"

"You can explain that to Detective Covington again when we go to the station to give him our statements this afternoon," Teddy said. "Right now, we need to let them get your friend out from under that contraption before children start wandering over."

"Children!" the professor exclaimed. "We need to go to Ryan's company and speak to his son immediately. The boy should hear the news of his father's death from a friend of the family, not perfect strangers."

"That's an excellent idea, Uncle," Cornelia said, "But, let me check with Detective Covington and make sure he has no objections to our leaving."

Since Detective Covington still considered the death an accident, he was happy to send them off. In fact, he seemed to be in no hurry to see the professor again.

* * *

At the front office of Browder Farm Equipment, they were greeted by an employee young enough to still have some peach fuzz on his cheeks. "May I help you, sir?"

"Yes," the professor said. "I'm looking for Ryan Browder, Junior. Is he here today?"

"I'm afraid that Mr. Browder isn't with the company anymore," the young man said.

The old man turned nearly as white as his beard. "What? Why would the son of the owner leave the company?"

"It wasn't Mr. Browder, Junior's decision, sir. His father dismissed him."

"When did this happen?"

Even at his advanced age, the professor had an aura of authority about him that cowed the young man into taking a step back.

The lad tugged at his collar, unsure of whom he was addressing or how much he should reveal about his employer's personal affairs. "Yesterday," he said.

"That's ridiculous. Why would Ryan fire his own son?"

Cornelia interrupted. "There's been an accident at the State Fair. We need to speak to Mr. Browder, Junior. Where would we find him?"

"At his mother's house, I suppose."

"At his mother's? She has a house of her own?"

A flush crept above the tight collar. "The first Mrs. Browder, yes. Mr. Browder, Senior, built a more modern house when he married the second Mrs. Browder. It's quite a showplace."

Professor Pettijohn huffed.

Cornelia could see that her uncle was building up a head of steam and steered him toward the door before he could launch into a dissertation on whatever he'd gotten from the boy's statement.

"Showplace," the professor muttered as they left the factory. "That doesn't sound at all like the Ryan Browder I remember."

"I should think an engineer would want a modern home," Teddy said.

The professor stopped and glared at her. "Modern, yes. One of the qualities I looked for in my engineering students was a desire to innovate. An engineer has to be interested in creating more efficient designs, but 'showplace' implies something entirely different. And another thing: I don't know what to make of him leaving his wife and family. Ryan and Maude Browder built this factory together. Maude, Mrs. Browder, ran the business office until her son graduated from college."

"Well, I hope you don't get into that with his son, Uncle," Cornelia said. "There was obviously some friction between them. I can't imagine how I would have felt if I had last parted with my father on bad terms."

The professor stroked his silver whiskers. "You know, Corny, Junior might not have inherited his mother's skill at managing the business. He's a personable young man, but it wouldn't be the first time a son turned on his father over money."

"Don't call me Corny."

Teddy giggled. "Give it up dear, your uncle finds the nickname endearing and isn't going to change at his age."

Cornelia sighed. "There was nothing at the Fairgrounds to suggest your friend's death was anything other than an unfortunate accident."

"He was murdered," the professor insisted. "No student of mine would take the safety bar off and turn his back on a disc harrower. I taught them better than that."

"Maybe he was distracted," Cornelia suggested. "It couldn't have been easy to fire his son."

The professor's lips pressed so tightly together that his mouth disappeared into his thick white beard. He squared his shoulders and marched to the car without another word. Every attempt his niece made to break the stony silence hung unanswered in the air as they drove across town to see Ryan Junior.

* * *

Professor Pettijohn took off his fedora and brushed a stray lock of snowy hair back into place. He hesitated a moment before knocking on the heavy oak door.

"Is there something wrong, Uncle?" Cornelia asked.

"I haven't seen Maude Browder since Junior's graduation. She and Ryan were still married then. Ryan never saw fit to tell me about leaving his family. I'm not sure what had happened between them, or how Maude will take the news of his death."

Cornelia put a hand on his shoulder. "There's only one way to find out." She reached out and pulled the brass bell.

"That wasn't kind," Teddy said.

Cornelia's square jaw tightened. "Sometimes the greatest kindness is to act decisively, Teddy. I thought you would have learned that by now."

Teddy kicked her in the ankle. "Sometimes decisive action just causes unnecessary pain."

The door opened before Cornelia could come up with a scathing retort.

A sturdy woman with warm brown eyes peered at them over gold-rimmed glasses. She was wearing a simple shirtwaist dress adorned by a cameo brooch at the throat. Her dark brown hair was streaked with gray. Cornelia surmised she was a few years younger than Teddy.

"Mrs. Browder," the professor said, "I don't know if you recall me, but..."

"Professor Pettijohn! Nonsense. You'd be a very difficult man to forget."

The professor stood a little straighter. "I'm sorry to trouble you at home, but I'm looking for young Ryan. Is he here?"

"My husband no longer lives here," she said. "I can give you his address, but at this hour he's most likely at the Fairgrounds."

"I meant Ryan Junior," the professor said, color creeping into his cheeks. "I heard..."

"There's no need to be uncomfortable, sir," she assured him. "Please, do come in."

She led them to a spacious parlor. "You were so very kind to me at our wedding, Professor. I do hope you aren't put off by the failure of my marriage. It was all years ago, and I have become quite accustomed to being a divorced woman. Though, sadly, my life isn't nearly as scandalous as the magazine stories would suggest. Indianapolis offers so few opportunities for mingling with the swell crowd."

Cornelia admired the way Mrs. Browder put her uncle at ease. She could see why he was so surprised that his friend would have abandoned such an intelligent and charming wife. She was also certain Teddy could have found that 'swell crowd' in Indianapolis for Mrs. Browder. In fact, Teddy's skill at finding parties with illegal alcohol was so well-honed that she could find the local bootlegger in whatever town they visited.

"Is your son at home?" the professor asked. "It is important that I see him right away."

"I've only just returned from some errands," she said. "If you'll excuse me, I'll have Hilda check."

Professor Pettijohn paced the parlor floor as he waited for Mrs. Browder to return.

"Do sit down, Uncle," Cornelia said, "You're wearing a trench in the rug."

"How can you be so calm?"

"I'm not calm," Cornelia replied, "but the time waiting would be better spent figuring out what you are going to say. You can't come into his home and accuse him of murdering his father."

The professor started to say something but stopped when the parlor door opened and a younger, leaner version of Ryan Browder walked into the room.

"Were you saying something about Father?"

The professor looked at him and frowned. He didn't look at all like a man who had just murdered his father in cold blood.

"Where were you early this morning?"

Ryan Junior half-smiled. "And good morning to you too, sir. Our housekeeper tells me that an old friend of my father's had some urgent business with me. Just who are you and what concern are my whereabouts to you?"

"I'm Professor Percival Pettijohn, retired. Your father was a student of mine, some years ago."

Junior's eyes widened as he looked at the professor's slightly stooped shoulders and snowy hair. The old coot was remarkably well preserved. His father hadn't been a student in more than forty years.

"I think I met you once," Ryan Junior said, "when I was five or six."

"Yes. Your father brought you with him to the retirement party my former students threw for me."

A trace of a smile played on Junior's face before he grew serious again. "Those were happier times, Professor. Now, if you must know, I was sleeping in for the first time in years. Rather enjoyed my first morning as a dew-dropper. Until Hilda woke me."

"For a man who has just been fired, you don't seem very concerned," the professor said.

"You're well informed," Ryan Junior said. "Are you here to offer me a job?"

"I went to the factory looking for you, because there's been an incident at the Fairgrounds. It was rather a shock to discover your father had discharged you."

Ryan Junior gave a bitter laugh. "I wish I could say it was a surprise to me, but Father has threatened to fire me so often that he had to eventually go through with it. Once he figures out that he will have to hire at least two men to replace me and pay them higher wages, he'll come around."

"I'm afraid he won't," the professor said. "We went to see him demonstrate his new disc harrower at the Fair this morning and discovered him under the blades."

Junior sank into the nearest chair, his face ashen. "Is he badly injured?"

"He's dead, Mr. Browder."

Maude took in a sharp breath and her hand flew to her mouth.

"I don't understand," the young man stammered. "He is always so careful with designing safety features into his equipment. How could he get trapped under the blades?"

"The police seem to think it was an accident," the professor replied. "I'm more inclined to agree with you. The Ryan Browder I knew wouldn't remove the safety bar on a harrower and turn his back to the blades."

"You think he was murdered." It was a statement, not a question. Ryan Junior was watching the professor's face intently. "Do you think I killed him for firing me?"

"You think very highly of your skills," Cornelia said. "But why would he fire you if you are so valuable to the company?"

The young man's voice was calm, but his face revealed the anger their suspicions provoked. "Father thinks we can run the company the way he did when he built every machine by hand and personally delivered it to a local farmer using a pair of draft horses. I live in the twentieth century. We are competing with companies all over the nation and in half a dozen other countries."

"You were fighting with your father because he was old fashioned?" the professor said. "That doesn't sound like the man I remember."

"Father was angry because he wanted to retool his entire workshop to build a new harvester he's designed. I told him that he was over his research and development budget and the project would have to wait until we saw the fall sales figures."

"It is his company," the professor said.

"Yes, half his anyway. My mother owns almost as many shares as he does. He doesn't have so much power that he can break contracts to do whatever he pleases. He wanted to take money from the marketing budget to cover his project. The discussion turned into a fight after I told him that I had a contract to sponsor the farm reports being broadcast from the State Fair."

His eyes lit up as he talked, and he stood. "We've built a special glass broadcast booth with our company logo, and are committed to a huge advertising push as we head into the harvest season. The money he wants to use is already spent."

"No wonder he fired you, making those kind of expenditures without his consent," Cornelia said.

"My job is to make decisions. Father has no business sense."

Ryan Junior must have seen the shock in their faces. He paused and looked at Maude, who came over and put an arm around her son's waist.

"Ryan Junior has been running the company since the day he graduated from college," she said proudly, "and doing a fine job of it, too."

"I learned from the best," he said. "Mother took over running the factory before I was born. My crib was in her office. I worked there every day after school and all day in the summers. At one time or another, I've done every job in the plant. All Father has ever done is design and build new machines."

"You don't give him much credit for those designs," the professor said. "There wouldn't be much of a business without them."

"Oh, don't get me wrong, Professor. Father is very good at what he does. You won't find better farm equipment than what we build. But he would have bankrupted us if he were left to his own devices. That's a fact that the new Mrs. Browder hasn't quite come to terms with."

"I hear that she lives in a showplace," the professor said.

"Oh, yes. The house was designed by the late Howard Van Doren Shaw."

Teddy's eyes widened. "The Chicago architect? It must be truly impressive."

"Oh, yes, and costly. She refuses to live below the means she is accustomed to," young Ryan said. "She's quite the socialite."

"Ryan circulating in high society?" the Professor said. "He really did change. He preferred the company of farmers when he was my student."

"The country club was my suggestion," Ryan Junior said. "I thought it would help bring us more trade. I went to college with a fellow who put in a word for Father. I rather wish I hadn't asked. It was his sister that Father married. Not that it matters now."

Maude patted his arm. "No, it doesn't."

"Has anyone told Florence about Father yet?"

"I believe Detective Covington was planning to make the notification," Cornelia said. Naturally, the current wife would receive the visit – not the one who had spent her life with the deceased. Ryan Junior might rue his suggestion to his father, but what had followed had been his father's choice. She wondered if Ryan Senior had rued what he lost.

* * *

The trio stayed a little longer, then left to make their written statements at the police station. Once they were finished, they piled back into Cornelia's Dodge Brothers touring sedan.

Cornelia helped her uncle into the back, then slid behind the steering wheel. "Where shall we head now?"

"I think we should pay a condolence call to the new Mrs. Browder," Teddy said.

"You just want to see this house."

"Of course I do. And the widow," her companion replied. "We wouldn't want to be rude in her time of sorrow."

"Oh, and you want to be nosy, too," Cornelia muttered with a half-smile. Most of the adventures in her life had been instigated by Teddy's insatiable curiosity.

* * *

The late Ryan Browder's home was hardly the modern wonder she had expected. It sat back from the street behind a tree-lined circular drive on a lot that must have covered at least five acres. The brick and stone structure bore a greater resemblance to the country manors Cornelia had seen in England during the Great War than to the clean-lined architecture of Frank Lloyd Wright.

"Glorious," Teddy said. "If I'd stayed in finishing school, I might live in a house like that now."

"You ran away from finishing school."

"I didn't want the arranged marriage that would have been my diploma."

"Was a farmhouse in rural Kentucky what you had in mind?"

"No, but surprise is part of the fun in life," she replied as they approached the front door.

Maude Browder had a housekeeper. The new Mrs. Browder had a butler in full livery who left them waiting in the foyer while he went to see if his mistress was at home.

When he returned, he escorted them through the drawing room and out onto a stone paved patio that lead to back yard, dominated by a pair of lawn tennis courts. A pretty young woman sat at a small table reminiscent of those at Paris cafés, dabbing at her eyes with a lacy handkerchief. She still wore her tennis whites and a broad bandana around bleached blond hair. An athletic young man with dark hair and rakish good looks was trying to console her. He was also in whites, and his tennis racket lay on the table beside a sweating pitcher of lemonade.

Pettijohn bowed. "My apologies, madam, for our having to meet under these sad circumstances. I'm Percival Pettijohn, professor emeritus of the University of Kentucky. Your husband was one of my best students."

Florence Browder leaned forward to clasp his hand. "Yes, George mentioned that when he brought your card. He also said that you... found... Ryan?"

"To our great sorrow," Pettijohn said with a solemnness of tone. "This is my niece, Cornelia Pettijohn, and her friend, Theodora Lawless. They are both nurses and tried to help your husband, but it was already too late."

The young woman muffled a sob. "That beastly detective who came by said it was quick. That he didn't suffer. It was the only good thing he said."

Her companion scowled. "He practically accused her of running him down with his own machine. Wanted to know where she was this morning. Where I was, for that matter."

After seeing this young swain with Florence, Cornelia wasn't surprised that Detective Covington had become suspicious. What husband in his right mind would trust his young wife alone with this charmer? For that matter, what sort of wife would entertain young men in her husband's absence?

"He treated us like common criminals," the blonde woman said, wiping her eyes again and smudging her mascara further. "I've called my attorney, believe you me. I plan to file a complaint about his rudeness. At least he didn't question us in front of Daniel. Oh, Daniel!" Her sobs began afresh. "He has no father now."

"Ryan has another child?" the professor said. "I didn't know."

"Daniel's only a toddler. He's with his nanny. I didn't want him to see me like this. At least he's too young to understand what's going on."

Cornelia wasn't so sure she understood what was going on in this household; certainly more than met the eye. Otherwise, Mrs. Browder wouldn't have called her attorney so quickly.

"I told Detective Covington that if my husband was murdered, he should be looking closer at Ryan's first son," Florence added. "Did you know Ryan fired him for mishandling company funds?"

"Oh, dear," Teddy said. "He was stealing from the company?"

Florence looked over at Teddy, who seemed genuinely friendly. She seemed to think for a moment, and then admitted, "Ryan didn't mention true theft. But Junior was spending money earmarked for Ryan's important work on frivolous things, like radio sponsorships and hiring new people. Probably cronies of his."

"What did the detective make of that?"

"He said he would make inquiries. I hope he is at least half as rude with that selfish lout as he was with me."

"You don't get on with your stepson?" Cornelia said.

"I did at first. He and Charley, my brother Charles, are fraternity brothers. We used to run together." She dabbed her eyes and gave an exaggerated sigh. "Since he's taken over the company finances, Ryan Junior thinks the whole factory belongs to him. He really got in a lather when his father decided to change the will and leave his shares to Daniel."

"Ryan disinherited his older son?" The professor stared in disbelief at the young woman.

"Mr. Wilham, our attorney, said that Ryan hadn't signed the new will. But Ryan Junior knew his father was going to see that Daniel got his fair share of the company."

It didn't seem fair to Cornelia that the son who spent his whole life being groomed to run the company would be made second fiddle to a toddler. But she didn't say that aloud. "Had your husband neglected to make a new will since his family circumstances changed?"

Florence didn't meet her gaze. "He's made several since we married. The last was just after Daniel was born. In that one, his shares were split between his sons. That's hardly fair. Ryan Junior will inherit his mother's shares. He'll be three times better off than his brother."

"Did you tell Detective Covington about the new will?"

"Of course." Florence said. "I'm not going to let Ryan Junior cheat his brother out of his rightful share of the estate. Mr. Wilham says we might be able to break the will."

All traces of being grief-stricken had vanished. Under that mop of bobbed hair, Cornelia could almost see the wheels turning inside the current Mrs. Browder's head. She wondered if young Ryan knew his step-mother's machinations were behind many of his troubles with his father. Still, she couldn't see Florence killing her husband before the new will was signed. Unless he had figured out what she was doing.

* * *

They returned to Maude Browder's house to find a small gathering. Several of the factory's employees had come to pay their respects to the family. Cornelia thought it was very telling that they had come to see Maude before visiting Florence. There was little chance for her to say anything to Maude about her visit to the new Mrs. Browder. Every few minutes, another employee arrived with flowers or a covered dish. Maude knew all of them well enough to ask by name after family members not accompanying them.

Cornelia noticed that Ryan Junior was equally familiar with the factory staff, which lent an air of credibility to his earlier statements about growing up at the factory. He was having a more difficult time talking than his mother had. More than once, his voice broke when he spoke about his father. She found it difficult to believe that he was a murderer.

Detective Covington arrived with another officer Cornelia remembered seeing at the Fairgrounds, though she couldn't recall his name. He was a tall, lean, young man and looked acutely uncomfortable having to accompany Covington. Cornelia wasn't surprised. Covington reminded her of a drill sergeant with his close-cropped hair and blunt manner.

"I paid a visit to the factory," Covington said, approaching Ryan Junior, "and did a little checking of my own. Mr. Browder, I understand you were advertising for an open engineering position with the department at Purdue."

"Yes. What of it?"

"Your ad was prescient, sir, given recent events."

"It had nothing to do with prescience. We needed a new engineer, possibly two."

"Was your father planning on retirement?"

"Oh, no. He planned to keel over at his drafting desk. But he had begun spending less time in the office. He had a new wife, a child he wanted to spend leisure time with," Ryan Junior said, the latter with bitterness. "And he had even discussed visiting Paris in the spring. Plus, I thought some new blood might be useful."

"In what way?" Professor Pettijohn asked, eyebrows rising.

"There have been several advances in the last few years. I thought it was best to keep up with the times in technology."

Pettijohn sputtered and opened his mouth but Teddy put her arm in his. "You mean that he had stopped learning? How tragic for an engineer," Teddy said. "Uncle Percival here loves getting the newest gadgets and examining them. You should see how adept he is at making motion pictures."

Ryan Junior must have realized he was offending his father's mentor. "I'm sure he was still interested in learning. He just didn't seem to have time any more. There are several unopened engineering journals piling up on his desk. Besides, the company is growing and needs more than one engineer."

"So you are saying that you were just being practical," Covington said, his dark eyes narrowing, "and the timing of your advertisement had nothing to do with your father's new will?"

Ryan Junior's face drained of color. "Are you accusing me of murdering my father for money?"

The words came out much louder than he had intended.

All around him conversation stopped and heads turned to witness what was said next.

Covington flinched but his voice remained steady.

"I have seen the unsigned will and the one it would have replaced," he said. "It was quite a lot of money, Mr. Browder. More importantly, it was control of the company. Yesterday, your father fired you and today he intended to sign a new will leaving everything to your half-brother. I would call that a motive for murder. Wouldn't you?"

"I did not kill my father."

"I hope you don't have any plans to leave town, Mr. Browder. We don't have enough evidence yet to prove that the professor here was right about your father's death being murder. But, one witness has said they heard someone running away. I assure you, my men are questioning everyone who was anywhere near that exhibit. Sooner or later, we are going to find a witness who actually saw what happened. When we do..."

* * *

"I can't see young Browder killing his father," Pettijohn said, once they were back at the home of Genevieve Gray, Pettijohn's niece and Cornelia's cousin. Genevieve had left them pot pies and a note letting them know that she had gone to see the Claypool

Trio perform at the State Fair, which made Teddy sigh wistfully. She loved live music.

"I agree, Uncle, but the police have to look at who had opportunity and motive." Cornelia took his empty dish and took it to the sink with her own.

"He had a good reason," the professor said. "Although I hope that, in the end, his sense of fairness would prevail. Young Daniel will inherit his mother's home and whatever money she has left at the end of her extravagant life. Junior has worked for the company his entire life."

"Perhaps Florence's friend, the cake-eater, did it," Teddy said. "He may have wanted her for himself. And the opening day of the Fair made a good opportunity."

"That dolt? I doubt he's ever been on a real farm, much less be familiar with the equipment," the Professor sneered. "The same could be said for the current Mrs. Browder. She might want the factory for her son but doesn't look like the type who would know about the machines they build there. Besides, she wouldn't do it before the new will was signed."

"Ryan Senior would be unlikely to turn his back on that young swain." Cornelia took Teddy's dish. "The killer would have to be someone he trusted, someone who also knew how to drop the machine on him at just the right moment. I hate to admit it but that sounds like Ryan Junior."

"Or his mother," Teddy said.

"What?" the Pettijohns said in unison.

"I just said that Maude Browder was as familiar with the equipment as her son," Teddy said a little more timidly than usual. "I overheard her talking to one of the employees this afternoon, making suggestions about how to solve a problem he was having with a harvester. He seemed to think she knew what she was talking about."

* * *

Cornelia tossed and turned. Part of her wished her uncle had not insisted that Browder was murdered. The police might not have suspected homicide. They still didn't have proof that it was anything more than an accident. If she took Uncle Percival home tomorrow, the police might still drop the case. She got up and sat by the window, looking out over the twinkling lights of the city. She couldn't shake the thought of someone deliberately dropping that harrower on Ryan Browder. Cornelia liked both Ryan Junior and Maude Browder, but was that reason enough to walk away from a murder?

Shortly after daylight Cornelia made her decision. She went downstairs, picked up the phone and called Detective Covington.

* * *

Detective Covington pulled into the driveway of Maude Browder's house just as Cornelia's Dodge rounded the corner. She hadn't told anyone, not even Teddy, that this was a prearranged meeting. If her plan backfired, she alone would deal with the consequences.

Today, a black wreath hung over the door and the drapes were all closed. They could hear voices from inside. Loud ones.

"I'm telling you, I wasn't there!" Ryan Junior's voice.

"Your car was spotted at the Fairgrounds," Covington boomed. "We can place you at the scene of the crime."

"We should get in there," Cornelia said, pushing the door open. Hilda, the housekeeper, wasn't there. She was at the edge of the parlor, twisting her dust rag in her hands.

"My car? Who says my car was there?"

"I do!" thundered Cornelia, causing everyone to jump, including Teddy and the professor. "I didn't realize it until we visited last night and saw it. A red Bay State convertible with a black top. Ding on the right fender. Pulled out just as I was parking. Not a common car around here."

Ryan Junior stared at her, his face slack. "It couldn't have been there. I was here, asleep."

"Are you suggesting a stranger stole your car and drove it to the Fairgrounds with the intention of killing your father?"

"Cornelia," the professor said, "Let's not be too hasty. There might have been a similar car in such a large town. I don't recall seeing the vehicle you're describing."

"You were looking for your friend. I was looking for a place to park. I saw it," Cornelia said.

"There you are," Covington said. "A witness. You had a reason to kill your father – to stop him from changing his will.

99

And you knew how to operate his machines. No one else involved with him does."

"That's not true!" Maude cried. "It's not true."

Covington turned to look at her. "His current wife would have wanted him alive to sign the new will. I've looked into the background of her sporting pal. He's a tennis instructor with no background in machines at all. Only your son had a reason to want him dead AND knew how to rig an accident with farm machinery. No one else involved did."

"I did," Maude said.

"You did?" Covington asked.

"She ran the office," Ryan Junior quickly said, "but she never used the machinery. She couldn't do that."

"Yes, I did." Maude was firm. "Who do you think helped him assemble his early designs? I spent many a day holding up a metal arm or working a lever as he made an adjustment."

"She's just trying to protect me, detective," Ryan Junior gasped. "You're right. I did it. And she's trying to keep me out of prison."

"You said you were sleeping and your mother said she was out running errands," Covington said. "Neither of you can alibi the other."

"I'm telling you, I did it!" Junior grabbed Covington's arm. "I went to the Fairgrounds and asked for my job back. Father laughed and turned his back. I was furious and... and... I dropped the harrower on him. It nearly cut him in half."

Covington shook loose and turned back to Maude. "And your story, ma'am?"

Maude's eyes filled with tears. "Junior put his whole life into the company. He gave everything – I gave everything – to make his father proud. It was one thing to abandon us but to put the company we built as a family into the hands of that gold-digger? I went to the Fairgrounds to talk some sense into him. He wouldn't listen. He just told me that I could come watch him sign the new will if I wanted. He turned around to pick up his wrench and I released the safety. Nearly took his head off. Not that he hadn't lost it already." She broke into weeping and sat down.

* * *

What had started as an adventure had turned into a tragedy. Professor Pettijohn, Cornelia and Teddy left Indianapolis, heading south, right after the funeral. The mood in the car was so somber that they didn't speak until they crossed the state line into Kentucky. It was the professor who finally struck up a conversation.

"Cornelia," he said. "I forgot to tell you. I've had the harrower that killed Ryan shipped to your farm."

She almost let go of the steering wheel. "You did what?"

"Ryan Junior didn't want to keep it around. He couldn't very well put the machine that killed his father on the showroom floor. I offered to take it off his hands. I knew it would be fine with you, since you aren't the silly superstitious type."

Cornelia could hear Teddy chuckling.

"He's right, dear. And I'm sure the blood will wash off."

AUTHORS' NOTE

Teddy and Cornelia, who also appeared in *Hoosier Hoops and Hijinks*, were inspired by Sarah's great-great-aunt, who served in the Army Nurse Corps at Brest during World War I. 'Aunt Dess' is a family legend due to her intrepid nature and stubborn personality. Uncle Percival Pettijohn first appears in *Concealed in Ash*, and Sarah fell in love with him. As a retired professor of engineering at an agricultural college, he has a great interest in the newest farming machinery, and the Indiana State Fairs were a perfect lure.

Sarah Glenn and Gwen Mayo

Murder on Indiana Avenue
Andrea Smith

The poster at the door made me grin. It was big with words in bold type:

Stardust Lounge Presents Chicago Jazz Vocalist Eve Dawson, July 25 and 26, 1936. 8 p.m., 521 Indiana Avenue. One dollar seventy-five cents at the door.

"That's quite a cover, Pound Cake," I said to my wife, Eve. I called her that because her skin was the same pretty shade of brown as the outside of a perfectly baked cake. "Lester must be doing all right to charge so much."

Eve squeezed my hand. "Am I dreaming? Are we really playing Indiana Avenue? Like Duke Ellington?"

We went into the club, an intimate room with gold-laced wallpaper and gold silk draperies. A curved mahogany bar snaked from the entrance to near the stage. The ceiling was painted with twinkling stars. We wound our way through white-cloth draped tables to the bandstand where Eve would be in the spotlight. The jazz rhythms that had greeted us at the club's open door were coming from a sax player, bass, two horns and a drummer.

"There's a Steinway," Eve whispered. "Waiting for your gifted hands."

We went to the band area and I stuck out my hand to the sax player. "Gabriel Dawson. My wife, Eve. We're playing with you guys tonight."

He was chunky with reddish-brown skin. He rested his sax on his knee and looked me up and down, trying to decide if I was friend or foe. Finally he shook my hand.

"Porter James. You the Chicago folks Lester been raving about." He squinted at Eve. "Says your voice is sassy as Holiday's."

Eve glowed at the compliment. "Don't consider myself in her league but it's not for lack of trying."

"My wife is modest," I said. "Where can we find Lester? We want to let him know we're here. After that maybe we can go over the set."

"There you go, all business," Eve teased. "Plenty of time for rehearsal."

"Down there on the right." Porter pointed to a hallway left of the bar.

At the end of the hall there was a door with a gold nameplate that read: Lester Sanders, Proprietor.

Fancy and official.

I knocked.

"Enter," Lester's booming voice ordered.

We did, and there was Lester sitting at a huge desk holding court with two white men in expensive tailored suits. One had a scatter of blonde hair, the other was dark haired with a thick mustache to match.

"Gabe! You ugly dog! Come on in, we're just finishing."

I touched Eve's tiny waist and guided her into the office.

The two men glanced at us then at Lester as if waiting for a signal. Finally the blond man smiled and said, "You don't want to drag your feet on this too long. I wouldn't let it pass."

Lester drummed his thick fingers on the desk. "Some decisions take me more than a minute but I won't be too long deciding."

The men stood. "Fair enough," the blond one said. He nodded at us and they left.

"Look at the colored boy cutting deals," I teased.

Lester laughed and bounded from behind his desk. Eve took off the baby blue cotton gloves that matched her summer dress and reached out a hand. Lester ignored it and swooped her into a bear hug.

"How'd this old hound talk a pretty lady like you into marrying him?" Lester asked playfully. "Must have cost him every piece of his Chicago real estate."

Eve smiled. "Oh, he did better than that. He wrote me songs and I knew our melodies would be unforgettable."

I found myself grinning again, remembering when we'd first met. It was as if I'd known Eve all my life. After a year of marriage, most times I still can't believe she chose me.

"Where's your missus? Is she real or just more of your big talk?" I teased Lester.

"Rosalee tutors after she's done teaching over at Crispus Attucks High School," Lester said, pride in his voice. "She'll be here for the show. We can grab a steak afterwards at the best restaurant on The Avenue."

"That band of yours any good?" I asked.

Lester stuck out his chest. "Man, you know I hire only the best. That's why you're here." He stared at Eve. "Don't want to make you nervous but some mighty important people gonna drop in to see if your singing lives up to my bragging."

He winked at me.

"Who would that be?" Eve's voice was calm but her eyes sparkled like they did when she created a new melody.

"Alice Brown, who owns The Crystal Room in the Walker Building. Biggest club on The Avenue."

Eve looked at me. "We'd better go over the sets. Make sure we give her something to hear and see."

I rolled my eyes at the ceiling. "What happened to we have plenty of time before rehearsal?"

Back out with the band, I warned Porter: "My lady never performs a set in the same order. She goes with how she feels." Then I slid onto the piano bench.

After two songs, Porter said, "Lester wasn't speaking out of turn. Didn't expect such a big voice from such a tiny woman. It's special the way you phrase notes. Yeah, folks gonna take notice tonight."

"That's kind of you, Mr. James." She turned to me. "Do we have time to go to that hotel Lester has for us and freshen up for the show?"

I took my watch from my suit coat pocket. "Long as you don't try on fifty gowns before you figure the first one was perfect."

Eve made a face. "Oh, hush." She searched around the piano

bench. "Shoot. I think I left my gloves in Lester's office."

I started to move but she waved me off. "I'm not helpless." She twirled on her stacked heels and trotted away.

I went over to the bartender to get directions to the Fairmont Hotel. He was telling me how Louis Armstrong was staying there next weekend when Eve came rushing back wearing an expression that said she'd seen a monster.

My heartbeat picked up speed. "Sugar, what's wrong?"

She waved her gloves. "On the desk right where I laid them. Let's get to the hotel, darling. We can't be late for our first Avenue gig."

Outside, the truth tumbled out.

"Lester's office door was open and I thought he was in there alone so I didn't knock. Just went right on in. Gabe, that man with the mustache was beating up on Lester!"

My body went rigid. "He didn't try to hurt you did he?" I turned back toward the door. "We'll go..."

"No!" She grabbed my arm to stop me. "He left when he saw me."

"He didn't come past me."

"He must have gone out a back entrance. I asked Lester if he was all right, if he wanted me to get you and he laughed and said absolutely not and that he would see us here for the show. What are we going to do?"

I took in a breath. "Nothing. Lester's stubborn and proud. I won't do a thing unless he asks me to."

* * *

The Stardust was overflowing when we got back. Lester took us to his special table and introduced us to Rosalee, a nice-looking woman with her hair in a topknot. She wore a business suit, which was plain compared to the other ladies' frilly party gowns.

After we chatted a while, Lester's MC took the stage to introduce us.

Porter, now wearing a tux and with his hair slicked down, winked at Eve. She looked like a goddess in her gold, strapless gown. She closed her eyes for a beat, then that sultry alto voice broke into an upbeat jam I'd written for her.

Do I love you? You know I do. I do. Darling, I do.

Love you more than the sky is blue. I do. Darling, I dooooo…

Joy at Eve leading with my song came out in my fingers that skipped across the piano keys. Porter jumped in, blowing a sweet riff on his sax. Folks clapped and some got to their feet to dance, leaving the troubles of the day behind for a time. Then like a needle skidding on a phonograph…

"Police!!!! Everybody stay right where you are!"

The band stopped. Ladies screamed as police in uniforms and plain clothes swarmed the tables, knocking over the elegant wine glasses.

Two plain clothes cops stormed the stage. One asked, "Which one of you boys is Lester?" He was wearing a fedora. Sweat trickled down each side of his face.

"That would be me," Lester said, striding toward us. He was calm. Like he was used to the harassment. "My license is up to date."

Before Lester could reach us, four cops slammed him to the ground and twisted his thick wrists into handcuffs. Rosalee screamed. Eve's hand flew to her mouth. It was all I could do to stay rooted in my spot.

The police yanked Lester to his feet and the fedora-wearing cop said, "This ain't about a license. Show us your back entrance."

Lester told Porter to go back to playing. I told Eve to stay with Rosalee. She gave me a look that said I might as well have been talking to a sack of flour. They were behind me when I followed Lester and the cops.

In the alley, a few feet from the door, were more cops standing over a body. When we got closer I could see it was Lester's visitor with the mustache. The man Eve said hit Lester.

"You know him?" the cop asked Lester.

"I know who he is. Doesn't mean I had anything to do with this."

Fedora got in Lester's face. "We got a tip that says different. Somebody saw you shoot him."

Lester knew not to make a move. He just said, "Be pretty stupid of me to kill a man and leave his body behind my place."

The cop hitched his pants. "Did anybody say you was smart?"

"Who gave you this tip?" Eve said.

The cop turned a scowl on Eve. "You are?"

Eve flipped her gold silk shawl over her shoulder. "A friend."

Fedora's mouth twisted into a smirk.

"Take him," he ordered his cops.

* * *

The Stardust cleared out fast. Porter said he would lock up; we told him we would take Rosalee home, which was a russet brick bungalow on Vermont Street. She led us into a small, clean parlor with table tops filled with pictures of her and Lester wearing wedding finery and deeply-in-love smiles. Rosalee collapsed into a soft flowered chair.

"Can we get you anything?" Eve asked.

Rosalee stared straight ahead, trancelike. "Lester didn't do this. All he ever does is help people. Everybody comes to him when they're in trouble. Lord, my folks are going to tell me I told you so. They weren't happy about me marrying Lester. They don't understand this jazz stuff. They think it's low class."

Rosalee's eyes widened as if she realized she might have said the wrong thing.

"Sorry. I didn't mean..." Her voice trailed off.

"No need to be," Eve said in a patient tone. "I'm proud of the voice God gave me. Music can get you through hard times. Jazz is sorrow being made happy. There were two men with Lester when we got to his office. Do you know what he was meeting with them about?"

Rosalee shook her head. "He's been going on about some union deal. We have to get our lawyer. We have to get Lester out before those cops hurt him."

* * *

At nine the next morning, we were at the Indianapolis Jail on Washington Street. I told an angry-looking cop that Eve was Lester's sister and we'd come in place of Lester's wife. Two hours later they shuffled me into a room where I had to talk to Lester on a phone with us separated by glass.

I was glad Eve hadn't been able to come back. The right side of Lester's face was big as a grapefruit and his right eye swollen shut.

Cops had had their fun.

"It's an improvement on your ugly mug, my man," I said, laughing.

Lester tried to smile but his swollen lips couldn't cooperate. "Sure I never looked better. Rosalee?"

"We saw her home. She's holding up, I think. I told her we'd talk to your lawyer."

Lester bobbed his head. "Alfred Carr. A good man. He's helping me with a deal and he got some of my guys out of a jam before. His office is in the Walker building."

We eyed each other a minute.

"What's really going on?" I asked.

He focused his open eye on me. "You asking me if I did it? You think I killed a man?"

"Lester..."

"You've known me since we were sixteen and jamming in Chicago. You think I'm capable of killing?"

"Come on, you know better. Eve saw him hit you."

"A little disagreement."

"So he hit you for nothing."

He didn't get a chance to answer because the two guards came up behind him and one snarled, "Time's up."

Before they snatched the phone from him, Lester got out, "Don't worry about me. Just look after Rosalee."

When I got back to the waiting area, I replayed the visit for Eve.

Eve clucked her tongue. "You mean your smooth talk only works with me? Well, maybe this lawyer will have better luck with him than you did."

* * *

The yellow brick Walker Building was shaped like a slice of pie. Set on an angle right at the tip of Indiana Avenue, the four-story structure took up a huge chunk of the street.

"It's one thing to hear about a place, but to actually see it yourself is something else," Eve said, craning her neck to take in as much of the ornate lobby as she could. "Just think, Madam Walker made a million dollars with her hair preparations."

"Yep. Now you can get whatever service you need from

Negro businesses, including that of Attorney Alfred Carr in Suite 421," I said, moving Eve toward the elevator. "No time for admiring woodwork."

A high-pitched voice answered our knock on Suite 421. "Come in, please."

A slight, fair-skinned Negro man was behind a neat desk. A small fan on a file cabinet behind him whirled mightily to cool the hot office to no effect.

I apologized for just showing up and explained, "Lester Sanders sent us."

Carr waved his hand at the two wooden chairs in front of his desk. "Yes, I heard about his misfortune."

"Can you help him?"

Carr put a pad of paper on his clean desk. Made me wonder just how many clients he had.

Carr lifted just his eyes to look at me. "This isn't some club fight. This is murder and someone claims to have seen him do it."

"How do we know the police are telling the truth? As his lawyer can't you demand to know his accuser's name?" Eve asked.

Carr gave her a patient look. "I know Lester couldn't have done this. I just want you to know it won't be easy. Cops in this town..." he shook his head. "Let's just say innocence is the last thing they care about."

"Do whatever it takes," I said.

Carr stared at me a minute. "If we get bail, it's going to be costly."

"You get him out," I said. "We'll take care of the money." I stood up, reached across the desk to shake his hand. "We'll be at Lester's house later this afternoon."

"I'll come see you," Carr said.

In the elevator, Eve said, "He didn't sound too hopeful."

"Maybe he's just being honest. Odds aren't on Lester's side."

"My mother taught me to ignore the odds. If we had rolled over because of the odds, my family would still be in a shack in Memphis and I wouldn't be singing."

"And that, Pound Cake, would be a tragedy," I said.

We were almost at the front entrance when Eve came to an abrupt stop. "Look, Walker's Beauty School. I think I'll get my hair done."

"Now? But your hair looks just fine."

"Can't just look fine, silly. It has to look spectacular. Besides you can learn all kinds of things in a beauty shop."

She took my arm and led me to the shop. I took a seat in the reception area near the window but close enough to the first chair where Eve was being attended so I could hear the conversation. I picked up *The Record*, the Negro weekly newspaper, from the stacks on the table in front of me. My gut tightened at the front page headline:

Stardust Lounge Owner Faces Murder Charge

Stardust Lounge owner Lester Sanders was arrested on suspicion of murdering William Kramer, business partner of Martin O'Hara. The partners have interests in multiple businesses. Police say an anonymous tipster claimed to have seen Sanders shoot Kramer. Police have not located the murder weapon and have not released a motive.

I pictured Lester's swollen face and Rosalee's tearful one.

"Isn't that something about that club owner being arrested?" Eve said to the woman doing her hair. "That kind of thing happen often in this city?"

"Chiiiiiiile, Indianapolis can be rough at times. Such a fine-looking man, that Lester Sanders. Can't imagine him doing something like that. Do you want your hair bumped or in an up do? You have the cheekbones for a French roll." The woman lifted Eve's thick hair back from her face.

Eve peeked at herself in the mirror. "Hmmm. I'll go with up."

"Maybe that Mona Bishop can help him," a stylist in the chair behind Eve said, giggling. The hot comb she was running through her client's hair sizzled as it straightened the natural curls.

"Oh, I don't know about that. I heard their falling out was pretty ugly," Eve's stylist said.

"Who's Mona Bishop?" Eve asked.

"Owns two clubs and the Southern Cookery restaurant. She's not as rich as Harold and Oscar Simpson... those brothers own half of Indiana Avenue... but she makes a ton of money. Know what they say about a woman scorned and all."

"Do tell," Eve coaxed.

"Honey, they was quite the item for years. I got it on good authority she gave him the seed money for his club. Imagine how she felt when that fine man married that school teacher."

Eve's eyes locked with mine. "Must have cut her heart to pieces."

"I heard a few plates went to flying in that restaurant. What do you think?" the hairdresser said, twirling Eve's chair around to face the mirror.

Eve smiled at the reflection. I couldn't help but think the updo would have been perfect for tonight's show if we'd been giving it.

"Beautiful," Eve said.

"Twenty-five cents," the stylist said.

I stood, gave her fifty cents.

She gave me a puzzled look. "Where you folks from again?"

"Oh, a little ways north," Eve said. "Thanks for the styling."

When we were back in the car, I showed Eve the newspaper article about Lester's arrest.

"Sure doesn't say much about Kramer or this O'Hara. And why didn't you tell me about Lester and Mona Bishop?" Eve asked.

I turned towards her. "Because Lester never told me about it."

"What kind of friend are you that you don't know these things?"

"Pound Cake, there may be a lot of things I don't know about Lester, but I know for sure he didn't kill that man."

Eve was silent a minute. Then she said, "We should go see this Mona Bishop. If she cared about him once maybe she'll help him. Maybe she knows something about this Kramer and O'Hara. We could see if she's at her restaurant."

The word restaurant made my stomach gurgle. We hadn't eaten since we were on the road yesterday. "You get no argument from me. I could eat a table right now."

"Gabe?"

"Yes, love?"

"Don't you ever even think about cheating on me."

I tried to keep a straight face when I said, "You expect me to ignore the pretty ladies who flirt when we're on the road?"

She punched me on the arm. "Find that Southern Cookery on your map, man."

* * *

The aroma of fresh baked bread brought my taste buds to attention when we stepped into the Southern Cookery. A young woman was stacking menus at the hostess stand. "Can't say how long a wait it will be," she said right away without even looking at us.

"We have time," Eve said. "But we were wondering if Miss Bishop is here?"

The hostess lifted her eyes and gave us a skeptical once over. "Come again?"

"A friend told us we had to eat here when we came to town and to make sure we personally said hello to Mona," Eve said matter-of-factly and swiveled her head to take in the place. "So is she here?"

"She's here. I'll seat you and see if she's available."

"Splendid," Eve said.

I ordered the meal I would have had at dinner with Lester the night before – steak smothered with sautéed onions, mashed potatoes and the smoothest brown gravy I'd had in a long time. Eve had a knack for cooking and I was fair, but being on the road neither one of us got to use those skills much. She ordered a smothered pork chop and rice. We both had sweet tea.

"It seems we have a mutual friend."

We looked up at who the smoky voice came from. Mona Bishop was tall and shapely. She wore a white dress splashed with red flowers, lipstick the same color as the flowers contrasting her cinnamon skin. She had a bearing like she owned the world. I sprang to my feet.

"A gentleman who stands up for a lady. Not many of you around these days. Please, do sit down and finish your lunch," Mona Bishop said. "I hope that steak was prepared to your liking."

I glanced down at the bone on my plate, all that was left of my meal. "Well done but tender like I ordered. Gabe and Eve Dawson. Friends of Lester Sanders."

Mona Bishop looked from me to Eve.

"The couple that played Lester's last night." She smiled at Eve. "Heard you had folks on their feet for what little of the show there was."

"We're trying to help Lester," I said.

Mona Bishop folded her arms. "Are you a miracle worker? They say he killed a man."

"You think Lester is capable of such a thing?" Eve asked.

The two women locked eyes a minute.

"Didn't say that," Mona Bishop said. "But once you get into trouble in this city, it's hard to get out. Then there's the little matter somebody said they saw him do it. That's even harder."

Eve pressed her lips together. "Do you know anything about the man they say Lester killed or his business partner?"

"Only what I've heard."

"That is?" Eve asked.

Mona Bishop gave a sophisticated laugh. "My, you're full of questions. Sounds like you want to do the cops' job."

Eve took a deep breath. "When I was twelve, police dragged my brother away in the middle of the night. They said he'd robbed a store and killed the owner. My brother was home with us that night, but they wouldn't believe us. He was only nine. We never found out where they took him. Never saw him again."

Mona Bishop was silent. Then she said, "Wish I could help but I really don't know anything. Enjoy your lunch. It's on the house."

With that, she sashayed away.

I reached across the table and covered Eve's hand with mine. Sad it was all I could offer to help with a hurt that would never go away.

* * *

With full stomachs but no answers, we went back to Rosalee's to wait for Alfred Carr. Rosalee's eyes were red; she was wearing the same dress from yesterday. But her tone was happy.

"Come on in the kitchen. I'm fixing Lester's favorite meal for when he gets home today. You folks must be starving."

Eve and I exchanged a glance.

"We had lunch already," Eve said. "Mr. Carr is supposed to drop by and let us know what he learned about Lester's case."

"Lester's going to gobble up this meal. Best meat loaf I've ever cooked," Rosalee said as if she hadn't heard Eve.

The doorbell rang almost making me jump. "I'll get it."

I opened the door to Alfred Carr. His hangdog expression told me he didn't have good news, but I was going to let him tell it.

"Lester?" Rosalee called coming into the parlor. Puzzlement replaced her smile when she saw only Carr standing there. "Where's Lester? I... I thought you were getting him out?"

Carr cast his gaze downward. "I'm sorry. No bail. And they filed murder one charges. That's the death penalty in Indiana."

Rosalee let out a wail and dropped to her knees. Eve and I both sprang to her side. We helped her up and guided her upstairs to the bedroom. I left Eve to settle her and went back down to grill Carr.

"That's it?" I asked.

Carr clutched his briefcase. "We may have a defense. Lester was worried about his club. He had a temporary breakdown."

"You think cops buying that?" Was the man's lawyering skills really this bad?

"It may be all Lester has," Carr said. "I'll be at my office."

All I could do was shake my head as I watched him high-tail it out.

"What now, Gabe?" Eve asked from the stairs. "We can't just let them make Lester pay for something he didn't do."

I searched my brain for an answer.

"I've been thinking about our visit with Mona Bishop," Eve said. "Doesn't it seem odd she wouldn't know anything about this Kramer and O'Hara? Well-off, well-connected woman would seem to make it her business to know people like them."

"It would seem," I agreed.

"What time is it, darling?"

I took out my watch. "Two-thirty. Why?"

* * *

The why was Eve thought it a good idea to get a first-hand look at O'Hara's operation. I got his office address from the phone book, and we were now parked a little ways from it behind the taxis lining Meridian Street.

"Just what do you plan to say to the man if he's in there?" I asked.

Eve gave me an impish smile. "We need a manager?"

"Here I thought I was doing a pretty good job at that." I reached for the door handle when Eve touched my arm.

"Look," she whispered.

Mona Bishop was coming out of O'Hara's office.

"Somebody lied to us," Eve said.

We watched Mona get in a taxi and get sped away.

I moved to get out again. Eve stopped me again.

Now O'Hara scurried out.

"And somebody's in a hurry," Eve said.

O'Hara got into a Chevrolet parked two cars in front of us.

"We have to follow him, Gabe."

When the car pulled out, I eased out behind it. Tailing O'Hara led us to the Stardust. We waited for him to go in, then got out and slipped inside. We watched him bounce to the front where Porter James was sitting at a table, cleaning his sax. We ducked into the coat room, trading not being seen for being able to hear what was being said. O'Hara took an envelope from inside his suit jacket and handed it to Porter, slapped the sax player on the back. Then he trotted back up front and out the door.

"Mona and Porter working with O'Hara?" Eve whispered. "We need to tell Carr."

We found a diner with a payphone close by and I called the lawyer.

"I'll look into it right away," was all he offered.

Of course, Carr's response wasn't enough for my lovely Eve.

"While he's looking, maybe we can get that Bishop woman to tell the truth."

* * *

The Saturday evening crowd was filling up Mona Bishop's Cotton Candy club. It wasn't as high-end as Lester's place and the band that was playing a Cab Calloway jam couldn't match Porter's. I wondered if she resented Lester's club doing so well.

Dressed in shimmering silver, Mona was at the bar, legs crossed and smoking a cigarette. She laid her confident smile on us. "Look who decided to join us tonight. Carlton, drinks for this elegant couple."

I waved him off.

"They refused Lester bail," Eve said.

Mona's expression was blank. "That's too bad."

"Is that what O'Hara said, too?"

Mona took a drag on her cigarette. Slowly blew out the smoke. "How would I know what he would say?"

"Maybe because you paid him a visit today?"

Mona squared her shoulders. "Says who, honey?"

Eve squared hers. "We saw you leaving his office."

Mona's eyes hardened at Eve. "You two make a habit of following people?"

"You make a habit of framing people for murder?"

Mona stabbed her cigarette out in the glass ashtray. "And what do I get out of doing that?"

Eve said, "Oh, I don't know, revenge because Lester married another woman?"

Mona stared at Eve.

Then she surprised me by bursting into laughter. "You think I double-crossed Lester because he broke my heart? Lady, you're so wrong, you..."

She didn't finish the sentence.

Craaaaaaaaaaaaaaaaasssshhhhhhhhhh!!!!!

The sound of shattered glass came first. Then tables nearest the entrance went up in flames. Mona Bishop almost tumbled from the barstool, stood looking hypnotized at the fire. No one moved to try and put the fire out, people just fought their way to the side exit. I figured that was a good idea and grabbed Eve and Mona by their arms. "This way. Hurry."

Outside we weren't met with the sounds of sirens. It seemed the fire department was in no rush to save a business on The Avenue. So we stood across the street from the club with the rest of the shocked onlookers and watched thick black smoke clog the early evening sky.

* * *

For the first time since we'd met her, Mona's haughty self-assurance was gone. She stood with her arms crossed hugging herself. Mumbled, "That vindictive…"

"O'Hara?" Eve asked.

Mona's gaze was locked on her smoldering club. "That lowlife threatened to have our licenses yanked if we didn't cut him in. Lester's business was going to triple if his union deal worked out. Union musicians meant he could book better acts and charge more."

"That's what he meant when he told Lester it was an opportunity he couldn't pass up?" Eve said.

"What?" Mona asked.

"We saw O'Hara and Kramer meeting with Lester. That's what O'Hara told him. You couldn't go to the police?"

Mona clicked her tongue. "Honey, cops getting their cut, too. I didn't tell Lester but I was already talking to the Simpson Brothers about selling them both my clubs and keeping Southern Cookery. Made up my mind when Lester got in trouble. I signed the papers today and told O'Hara he could stop hounding me because I don't own them anymore. Guess it made him mad enough to have my place burned down. He just wants everything."

"It was all business with you and Lester? People said you went into a rage when he married."

Now Mona looked at Eve. "Ugly gossip. Being a woman in this business is no jam session. Lester looked out for me. He's a good friend. If I find out who that scum paid to burn Cotton Candy, I'm going to make sure they rot in jail."

"We think we know," I said, and told her about Porter meeting O'Hara.

"Where's your car? Let's go get him right now," Mona said.

"You think O'Hara paid Porter to kill Kramer?" I asked. "Why kill his own partner?"

Mona stuck her chin out. "Because of me."

We waited for her to continue.

"You wondered why I wasn't pining over Lester. Bill Kramer was why. We'd been together for months. He was trying to get

O'Hara to leave me and my club alone. I didn't think it would get him killed."

* * *

Porter was packing his sax when we got back to the Stardust. "You seem in a rush," I said.

Porter grinned. "Might have a gig at the Tulip House. Don't know if we ever going to open here again and I got to eat."

"O'Hara didn't pay enough?" Mona snarled.

Porter blinked rapidly. "Sorry, Miss Bishop. I don't know what you're talking about."

"The Dawsons saw him paying you off."

Porter kept packing his instrument. "I did some work for O'Hara. Like I said, man's got to eat."

"Burning down my place kind of work?"

Porter's gaze jumped from me to Eve to Mona. "You accusing the wrong man." He dropped the mouthpiece of his sax and bent to pick it up.

At that moment, Mona rushed toward Porter, reached in his pants pocket and snatched out a wad of cash.

"How'd you earn this?"

Porter grabbed the money. "That's my business. Busted my chops for Lester when he was struggling. He get on his feet and what's the first thing he wants to do? Jump into the union. He knew I couldn't get in."

"You didn't give it a chance," Mona said.

Porter shoved the money back in his pocket. Kept his eyes on us while he closed his sax case. "Mine was the first name Lester gave 'em and they turned me down."

"You killed Kramer to frame Lester over the union when all he did was try to help you?" I said.

Porter's shook his head almost violently. "Naw, naw. You not putting no murder on me."

"Hello?" someone called.

We turned to see Carr zig-zagging among the tables. "Thought I might find you here."

"You're just in time," I said. "Porter was about to tell us why O'Hara gave him a bunch of money. Payoff for a murder maybe?"

Carr's voice deepened with more confidence than we'd heard before. "Well, the police might want to know that too." He turned to Mona. "Shame what happened to your club just as you were about to sell to the Simpsons."

"Naw, not happening that way because I didn't kill nobody," Porter said.

"What did you say?" Eve asked.

"I didn't kill nobody," Porter said again.

"You, Mr. Carr."

Carr looked confused. "I'm sure police will consider the payoff a reason to question Mr. Porter about Kramer's murder."

Eve moved closer to me. "Mona, did you tell anyone besides us and O'Hara you sold the clubs?"

"I certainly did not," Mona said.

Eve gave Carr a fiery stare. Stepped toward him. "The only way you could know is if O'Hara told you."

Carr smiled, whipped out a pistol, grabbed Eve to him and put the gun to her temple.

The tendons in my neck tightened. "Take your hands off her."

"Lester said you're a good man. Why would you do this to him?" Eve asked.

"Look around, dear. Not all of us are making tons of money off the Avenue night life. I was about to lose my practice because of this Depression. My home. O'Hara's deal gave me a chance to save it. All I had to do was make sure the union turned down Lester's musicians. The deal would fall through and his business would get so bad he'd have to cut O'Hara in."

Carr squeezed Eve's neck. "Things were going as planned until Kramer lost his mind over Ms. Bishop. He was convincing O'Hara to back off. Where would that leave me?"

"Under the jail, I hope," Eve said.

Carr's smile was almost demonic. "The police have their killer. I made sure of that when I had Kramer meet me behind Lester's. Next I'll help them find the gun. I could kill you all but there's no need. The police aren't going to believe Lester's friends who'll do anything to save him. I'll be long gone if they do decide what you claim has any merit."

I planted my feet wide, readying for an opening to attack. My movement made Carr jump.

"I will put a bullet in her like I did in that love-struck fool."

"You're not leaving with my wife," I said.

He pressed the gun harder, making Eve cry out. "Oh, I am."

"Not living," Eve said. Then she swung the heel of her stacked shoe back into his leg.

"Ommph," Carr grunted.

It gave me a second to spring. There was a loud pop and I was knocked off my feet. My arm felt like it was on fire.

From the floor I saw Porter leap at Carr.

Carr and Eve went down and the gun flew from Carr's hands. Porter slammed Carr's head into the floor. Over and over. I think every slam was for what Carr had just confessed to taking from him.

* * *

Long hours later the cops put Carr in Lester's place. I swear I saw a tear in Lester's swollen eye when we picked him up. Rosalee did cry when we delivered her husband.

"We'll never be able to repay you," Rosalee said, clinging to Lester. "Are you going to be all right?" she asked me.

"Not even a bullet can keep me down," I said, rubbing my bandaged arm. "Lester, why didn't you tell us about O'Hara's shakedown?"

Lester shrugged. "Figured I could work through my problem myself like I've always done."

"Told you he was stubborn," I said to Eve.

"I have to know, why did Kramer hit you?" Eve asked Lester.

"Fool thought I was trying to get back with Mona because he saw us together. We were just trying to find a way from under O'Hara's thumb."

Lester shook his head. "Can't get over Carr. Porter. People I trusted. Hadn't been for your sharp-eyed lady, I'd be rotting in jail."

* * *

The doctor ordered me off the piano for two months, so we were enjoying the rare occasion of being in our own house in Chicago. Eve came in with the mail, the crisp smell of September on her coat.

"You have a letter from Lester."

I looked up from my newspaper. "So open it, Pound Cake."

Her smile grew as she read it. "Ms. Brown wants us to headline the Crystal Room at Christmas. Lester says it'll be the biggest show on The Avenue."

"Uh oh. Guess you'll need twelve new gowns."

"There you go exaggerating," Eve said, chuckling. "Well, maybe three or four."

AUTHOR'S NOTE

The 1930s are most often associated with the Depression. A terrible time of high unemployment and bread lines. But the 1930s were also a time of great creativity and artistic innovation, especially in the area of jazz music. Indiana Avenue in Indianapolis was at the forefront of the jazz music scene. During its heyday, Indiana Avenue crackled with energy, and hardworking and fun-loving patrons flocked to the opulent entertainment venues along the Avenue to witness some of the most well-respected jazz artists in history, including Duke Ellington, Cab Calloway and Louis Armstrong. They got to enjoy new talents who were just getting their start.

I usually write about a female Chicago police detective in a contemporary setting. But I love history and Indiana Avenue's colorful jazz scene seemed the perfect setting for a historical mystery. So in *Murder on the Avenue* I introduce Chicago jazz singer Eve Dawson and her husband, Gabriel, who travel to Indiana to perform in a friend's lavish club but find their gig interrupted by murder. The couple must summon detective skills they never knew they had to help a friend in need.

Take a stroll with Eve and Gabe to Indiana Avenue where jazz greats, aspiring artists and murder are all on the stage.

Andrea Smith

The Dark Core
Diana Catt

Sister Mary Francis immersed herself in the daily task of cleaning the main altar of Saints Peter and Paul Cathedral, her place of worship and source of inner peace for the last fifteen years. While performing this labor of love, she heard the heavy oaken outer front door open behind her. Several parishioners occasionally stopped by in the evening for some quiet, private prayer time. She frowned though, as the closing bang reverberated throughout the church.

Sister Mary glanced behind her to see if she knew the parishioner who had stopped by. She knew most of the members of their shrinking community by sight. Old Mrs. Snow would have struggled with the door and might have injured herself if it had gotten away from her, whereas Mr. Arckle wouldn't have even heard it slam or cared much about disturbing other worshipers. It was neither of them. She didn't recognize the young man standing in front of the votive candles.

She was hoping the visitor would be Father Malcolm, the elderly parish priest in charge of everything. She needed to thank him again for letting her borrow the parish car today for the youth group excursion to the Indiana War Memorial. Father Malcolm was great about letting the nuns drive, but he had frowned his disapproval of her newly purchased slacks. He preferred the traditional long black habits, though he would never openly challenge the Second Vatican Council's reforms.

She enjoyed the new freedom in attire the nuns had been given, but she dressed modestly and practiced moderation in her demeanor. She often prayed God would help her avoid the temptation to succumb to vanity and its subsequent consequences. She knew from experience what problems that could cause.

In the back of church, the panel of prayer candles cast flickering shadows on the pillars and pews of the great cathedral. She caught the scent of a freshly burnt match. She whispered a quick prayer in support of the young petitioner who lit the candle.

Sister Mary Francis had a close relationship with the youth of the community. She had taught most them as they progressed through their third year at Saints Peter and Paul School. Even after financial difficulties had caused the school to close five years ago, she had been allowed to stay on as head of the youth religious education program. She thanked God for the opportunity to stay in contact with all the children in the parish, for she felt her special mission in life was to keep the children safe through education and prayer. There were so many risks facing the innocent.

She carefully lowered one of the massive candlesticks from the altar and considered how it outsized the tiny candle she herself lit in the back of the church earlier in the evening. As part of her daily meditation ritual, she would stare at the tiny yellow-blue flame and pray for God to keep the innocent safe.

When she had carefully lowered the last of the candlesticks from the altar, she sensed that someone had joined her in the sacred chancel. She turned her head toward the soft footfalls on the carpet and only caught a glimpse of one of the heavy candlesticks seconds before it connected with her right temple. The sudden sharp pain to the side of her head pulsed through her body momentarily before she lost consciousness.

When Sister Mary Francis came to, she was lying on her back on a hard, cold floor. At first, all she could see was a single bare light bulb hanging at the end of a cobweb-covered cord straight overhead. Intense pain throbbed from the right side of her head, and she squeezed her eyes shut against the glare of the light and the pain. She touched her head and felt the sticky signal of blood. Lots of blood. She couldn't remember what happened or where she was. She slid open one eye.

Along the wall in front of her she could distinguish boxes stacked four high, labeled "song books." On top of the boxes were life-sized marble statues of Mary and Joseph. Now, at least, she knew her location. She'd helped bring those statues down here to the cellar storage room after Mr. and Mrs. Cunningham donated the modern wooden statues a few years ago.

She eased herself up onto her elbow to assess the damage. Her clothes were disheveled. Her cardigan mussed with dust and debris. Her blouse draped out from the waist of her slacks and two buttons had popped off near her chest. A shock of red trailed down her white cotton shirtfront. Pain in her right foot caused her to push up to a sitting position and examine the raw, angry wound on her right heel. Her stocking was torn and the shoe nowhere to be seen. She must have tumbled down the cellar stairs and somehow crawled into this room.

The door was only about six feet to her left and help could be reached at the top of the stairs. She struggled to stand in spite of her painful foot and pounding head and took a step toward the exit. Then a laugh from behind forced her heart to lurch.

Instinctively, she scrambled to reach the door but a young man beat her to it. She drew in a breath and tried to steady herself. It would be okay. She knew all the young people in the parish. He would help her. She took another breath and looked at the thin man. Barely a man, she decided. His hair hung below his ears in dark, wavy curls and he wore faded blue jeans. The upraised fist emblazoned on his T-shirt meant something to today's youth, but she couldn't remember what. Her gaze returned to his face. She should probably recognize him from grade school, but for the life of her, she couldn't place him.

"I've hurt myself," she said. "Please, help me."

"I'm going to send you to Hell where you belong," he said and backhanded her hard across the face.

The sudden blow sent her reeling backwards to her former position on the floor in the center of the room where she lay in shock. The only thing she recognized about this young man was danger. She knew danger well enough.

"Why did you do that?" she asked, holding her hand to her cheek and trying to rise from the floor.

He didn't answer, just slowly advanced toward her, his face filled with menace.

"Oh, God," she said, as a prayer.

He stopped his advance toward her and laughed. "God can't help you now. He might have intervened the last time but I've got you alone now."

Last time? What was he talking about? He couldn't be... No, he was too young. Eighteen, twenty at the most. The other must be at least sixty by now.

Dear God, help me.

"I don't know what you are talking about," she said, frantically pulling back up into a sitting position. "There was no last time. Who are you?"

He looked at her strangely. "Try and picture me younger," he said. "You liked me younger."

He stood between her and the door with his long legs wide apart, hands on his hips. He seemed quite confident that she should know him. His eyes locked onto hers with a tight unrelenting grip. Her pain seeped into her bones and remained there, disguised as fear.

Did she really know him? The nun stared hard at his features, trying to remember. He looked vaguely familiar. He had a square, clean-shaven jaw and piercing blue eyes. Maybe she remembered those eyes. He may have been a student of hers. She tried to imagine what this man would have looked like as a nine-year-old.

Finally, he said, "Come on now, Mrs. Hart. I know you favored Larry... wanting him for your special friend and all. But you almost picked me. I know you did."

"What are you talking about? Larry who?"

"Christ, lady!" he shouted, his eyes ablaze with anger. "You sent Larry to Hell, as surely as if you had put that rope around his neck yourself. How could you forget?"

Mrs. Hart? Larry? And suddenly she knew.

"Vincent? Are you Vincent Matthews?" she asked.

"I knew you'd remember," he replied. His scowl was replaced with a knowing smile and he nodded his head.

"Of course, I remember you, Vincent," she said, with a tenuous sense of relief, "and your friend Larry. I'm so sorry he died. He was such a sweet, happy child. You both were, of course, but he was always so fragile. I never understood what made him despair so, to take his own life. I pray..."

"You never understood? How could you not understand? You teased him, all of us, with those tight dresses you wore to class and inviting us over to do errands after school. God, Mrs. Hart, what's wrong with you?"

"But I'm not Mrs. Hart, Vincent. You do know me, though. I'm Sister Mary Francis, remember? I taught you and Larry in third grade. Surely you remember me?"

"Oh no, I remember the nun. You can't trick me. She always wore black. Head to toe. I know you're Mrs. Hart. You're hiding your curves in those drab clothes but you can't hide that red hair!"

Sister Mary's hand rose involuntarily to touch her short-cropped hair. Vincent had never before seen her hair. It had always been hidden by her habit. And yes, Mrs. Hart did have red hair. But surely the similarity between herself and the eighth grade teacher stopped there. She began to feel the fear taking hold of her again as she recalled how Vincent had been institutionalized after the suicide of his best friend.

"You remember Father Malcolm? He knows me, Vincent. He's upstairs somewhere right now. He'll tell you I'm not Mrs. Hart. Please Vincent, let's go find Father Malcolm."

He paused and looked at her closely.

"There's nothing wrong with my memory," Vincent said. "And why would I want to talk to that angry old man? Fire flying from his eyes. On and on about the wrath of God. Fun was evil on earth to him. But he was right about one thing. He was right about you."

Vincent pointed at her again. "That old priest told us you were bad. Evil. We both warned Larry to stay away from you. He died and the evil should die, too."

He moved toward her again, slowly, deliberately.

"But he'll tell you the truth, Vincent," she tried again. "He'll tell you who I am. Let's go find him." Sister Mary Francis stood up, aggravating the pain in her head and her foot, and tried to edge toward the door.

"No. That won't work," he said, still blocking her way.

"Think a minute now, Vincent. You wouldn't see Mrs. Hart working late at the church, would you? I don't think she even lives around here anymore. Why were you here anyway? To find Mrs. Hart?"

His shoulders dropped a little. "I just wanted to light a candle," he murmured. "I never stop thinking about him. We were here so much growing up. I wanted a good memory for a change."

Sister Mary Francis heard the quaver in Vincent's voice. She recognized the pain.

"I saw him crying here one time. I know it was because of you. I keep thinking of him in Hell, not able to get out. Forever and ever." He hung his head and said softly, "The doctors say I'm better. That's why they let me out. But they just don't know about Hell. You can never get out of Hell. Larry can never get out."

When he looked at her again he was smiling. "And then, I saw you and I figured there might be a way out after all! Swap you for Larry."

"God is forgiving, Vincent. You can't be sure..."

"No, no, no," he cried. "Larry is in HELL! It was suicide, remember? You forced it upon him. Had him touching you. You touching him. HE TOLD ME. Me. I was his friend. He wasn't strong enough to resist you."

Dear God, that poor child!

"I went to see him that morning," he continued. "I wanted to hear the details. I couldn't hardly stand it Saturday, when he was at your house, thinking about what you were having him do. And I guess he couldn't stand it either 'cause I found him. He already looked like a devil's monster, hanging there."

She felt her stomach turn. "I wish he had tried to talk to Father Malcolm or his parents," she said.

"That priest? Are you nuts? Never. He'd already warned us you were evil," Vincent said, wiping his eyes. "And he was right!"

Vincent leaned forward suddenly and whispered, "You should have picked me. I would have been stronger."

She cringed and backed away. It was hopeless. He could only see her as that woman. And maybe that was the way out.

"Wait," she said. "You're right, Vincent. But let God punish me in his own way. Let's go find Father Malcolm. I'll confess everything to him. He'll be very strict with me, you can be certain. You remember him."

Vincent looked thoughtful for a minute.

She held her breath but her hope vanished with his laugh. "Won't work. I wouldn't get to see Larry again. See, I plan to join you both in Hell to orchestrate the big switch."

A slight smile played at the corner of his mouth.

She backed away and began to tremble. She prayed with all her heart. *God, please help me. Don't let him hurt me.*

She made another desperate attempt to reach the door, but he grabbed her from behind, around the shoulders. He swung her around and struck her across the face, sending her flying backwards. The nun landed on a pile of old vestments in the corner. The impact sent dust swirling up around her. Vincent's tall figure blocked out the single light bulb behind him, creating a dusty halo and throwing his features into deep shadows.

Oh God, not again! Don't let it happen to me again.

Sister Mary Francis struggled to her knees, tried to scuttle away. He swung his fist and made solid contact. She was thrown backward by the blow, into a prone position on the floor. She felt blood running down the side of her mouth. This time the hurt went deep. It penetrated to her soul and she felt a darkness growing within her. He moved to hit her again but she rolled over just before impact. He hit the floor instead and cursed. She lurched to her feet and tried to run. She knocked over a row of metal folding chairs that were leaning against some boxes. The sound was deafening.

He continued his slow steady advance, seemingly oblivious to the noise. She bumped into the boxes of song books, dislodging the statue of Joseph perched on top. She screamed as it landed on her shoulder and knocked her to the floor. She frantically pushed the statue off of her. Sister Mary Francis was disoriented and lost track of the doorway out of the room. She backed away from her attacker until she reached a wall. She cowered against the barrier, focused only on his approach. His expression filled her with terror. She'd seen that look on a man's face before. Somewhere long ago, out of her past, that look had been there. She screamed as he closed in on her.

He shoved her down on her back and sat across her waist. He leaned forward and roughly placed his mouth on hers, stifling her screams. She beat on his chest with her fists and struggled under him, trying to turn her head away, to get him off of her.

"You should have picked me," he said, tears streaming down his face. "I know how to be a good friend."

His trembling hand found her breast and she remembered the innocent nine-year-old from long ago who had no power to fight the evil. But she was no longer nine.

She frantically reached around her for something, anything. She grabbed the corner of a heavy object by her head, out of eyesight. She struck at the evil, feeling the satisfaction of a solid connection. The evil fell sideways off of her and didn't move. The darkness within her turned to hate and she rose up on her knees, raised the object overhead and struck, hitting him again. The powerful need for revenge, for a release from the long-suppressed terror, surged through her and she hit him again. And again. Until she knew he was dead.

And she was glad.

In slow motion, she looked at her weapon before dropping the broken chunk of St. Joseph beside the man's body. It was same statue she had helped move to the basement long ago. It seemed like an eternity had passed since she had been that nun. She slowly moved through the doorway to the hall. She only half heard the footsteps descending the stairway. Father Malcolm and Mr. Glass, the janitor, appeared at the end of the dark corridor. The priest ran to her and put his arm around her.

"Are you all right, Mary?" he asked. "We heard screams."

The janitor passed them and entered the open door to the storage room.

"Better come here, Father," he called.

"Holy Mother of God," the priest whispered when he entered the room. "Take her upstairs and call an ambulance," he directed the janitor. "Call Officer Harding, too."

She heard the priest reciting the Last Rites over the body as the janitor escorted her upstairs. He seated her in the front pew of the cathedral and left to make the phone calls.

She stared into the flickering glow from a candle at the side of the altar. Deep in its center, in the heart of the flame, she searched for the comfort of her daily ritual prayer for the innocent. But she saw only cold, empty darkness.

AUTHOR'S NOTE

The Dark Core began in a Creative Writing class I took over 10 years ago at IUPUI. I wanted to set up a case of mistaken identity and I remembered an Elvis Presley/Mary Tyler Moore movie called *Change of Habit* I saw as a kid. MTM played a nun working undercover at a clinic where Elvis was a doctor and he didn't realize she was a nun. *The Dark Core* is not a romance, however.

I used the 1960s time frame, when nuns were given the option of wearing lay clothing instead of their traditional habit, in order to set up a situation of mistaken identity. The dark psychological motivations for the characters are more universal in time.

Diana Catt

One Day at the SPA
B.K. Hart

SPA Agent Jack Sheridan was on his back staring up at the stars. He blinked and refocused his eyes. Thick clouds of smoke blew across his starry night creating a hazy, dust and particle-filled sky. Then, the wind shifted and he saw the stars again. He lifted his hand toward his face, feeling the muscles protest along his arm and back. His fingertips made contact with the blood coating his face, and he ran his index finger across the bridge of his nose. It didn't feel broken.

He heard a moan from his left and let his eyes shift toward the noise. Sergeant Patrick Sandusky was face down in the gravel yard, fingers moving on his outstretched hand.

That's a good sign, he thought. At least the man's alive.

"Sandy?" he rasped. He forced himself into a sitting position, rolled to his knees, and began to crawl toward him.

Fifty yards away, what used to be a white Cadillac was burning bright orange. Within the ring of firelight, he could see two men. They were face down in the dirt. It was too late to help either of them.

He ran his hands over the sergeant's big shoulders and down his legs. Nothing felt broken or out of place. Jack gripped Sandy by the shoulder and slowly rolled him over. There were deep gashes where rocks had cut into his face. He began to check the dilation of his friend's pupils when Sandy spoke.

"If you're getting friendly with me, we should get a room," he grunted.

"Can you get up? We need to get going," Jack said.

"What happened?" Sandy asked. He rose to his feet and looked over at the flaming vehicle. Spotting the two men on the ground, he said, "Jesus, should we check them?"

"No point. There's no way they could have survived a blast at that distance."

"Bomb?" Sandy asked, limping toward the passenger door of the dark blue Ford LTD. It was standard agency issue and built like a tank.

"Grenade started it but I think the gas tank helped it along."

"The bonds?" Sandy asked.

"They took them."

Sandy grunted.

Jack remembered seeing a large dark vehicle barreling down the drive and two armed men emerging from the cornfield. Sandy had pulled his service revolver and started forward when Jack spun him by the shoulder and shoved him down behind an abandoned tractor in the farmyard. The shock wave from the blast knocked them both off their feet and bounced them along the ground like wind blowing tumbleweeds across the plains.

"My face feels like I shaved with a machete. How bad is it?" asked Sandy.

"Ugly. Same as always," Jack replied. He slid the seatbelt on, while his hand fumbled on the seat between them picking up a thick walkie-talkie shaped mobile telephone. He handed it over to Sandy. "See if you can get HQ on this thing."

"I don't think we can get a signal out here," Sandy said. He dutifully followed his commanding officer's instructions and keyed in a number. There was a hollow, tinny ringing, then dead air. "I'll try again when we get closer to the city."

They drove in silence down the dark county roads, passing no one.

"What's the plan?" Sandy finally asked.

"Report in," Jack said, "and find out how the hell Otto Strauss found out we were at that farm."

* * *

The offices of the Stateside Procurement Agency had moved into the south tower of the World Trade Center four months after the tower had been completed. The new offices were located on the 72nd floor, which seemed auspicious since they had moved in the same year. Executive Director Richard Pointer sat behind a large mahogany desk. A newspaper was spread before him. He mumbled and cursed under his breath, shaking out the creases in the paper as he read. An impressive view of the East River reflected upon the water's surface as the sun's golden fingers painted the sky in rich orange and pink hues, burning away the husky purples from the night. Its beauty was wasted on the office's occupant that morning.

Jack Sheridan stood watching, silent in the doorway. He rapped his knuckles along the doorframe, announcing his arrival. He'd had time to think. The more he thought, the angrier he got. He had been set up.

Otto Strauss wasn't simply driving by an abandoned farmhouse in the middle of upstate New York on his way to save puppies at some animal shelter. Indeed, it would be more likely for him to blow up those puppies. Last night, Jack had almost been one of those puppies and he wasn't very happy about this realization.

Richard Pointer shook out his paper and snapped it shut, a look of disgust passing over his features.

"That damn Nixon is going to get himself impeached! I don't know what the hell I was thinking voting for the imbecile. He's the President of the United States of America and he's running around making excuses and getting caught in lies." Pointer slammed a hand on his desk for clarity. "What he should've done is said, 'Yeah, I authorized it, so what? You want this country safe or you want it taken over by a bunch of communist pigs?'"

"I am pretty sure most of the country doesn't view the Democratic Party as communist pigs," Jack said quietly then added, "Sir."

Richard ignored his comment. "With all the changes in technology, people should be smarter. Look at this terminal. It's cutting edge technology and while it isn't mobile yet, I can access information for most of the U.S. Government. Hell, all our agencies are using mobile telephone devices these days. You can get money out of a machine instead of using one of those girls at the bank. I've done it! By the end of the century, you'll be able to get money from an automated machine in places like McMurdo Station in Antarctica."

Jack Sheridan glanced at the monitor screen behind Richard Pointer. It was a thick, green window with a hard, off-white casing. He knew from experience that the average terminal weighed in around eighty pounds, requiring two men to move it in a safe and controlled manner. *Jack had a brief flash of running across McMurdo Station under enemy fire carrying a three- pound mobile device in one hand and a military issue rifle in the other, eighty pounds of bulky terminal strapped on his back.* The corner of his mouth quirked, resisting a smile. He simply couldn't see it.

"Sir," Jack began, his own military training requiring deference to a superior officer.

"Call me Richard or Pointer, I don't care. We're an informal group here. Every person in this office came from some other agency or has a military background. We'd be sir-ing, ma'am-ing, and saluting all over the place. Nobody has time for that."

"I understand, sir. Old habits die hard. Have you been able..."

"How's Sandusky? Special Forces isn't going to be happy that we sent one of their boys back all banged up. If you're going to keep utilizing his services, we're going to have to steal him away from the Army."

"He's just a little scraped. Took him to ICU and they put in a few stitches, gave him some aspirin and sent him home. He's one of the few people I can count on to cover my back, sir. I trust him. Did you get any information on Otto Strauss?"

"Well, yes, I did. Do you know for sure it was Strauss?" Pointer leaned back, steepling his fingers in front of his face.

Jack gave a grunt.

"We were on visual recognition terms over in Vietnam, and not always on the same side of the fence. Otto Strauss only has interest in projects with large quantities of money for himself. And he's not a nice guy."

"I can see that," Pointer said, dragging a file from the corner of his desk and leaning over it intently. "I didn't have a lot of time this morning, and you can't call just anybody in the middle of the night, but I checked with some contacts. It appears Strauss may be working for the German government at the moment, which side isn't exactly clear. He's sort of a free trade kind of guy, isn't he?"

"I'd call him a mercenary. I already know his background. I want to know where he is now and how I get my bonds back."

"I can't tell you that. What I can tell you is Germany hasn't been very happy since we went off the gold standard. They, like the Arabs we just got the bonds back from, have been seeking some kind of security against the Deutsche Mark losing value. They think the U.S. is going to deluge the market with paper dragons. You know, dollar bills not backed by gold."

Pointer pulled open a desk drawer and drew out an ashtray. He tamped down a pack of Lucky Strikes and slid a single out of the pack, cupping his hand over the end while he lit it. He raised an eyebrow and offered the pack up for Jack, who declined.

"Saudi King Faisal held those bonds for three years. It took an oil embargo and half their face value in gold bars to get them back. If East Germany got hold of the 1934 bonds, it's hard telling what they'd ask for. We're talking military reinforcement, coerced trade negotiations, a coup against the Soviet Union or worse. If Brezhnev suddenly found a few million dollars of U.S. gold, he could push for stronger Soviet representation in the Helsinki negotiations."

"That helps me find Strauss how?" Jack asked, hiding his irritation.

"It means we probably know where the bonds are going." Richard patted the air in a calming manner. "Jack, these bonds have been traded back and forth, held as collateral or hostage, depending on your point of view, since they were printed. They've become even more valuable since the U.S. is required to back them with gold. It's one of the few instruments Nixon's break-up of the Bretton Woods gold standard couldn't touch. Since the bonds were being held by Faisal in 1971, we were stuck with them as valid securing instruments."

He blew out a stream of smoke waiting to see if Jack would make the connection. "My point, boy, is those bonds are like a turd flotilla, they just keep floating to the top. They can only be traded in an exclusive market. You can't walk a half million dollar bond into a local bank and cash it. They require verification and validation, and there are only a handful of collectors who are qualified to do that."

"So, we do nothing?" Jack shook his head, opening his mouth to protest when the phone on Richard's desk began to ring. Jack motioned for Richard to answer the call.

Richard answered his telephone formally, including the agency name as well as his title. Jack found this a bit ironic, considering how informal the man had been with him this morning. As he listened to the exchange, he noticed a subtle change in the executive director's voice, and Jack looked up to see Richard Pointer jotting down information in a type of short hand. This side of the conversation sounded cryptic, but Jack came to acute attention when he heard the next question.

"How many of the bonds do they want to sell?"

* * *

Otto Strauss studied a map stretched before him across the console of his purposefully non-descript Chevy. He had been unable to secure an appointment with the collector until six this evening. It was just as well since he intended to spend that time scanning for an escape route should he need it. He wanted to get ahead of the curator and, if possible, check out his residence before the meeting.

Otto had been told the collector, Jacob Feinstein, worked out of Syracuse and had spent the night driving in that direction. This morning Feinstein had instructed him to meet at an estate located on Oak Hill Road almost in New York. Change of plans. Otto had turned his vehicle around to head in the opposite direction. It would take him at least two hours to make the trip from his current location, and he wouldn't have much time to check the lay of the land before the appointed meeting.

Otto was meeting his second team in the next hour at a hotel off Route 22. The associates from the evening before had already been relieved of duty as he had no interest in leaving behind individuals who could link him to the bonds in any way.

Thunder rumbled overhead and in the distance a streak of lightning flashed across the sky. It had been a beautiful morning, but clouds had rolled in just before noon, turning the landscape grey and dismal. Otto hated storms but the rain could be an ally.

He intended to use it as such today.

He reached for the black attaché he'd stolen the night before and opened it. A thick stack of certificates resided within. He slid one of the bonds out and looked it over carefully. He had studied the bonds he had been sent to retrieve via copies, renditions, and elaborate forgeries, but he had not seen a real one up close. Even now, he was uncertain. They didn't seem much different than some of the forgeries he had studied, which was why he was anxious to have them checked before returning to Germany. Germany had been deceived in 1968 by a batch of gold they had received from England. The gold had not lived up to the Good Delivery Standard and relations had been strained ever since. And rightly so, in Otto's opinion. The last thing he wanted was to pass delivery on a batch of faked gold certificates.

It could cost him his life.

The thought sent a flutter of anxiety through his stomach. It instantly turned into a flash of rage. This was how Otto Strauss had learned to deal with fear. Being afraid was not an option. Failure was not an option. He snatched the map from his console and threw it to the floor of the car. One hand tightened on the single bond he had pulled from the attaché. He forced the anger to subside, breathing in a slow and controlled manner. He twisted his neck until he heard it pop. The tension fell away from his shoulders and his heart calmed. Then, he slid the bond back inside its protective case with deliberate caution.

He turned on his FM radio and eased his car back onto the road. The song on the radio was *Money*, by Pink Floyd. "Money, get back/ I'm all right Jack keep your hands off of my stack."

That's right. Keep your hands off my stack, Otto thought. Not a stack of cash though, just a stack of bonds.

Fifty million dollars worth of Guaranteed Gold Bond Certificates.

* * *

Assistant Director Charles Edwin turned in his seat and put his hand over the console.

"Sergeant Sandusky. Good to meet you," he said.

"Sir," Sandusky said, shaking the outstretched hand. He shot a glance to the passenger seat and arched an eyebrow at Jack

Sheridan. It was unusual to see Jack in the passenger seat of any moving vehicle, and Sandusky had not been briefed on the current mission or its objectives. He had assumed it was in connection to last night, but he also knew better than to make assumptions.

Charles Edwin put the car into gear and began to drive. It was a little over an hour to the estate where Jacob Feinstein had arranged the exchange, and he intended to be there early. He wasted no time getting the car up to speed and onto the nearest highway.

"I waited to fill in Agent Sheridan until we had picked you up, so I didn't have to repeat myself. How much did Richard tell you about the bonds?" Charles asked.

"He said they were a turd flotilla," Jack said.

Charles let out a bark of laughter then sobered abruptly.

"That they are, indeed. The bonds were first printed as part of the Gold Reserve Act of 1934. Without going into a great deal of history here, they have been used as collateral for the United States Government since then in exchange for specific accommodations." Charles paused, as if searching for a better explanation. "For SPA, what that means is over the last half century, the agency has been assigned to retrieve the documents on average once every five years, give or take. The gentleman we're meeting today has been the curator in four of the last six recoveries, so he's intimately familiar with the documents."

"And he's trustworthy?" Jack asked.

"The man makes a 10 percent recovery fee in addition to any actual costs involved in the acquisition and this is just a side line for him. He's primarily a collector. He's a true patriot and he has special allegiance to the U.S. since he was a POW during WWII and feels the U.S. Government saved his life back in 1944. I consider him very trustworthy."

"And we know for sure the man who called him was Otto Strauss?" Jack asked.

"No. The man refused to be identified. Instead, he dropped a name Feinstein was familiar with and the rules of etiquette in the world of rare collections is, don't ask. If the referral is solid, it's good enough. Feinstein did however ask the man to describe the certificates in some detail and asked for the certificate series numbers. They matched what he recognized as the 1934 bond series, and he called us."

Charles drove along in silence for a few moments, adjusting his wiper blades to a higher speed in order to see through the heavy sheets of rain. Then, he continued.

"Right now, the Federal Reserve has fifty million dollars in gold bars loaded on a transport headed out of the country. It's stalled at the airport, grounded on the tarmac until we can get validation of the bonds." Charles said, "Feinstein would have been our next call once the certificates had been picked up because he's *our* guy. We would validate the certificates and the Treasury would clear the gold to leave U.S. soil. However, since we haven't been able to get our validation, the gold is just sitting there. I don't think I need to tell you how nervous this is making some people. And, the Arabs aren't happy about the turn of events either."

"Were you able to ID the bodies at the farmhouse?" Sandy asked from the backseat.

"We confirmed they were the envoy sent with the delivery. The Arabs are being very pushy about allowing the gold to leave. Their response has been to accuse the U.S. Government of fabricating the incident in order to welch on delivery. To be honest, if we had thought of that strategy we might have considered it but we didn't. Executive Director Pointer is due to retire in the next few years, and I'm next in line for the position. If this deal goes south, it's going to be my ass on the line. So I have a personal stake in making sure we get those bonds back."

"Why didn't they simply exchange the gold and the certificates at the same location, validate them on the spot? Wouldn't that have been easier?" Jack asked.

"Do you have any idea how much fifty million dollars in gold weighs? At the standard rate for today, we're talking almost ten tons. It's a major production to send that much gold out of the country, and there's only a select few personnel who get briefed on what is actually being hauled. The detail is hand-picked military guard. They get no advance notice which eliminates the chance of the cargo being hijacked somewhere along the route. It's a rather complicated ordeal."

"But the bonds are small and require a third party to validate so are easier to handle." Jack replied with a nod.

"Precisely."

"So, the mission is still to retrieve the bonds. What about Otto Strauss? Can he be eliminated?" Sandy asked.

"No." Jack and Charles said in unison, then exchanged looks.

Jack finished the explanation. "We prefer to take him alive. We need to know how he learned of the exchange and what he intended to do with the certificates."

"If it comes down to the certificates or Otto Strauss's life though, those bonds are our first priority," Charles said.

Jack turned in his seat to look at Sandy. "Strauss is a very dangerous man. Don't let him get the drop on you. If you have to take the shot, take it."

* * *

The estate at Oak Hill was a Georgian-style colonial home of russet brick. Its circular front steps sheltered by a long, covered porch painted in white and held up by matching columns of granite. A statue of a naked dancing woman stood in the center of the fountain in the middle of the courtyard. The panoramic view of the front drive could be seen from the wide plate glass window stretching the length of the porch.

The violent assault from the storm shook and rattled at the front glass window.

To the left of the home sat a three car garage. Several additional spaces were designated for parking beside the garage where a Rolls-Royce Silver Shadow sat parked. Trees lined the driveway, hiding most of the estate from the main road. The foliage thickened further away from the house, eventually blending into the wooded landscape surrounding the estate. Wind buffeted the trees, bending and separating the branches in odd and harsh angles.

Power flickered inside the home and faltered. A series of flashes illuminated the interior of the front hearth room, and its occupants jumped as the lightning was followed by a deafening reverberation of thunder, followed by a series of distant pops.

The lights flickered twice more and died.

"Well, this could make things difficult," a small, tinny voice said in the dark.

A warm female voice responded almost immediately, "Don't worry, Father, we have plenty of candles in the kitchen."

A light flared near the fireplace as she struck a match and lit the candles upon the mantel. Burgundy candles, thick and squat, let off the scent of berries. She lit a tapered candle from the mantel, and walked through to the kitchen. Firelight danced on the walls, casting the room in eerie liquid shadows, and another voice came out of the dark.

"This probably works better for us. We might need to move in closer, but there will be less chance Strauss will spot us," Jack Sheridan said.

"Makes everything easier for you," Jacob Feinstein said, "but I'm going to have some difficulties seeing the certificates in this lighting. Sophia, see if you can find an oil lamp in there."

An old hurricane lamp was located in the basement and set on the coffee table, near Jacob in the hearth room. The candles were placed strategically throughout the room to offer the best concealment for both Jack and Charles. Patrick had been sent to the Rolls-Royce just prior to the lights going out because it was the only place which could serve for outside surveillance and didn't require becoming soaked in the process.

The grey Chevrolet pulling into the courtyard was early. Three men in suits got out of the vehicle and ran up the short steps to the porch, disappearing from view for a moment to ring the doorbell. Jacob Feinstein rose from the settee and shuffled off to answer the door as Sophia reappeared to stand in the doorway to the kitchen, a dish towel clasped casually in one hand as if she had been drying dishes.

"Come in, come in." Jacob said, pulling the door open and standing aside. "We lost power about half hour ago. I'm not sure I can be much assistance to you today. Might be best if we reschedule for tomorrow."

A tall man in a grey raincoat removed his hat and stepped forward. He didn't introduce himself, simply addressing Jacob with an assumed air of authority. "It would be inconvenient. Take a look at them. If you feel unable to validate them, then we can make other arrangements."

Without saying a word, the two men who accompanied him shifted to positions near the door, one stepping toward the kitchen to linger a few feet from Sophia. Jacob glanced between the men, then back to the man in the grey coat. He had his hand out to shake, but the man who spoke was wearing dark driving gloves and seemed disinclined to take up Jacob's hand. Jacob shrugged and waved his hand to a seat near the sofa. Then he shuffled back to his seat and sat down.

"Who's the woman?" Raincoat Man asked.

"That's my daughter, Sophia." Jacob motioned for her to move forward into the light. "Some tea, perhaps?"

Sophia moved forward to the tea set. She looked very elegant in a mid-length angel sleeve shirt and her matching skirt, in gold and green tones. The skirt billowed as she walked, revealing it to be bell-bottomed slacks. She tucked the dishtowel into the side of her waistband and bent to pour.

"Let me see what you've got, Mister... " Jacob hesitated, since he had not been offered a name. "Sophia, don't go too far. I may need your eyes."

Raincoat Man reached inside his coat and brought out a sealed plastic pouch, opened it and pulled out a small stack of certificates. He leaned forward in his chair and handed them over to Jacob, who took them. He lifted a loupe from the chain around his neck and raised it to his eye. He grunted. Sorting the pages to move another to the front, he placed one page on the coffee table in front of him, nearer the hurricane lamp. He grunted again.

After several minutes, he leaned back and removed the loupe from his eye.

"Well," he said, his voice thin and reedy, "They are good. Very well done, in fact. I would be willing to give you a hundred dollars for each one you have."

The man scoffed, "A hundred dollars for a half million dollar certificate?"

"A forged half million dollar certificate," Jacob said merrily. "It's a quaint novelty, but you won't be able to take it to the bank."

There was a shuffle near the door as one of the men moved forward, handgun raised, and Otto Strauss's voice asked, "Why do you think they are faked?"

It was the moment Jack Sheridan had been waiting for. "Drop the weapon, Strauss."

The man near Jacob leapt to his feet, pulling a weapon as he did so. Sophia stepped away from the tea service, sliding a hand into the pocket hidden in her slacks, pulling her own revolver. The sound of a shot being fired sent everyone into a crouch. Jacob let out a yelp and lurched forward on the couch, sliding down the cushions and onto the floor. Sophia pulled her trigger, and Raincoat Man went down as she rushed to her father's side.

Charles slipped around the kitchen door and fired. The second goon near the door made a noise and reached out just as the front door was opened from the outside. Patrick Sandusky appeared, blocking his path.

Otto Strauss sprinted across the hearth room, dropping to the floor in a roll toward the front window. He kicked out and struck a side table which sent the burning candle toppling to the floor as he fired into the plate glass window. It shattered, spraying out onto the porch and scattering shards among the wind and the rain. Lurching to his feet, he flung his body though the open window.

Jack ran after Strauss, barely ducking in time as he saw the man turn and fire another shot back into the home. He heard the engine on the car start and then rev. Pumped with adrenaline, Jack felt his pulse quicken. He jumped through the window, slid on bits of broken glass and fell, ripping the knee from his slacks. From the corner of his eye, he saw Patrick take a shooter's stance and fire at the fleeing vehicle. Both men pursued the car at a full run as it cleared the trees along the driveway and disappeared. As they reached the edge of the courtyard on foot, there was an explosion. At the far end of the lane, what was left of the Chevrolet was now aflame, sideways in the road.

* * *

The ambulance came onto the estate through a service road to pick up Jacob Feinstein and take him to the hospital as the front drive was still blocked by the fire department, a wrecker and Otto Straus' vehicle. Jacob insisted his daughter stay at the house, assuring her it was a minor wound.

Charles Edwin had been placing calls to the Stateside Procurement Agency office for the last hour. The gold shipment was now permanently on hold upon the revelation that the certificates surrendered had been forged. It had been a bold move on the side of the Arabs to send false certificates. SPA now theorized that Otto Strauss might have been leaked information from the Arabs intentionally so the counterfeit documents could not be substantiated before the gold had left American soil.

Patrick Sandusky found the electricity had been sabotaged near the main transformer. What they originally thought had been taken down by lightning was proven to have been shot down at the main line. The electric company already had a crew on the grounds re-establishing the connection.

Jack Sheridan waited for the firemen to finish up, and for local law enforcement to take over the scene. He wanted to know what caused the vehicle to blow up, and he wanted to make sure Otto Strauss was the man in the vehicle. Unfortunately, he only got half of what he wanted. The car had been blown up via remote from C-4 left in the trunk. The rescue crew had found no bodies in the car. Subsequent questioning of Strauss' companions revealed an escape plan involving a secondary vehicle.

Otto Strauss was gone.

A glass company in New York City had already been dispatched to replace the shattered porch window. If you have enough money, you can buy anything. The Feinstein's did and they would be reimbursed by SPA. As a bonus, Jacob Feinstein would be allowed to keep the forged certificates as a collector item. It was a win in Jacob's eyes.

Sophia Feinstein came to stand beside Jack Sheridan. "He got away. And we don't have the bonds," Sophia said.

"Yes, but since they didn't get the gold, it's less significant. Otto Strauss and I will cross paths again," Jack said.

"It feels so... unfinished," Sophia said, "like Mr. Heavy and The Shanes."

Jack turned Sophia, looking perplexed. "Mr. Heavy and The Shanes?"

Sophia smiled. "It's an old movie. A middle-aged, kind of washed-up detective spends the entire movie chasing after *Mr. Heavy and The Shanes,* and it isn't until near the end that you start to get the feel that this thing he is searching for is a blues group, not an actual person. Anyway, the movie ends with the detective sitting at a bar, his back to the piano player who happens to be this young, black woman. And you hear the woman singing the words *Mr. Heavy and The Shanes strike again.* The detective turns and looks at the piano player and the movie ends."

Jack Sheridan's lips twist into a wry smile.

Sophia shrugs and says, "You never do find out what it all means. It just ends."

AUTHOR'S NOTE

I was inspired based on a novel I am working on called *Chasing The Paper Dragon*, which is modern-day thriller involving the agency, SPA, which even today almost nobody has heard about it. This was an opportunity to take some of our real U.S. history and marry it to the background of the bonds and the main objective of SPA. There is a rich history with the agency, and I wanted to explore John Sheridan, who is the main character in the short story. John is Jessica Sheridan's father, who is my lead character in *Paper Dragon*.

This was so much fun for me to write because I love the thriller and the characters, but I had to kill off Jessica's dad to make the story background work. And I always thought Jessica's dad would have been a really cool agent. He had to be to have such a strong daughter.

B.K. Hart

Lesson Learned
Victoria Stewart

After several tries to open my eyes, I could see Dr. Carter standing over my hospital bed. All the aromas of antiseptic, uneaten industrial food and floor cleaner assaulted my nose, adding to my lack of focus. Drugs could only do so much to ease the misery I was currently experiencing.

"Mr. and Mrs. Floyd, I'm glad both of you are here. The discharge plan is about complete." Turning to me, "You will be able to be released on Thursday, provided there aren't any further complications. Do either of you have any questions?"

"Will I be released to a rehab center?" I asked.

The pain medication was beginning to take effect. The sensation of floating was beginning to return. I was glad to see the rails up on the sides of the bed. I now could take a decent breath without the worry of passing out.

"It'll be the Mid-town Rehabilitation Center off North Capital Avenue. I think you should be able to go home from there within two or three months. I want you, at the very least, to be able to walk unassisted, and be able to go back and forth to the bathroom."

"Thanks Doc, I appreciate it. Right now I just feel helpless." At least that was what I wanted to say. Even to my ears, it sounded slurred and sloppy.

"You took an extremely hard fall down those basement stairs. I don't see how you were able to get upstairs before the EMT's got there." I could clearly see the doubt in the doctor's eyes but, as always, he didn't pry or force the issue. Now, as I lay there with such a broken body, I wished he had pried some, had forced the issue. I wish he found the real reason for all of the ambulance runs to our house, all the broken bones that had to be set, sometimes reset, and all the stitches that had been required over the years.

"Couldn't have without Jackie's help," I said with a smile that had to look disturbing since it was delivered through clenched teeth and a swollen jaw. I had no idea that broken ribs could be so excruciating. A pain that would not be forgotten. Ever.

"It is a good thing Jackie was there because you would have suffered permanent damage without immediate medical attention." Dr. Carter was now flipping the chart closed after he had made a few scribbles. Could anyone really read a doctor's scrawl?

"Since the leg was so badly damaged, will there be a limp?" Jackie asked with a frown, concerned as always with outward appearances. Over the years, we spent a small fortune on clothing designed to camouflage the numerous injuries. At least the ones that didn't require casts or crutches.

"The greatest chance for a limp would be because of the pin that was put in Robin's leg. But Dr. Jameson is the best orthopedic surgeon in the Midwest, so I'm pretty sure that there won't be a limp or any other signs of the accident. That is, of course, except for the scar that runs the length of the right thigh. It is amazing what we can do now in 1975 with all the current advancements. If this had happened a few years ago, Robin would have probably been confined permanently to a wheelchair."

"That's good. Thank you for all your help, Dr. Carter," Jackie said.

"I'll see you tomorrow, Robin." With a slight tip of the head, "Jackie."

Soon after the doctor left, so did Jackie. At this point there wasn't much left to say. Jackie's words were still resounding in my ears, the smell was seared into my memory. While waiting for the ambulance, as I drifted in and out of consciousness, there was the smell of toothpaste and mouthwash, and the heat of simmering, festering anger swirled around my ear. In a sickly sweet, soft voice, I was told, "If there is ever a next time...I'll kill you." Then pulling back from my ear, cupping my head and positioning my face so that we had direct eye contact, our brief conversation continued.

"Now nod if you understand." Though I lay broken and battered, I was quick to nod with a new found appreciation. I understood with a new clarity that what Jackie was saying was not an empty threat. It was an assurance, a promise that could and would be done.

"Okay, now let's get you untied and into the kitchen by the basement stairs. We don't have much time. We both know it only takes the ambulance ten minutes to get here. Although, the last time they did take longer." Jackie sighed. "I think they are tired of coming here so often. But this will be the last time that they will be called, right?"

"Right," I mewed like a weak kitten.

By the time I hopped to the kitchen, leaning heavily on Jackie and unceremoniously deposited on the floor, there was a pounding at the front door. The EMT's were two men that had been to our home before. I was always certain they understood it wasn't really my fault, that I had been forced into my circumstances. Just as they were closing the ambulance doors, I'm sure I heard one of them let slip a little chuckle, "Finally, justice." The other replied, "Amen to that, brother. Amen to that!"

As I look back, I now see they really did understand after all. My next memory was being rolled into the ER. The overhead lights passing quickly enough to make me even dizzier.

I wasn't sure I was ready to be alone to contemplate my behavior for the last fifteen years.

How can a person, who claims to love someone with such intensity that they wouldn't be able to survive without them, repeatedly cause such pain and agony?

If Jackie left me, I would never recover. But I also wouldn't leave. What we needed was a plan. No, what I needed was to stick to a plan. I'm finally ready to take responsibility for my actions and make amends. Since, as always, it was my fault, from that moment on I recommitted to Jackie so that abuse would not return to our home.

***

No one should ever be put in the position that Jackie was forced into. Victims are not considered the cause of their own victimization. Yet that was what had happened in our home for years. Peering into my bed stand mirror, the stark black truth stared back from the purplish green bruises. I could finally see who and what caused the unleashing of violence in our home. How could I be so arrogant and ignorant?

Looking back over all the years Jackie and I had shared, I could see that the enemy to our marriage was me. I wasn't too bad a mate. Life was even enjoyable – most of the time. But if liquor was added and I said the wrong thing, the situation rapidly deteriorated. It was as though when the two things combined, the liquor and the drinker, a wholly new being took control, less than human, more than beast. Transformation would follow quickly, turning the drinker into an unrecognizable, unyielding, and vicious creature.

Some drunks were fun, but not the one who lived in our home. It didn't matter what kind of liquor, all control would be gone, and then the abuse would begin. It would start with angry words, words that accused the innocent of awful, untrue things. Then it always worsened until there were things that were broken. Glass things, metal things, human things.

This brutal cycle had to stop because one or both of us would end up dead. We were soaring head-long into this, and one of us had to make it stop. It was clear now that this was solely within my power. Now, all I needed was the courage to do what had to be done.

I experienced periods when unpleasant memories surfaced in the past. I would see a bruise that had turned that sickly yellow and faded orange color. The unpleasantness would quickly pass. The remorse was short lived, calling into question whether it was true remorse or just empty words uttered to sooth me more that Jackie. As the years passed, the guilt was easier and easier to forget. This time though, I was experiencing flashbacks and wasn't sure they would ever stop. Even with the heavy medication, I kept being thrown back to that July morning.

Waking to find myself tied to the bed, my first thought was that I was having a nightmare. That mistake was quickly corrected. This was happening to me. Then came the first hit with the iron skillet. The room started to swirl. Jackie was careful not to knock me out, wanting me to fully experience all the pain and all the agony I could possibly withstand. There was no belittling or unfounded suspicion. Also different, though, was the pleading and begging. Seared into my mind was the absurd screeching. I finally realized these screams were emanating from me. The results of this lesson was a concussion which still makes me dizzy, four broken ribs that make breathing a challenge, a broken foot that has left me unable to bear any weight. A crushed right leg left me looking like a Frankenstein experiment. Nonetheless I found a new respect for Jackie that I would never forget.

Over the years we had come up with many creative stories to explain injuries. That is how abusive households work. We could see the disbelief in the faces of EMT's, and the emergency rooms doctors and the ever observant nurses, medical personnel we had seen repeatedly.

***

Nurse Debra seemed determined to inflict even more pain than I was already enduring, although she made no accusations, verbal or otherwise. Always the professional, the look on her face was condemning. Her mask of civility slipped for a moment. This occasion was different. She was on the verge of glee. I knew that I didn't deserve any compassion, and Nurse Debra was dead-on. It was easy to see the surprise on her face when she was getting my vitals, to hear that I had not been drinking and her quick assessment confirmed that I was definitely sober.

I was now paying for all the years I abused alcohol. The doctors explained that since I had such a high tolerance for alcohol, the pain medication wouldn't be as effective. I now understood why I must give up the bottle. The biggest motive still resounded in my ears... my choice, life or death. As soon as I could string a few words together I begged Jackie to collect all the liquor in the house and dump it.

The request had been a surprise I could tell, but it garnered a genuine smile from Jackie. It was the first real smile I had witnessed in a long time, and it was so pleasant and full of hope. That smile was what caught my attention so many years ago. It could take my breath away back then and I yearned for us to regain that wonderful feeling again. It gave me courage that things could be repaired. A new start could begin for the both of us from this point forward.

"Excuse me, are you Robin Floyd?"

"Yes." I was jolted from the past, startled to see the man standing at the foot of the bed.

"Good, I'm Detective Carr, with the Indianapolis Police Department."

"Yes sir," I said.

"I just have a few questions about the accident." The stocky officer sat down, pulling a chair close and opening a little flip top notebook. He looked me straight in the eye as he began. "The police department is starting a new division and we are now looking in to incidents that have been listed as possible domestic disputes."

He glanced down at his notes, then returned to meet my eyes. "We have had numerous reports of calls to your home over the last few years."

"Detective?" came a soft voice.

"Carr," he said, turning away from me.

"Yes, Detective Carr, I fell down the basement stairs and that is the whole story."

Glancing down at his notes, then returning his sharp eagle eyes to mine, he said "What we are seeing is a distinctive pattern, a pattern of possible domestic abuse."

"I know, but this time was different."

"Yes, Mr. Floyd, this time is different, the injured person is you. In the past, it has always been your wife. She always insists that it was an accident. The last time she was hospitalized I came to see if I could persuade her to make a statement but she was adamant that it was because of her clumsiness. I tried to get her to tell me the truth but she stuck to her story and wouldn't confide what really happened." I could see the frustration he had experienced with Jackie.

"I didn't know that you had met with her," Robin said.

"It's all part of this new program. We try to work with the victim to get a complaint that we can act on. But your wife wouldn't shift from any detail that she originally told the EMTs," Detective Carr said.

After a few minutes of flipping through his notebook, he started again. "According to the doctors, EMT's, and the ER staff, your case could be an abuse case. They didn't really want to report this. They are all very supportive of your wife, but with the new law they are required to report suspected cases of abuse. I can't really do anything if you insist that your injuries were caused by a fall. When I stopped by your house this morning, Mrs. Floyd showed me where the hand railing had come lose from the wall."

"Yes, I will fix that as soon as I'm able."

"It would be good if you did that. It looked as if the screws were loosened, not every day wear and tear. I need to ask, are you willing to tell me what really happened?"

"Really, Detective Carr, I fell. But I can assure you that there won't be any more emergency calls from our home again."

The chair scraped the floor as the detective rose to leave, except he didn't leave. He closed the door and returned to the side of the bed. His movements were like that of a cat, swift and silent. He was now close enough that I could smell stale coffee on his breath and feel the heat of his words.

He pressed his meaty hand on my bandaged leg, until he saw the panic in my eyes. "Okay, Mr. Floyd, I'm not going to open an official investigation but I'll keep a close watch out for any more calls."

"I swear there won't be. I've learned my lesson."

AUTHOR'S NOTE

Writers collect bits and pieces of casual conversation all the time and sometimes such bits and pieces can be developed into a short story or novel. The idea for *Lesson Learned* came from an experience a co-worker related to me several years ago. In that experience, neither the wife nor the husband concealed what had happened. It took place in the late fifties, so no action by law enforcement was taken, which was not unusual for the times despite the fact that their troubled relationship was well known in the community. The husband never did take another drink.

Victoria Stewart

James Dean and Me:
An Indiana Fable
Sherita Saffer Campbell

It was a hot end-of-summer day. I was sitting under my weeping willow tree drinking a mild whisky sour and feeling very sorry for myself. I was 75 and had outlived my husband. Our children were grown and gone. The grandchildren and great-grandchildren had lives of their own. Here I sat, craving some excitement. Then I glanced at the newspaper lying on my lap and read the weekend events. I was looking to fill my unoccupied weekend when I saw the headlines about the James Dean Festival in Fairmont.

Many years ago, when I was in my high school drama class, James Dean was my hero. He graduated from Fairmont High School while I was still in grade school. Fairmont was insignificant to me then, but James Dean changed all that.

Fairmont was just down the road from Muncie, my hometown. That is, it was just down the road as the crow flies, if it wanted to travel a squiggle path. But I had a free evening, so what the heck. I needed an adventure. I dumped my drink on the grass and headed in the house to get changed for the James Dean Festival.

I hopped in the car, set my GPS and headed for Fairmont. I chuckled a bit thinking about the first time I headed to Fairmont and a James Dean festival. That was light years back in time. I hadn't thought about those days for a long, long time. Too much pain? Dreams dashed?

I shook my head, gripped the wheel a little tighter. Maybe it was the whisky, maybe just my age, but that first trip I made to Fairmont so long ago began to unfold from my little tiny brain cells almost like I was directing a movie.

Back then I hadn't had my driver's license very long, didn't even own a car. I remember buying an Indiana map at the filling station. No GPS then. I tried to follow these weird little squiggly lines on the map. I took it home to see if my father, the greatest map-reader of all time, could help me. He was in the bathroom getting groomed for his band to play at the Moose Penthouse. Back then you said, "The band had to play." Now you have a gig.

Anyhow, I had my new little map in hand, and I walked into the bathroom to watch my dad shaving and humming a tune and pausing in his shave to write down the notes he was humming. I asked him to figure out the squiggly little lines.

"Just follow the map, for God's sake. You're in high school, you have a driver's license." And he went back to writing down musical notes. So I left.

There were no interstates then, like the one I was driving on today. No wide lanes. Just a lane that went one way and a lane that went the other way. No stop signs and just few speeding signs. I can't remember the speed limit then, but I remember being very careful. Cops were always watching teenagers. I pulled over and looked at the map. I had turned where it said. The road became one little lane, sort of. A little further on it got even narrower. I was passing fields of corn and beans. There were long fields of crops with few houses between them. This was God's country. James Dean country, like his soybean crop in *East of Eden*.

I kept following the road until I ended up in someone's driveway. While I studied the map to see where in the world I was, a man came out with a shotgun. He stared straight at me. I pealed out of there fast, as if I were at the country road in front of the private airport that we used for a drag strip. I burned rubber like an old pro. The gang and James Dean would have been proud.

I laughed out loud remembering that scene. And I made it to Fairmount then, I'd make it to the Festival today.

In my teen years, the whole world watched *East of Eden* and *Rebel without a Cause* and learned about James Dean. Then came his tragic accident. *Giant* was released after his death.

I cried when I heard.

As a teenager, I'd been enamored with him. After all, Dean was THE REBEL for our generation. His movies spoke to us and for us. Our parents were not so inclined. They howled at us just because he existed. He was a teenage hoodlum. Dear sweet innocents we were, we identified with the line in *Rebel without a Cause,* that "parents didn't understand anything about us." Our parents just raised their eyebrows. That one line embodied why Dean's movies were important to us.

My always-correct mother put her argument into one long sentence without even a breath. "Why did they have to do the chicken run to show bravery - that's stupid why would you do that to show you're brave?" she asked. I wanted to stop her before she exploded or imploded (my new word of the day). "Your uncles in WW2 were brave. The Jews in concentration camps were brave. Why hang a chicken on someone's front porch? That makes no sense to me." I sighed while she continued to hand pots and pans down for me to dry and continued her soliloquy. I quit listening.

You see for me, Dean represented the underdog. I understood him. He spoke to my generation. *East of Eden. Rebel without a Cause.* He was our rebel. He spoke to our condition with every word and every magnificent movement. We loved him. That was that.

James Dean was from a small town like mine. He became a success and was my inspiration. I wanted to be on Broadway. All of us, actually, in drama class, not just me, hoped we would to go to New York. Get on Broadway. The rest of the school hoped that we would make it big. Then we would become a part of our hero's life. They would come and visit us.

I smiled now as I remembered those long ago dreams we had. I dreamed to be in a James Dean movie. That was my goal.

Then came the end of the world. I mean the total end, the forever-and-ever end. The crash. Bang. And he was gone.

No James Dean. No starring role with him. He was supposedly killed on the Freeway, whatever that was, in

California. They had strange things in California that we didn't have in Indiana.

Except here's the thing: I couldn't believe he'd been killed. It had to be a Hollywood-style fake. He wanted a vacation and they wouldn't give him one. So he faked it. Or it was a publicity stunt for *Giant*, his new movie, which had not been released.

But, there was the funeral. A big deal. Then the burial later, in Fairmount. Much later. Some of us went there to be a part of it. That didn't work out too well. It was going to be a secret where they buried him. Crowds were so big. We gave up. We just wanted to make sure he was buried there. That he was dead.

Or not.

Years later, his grave site had become a shrine. So one night my friends and I, now grown men and women, went to see it at midnight. By now, many of my friends drifted away from our early certainty that he was not dead. It was eerie there, in the darkness. I swear, a big light sort of emerged out of the grave and moved around the cemetery. Then it went back into the grave. If he wasn't buried there, someone with a great deal of power was. We never went back. Like all good souls, we told others and they had the same experience. Someone with a magnificent spirit, or a clever theater illusionist, was buried there. Who knew for sure? But a light there was, I couldn't deny it.

Still, in the deepest part of my heart, I knew. I knew he wasn't dead and that I would see him and star with him in a movie, a TV drama, or in my real love, the stage. After all, he started on the stage. My dream never wavered. Of all his co-stars, he would pick me, and we would be together on stage and in movies. Just us.

After a while, some of my hero's New York friends announced they intended to make a movie about James Dean's life, to be set on location in Fairmount. And they were having tryouts at Fairmount High School. The school was in the middle of a field, which I thought was cool. A bean field. Soybeans again. Like in *East of Eden*. The gym was packed to the brim, and I was there. Every budding thespian in Indiana and the whole U.S.A. was there.

Only a favorite few were taken up to the stage. The first bunch had already filled out their applications and seemed to know each other. They weren't from Indiana. I don't remember the script but I waited a long time and finally had the chance to read a line or two. I did quite well, I thought. But no one paid any attention.

The chosen first folks on the stage, dressed to the nines, were already planning the performance. They tried very hard not to touch any Hoosiers or even stand close to us. They smiled at us a lot, though. I was called to the stage a second time and got to read several more lines. I remember being scared to death. A few of my friends also got called, though none of us was chosen. I returned home determined to practice the lines harder.

It was the same way when I returned the next week for the second, bigger tryouts. Before the second tryouts, I told my dad about my first journey, where I went and how much trouble I had. He raised total and complete hell. I wished I'd just told him I got to read a whole part. Or got good reviews. He'd have liked that. Maybe I would amount to something after all. But then he was counting out his musical notes again.

The movie was cancelled. I never heard the why and wherefore. There was an investigation. Nothing much came of it, except someone said the money was stolen by one of the managers. But somehow the gathering of wannabe actors and fans turned into a festival. Gradually, a few more things were added. More people trickled in. Eventually, the James Dean Festival came alive.

Over the years I switched from acting in local civic theater to writing. I never really regretted not pursuing an acting career. Besides, to me, acting meant the stage. Broadway. Being a star in New York. No regrets, except maybe when washing dishes or mopping floors. Stars didn't do that and in those moments my dreams would momentarily resurface. Writing, however, kept me busy. I wrote mysteries, poems; some things got published, some not.

But to make a living, I started a job that required research. I got good at it.

* * *

As I neared Fairmont, the movie reel in my mind ended. I guess if there were regrets, they must be buried now in that cemetery along with James Dean. I slowed the car and looked for a parking place. The annual James Dean Festival was now a big deal.

I walked around the festival looking at the booths, listening to the musicians. I wandered over to the stage to watch the actors playing James Dean's part in reenactments of his movies.

As I watched in rapture, smiling and nodding my head, I felt someone staring at me. "Lord," I thought, "it's just like the cemetery." I felt all shivery.

I slightly turned my head and saw this man look at me. He was smiling. Silver hair, twinkling eyes and a good-looking face like, well, you know, my hero. Even in old age, I was still smitten or crazy. Maybe both.

He smiled and turned to watch the acting.

I turned and waited a minute, then turned again. I stepped back behind someone and stared at the back of this silver-haired dude. It was like a profile of James Dean. There were lookalike James Deans wandering all over the festival. Some in contests, some just dressed up for the fun of it. They were all cool dudes.

Was he an actor watching a fellow performer? He sure had that smile down pat. The build, too. He should have been on the stage acting. Even the guy up there acting was watching him.

I followed him when the piece was over. He walked around and looked at the events going on. I'd read enough mysteries to pretend I knew how to shadow someone. So I did, shamelessly. Right to the car. I wrote down the license number. And watched him leave. Then I got in my car and followed him. I lost him at the stoplight. I drove around a while but no luck. By then, I was hungry, so I stopped at a little restaurant.

This restaurant was a holdover from James Dean's days. I sat down and ordered a burger, fries and a malt – a meal my doctor forbids me to have. I figured, once a year should be okay.

It was when I finished ordering lemon pie that I looked up and saw the silver-haired man.

"May I join you?"

I nodded, wary but very excited. Almost having a teenager crush, if you know what I mean. You never get over that, even when you are 75.

"I'll have the same," he told the waitress. "The James Dean Special," he and I said at the same time.

I smiled. He smiled and sat down. We gave each other one of those long careful looks. You know the kind, like you know more than he does or he knows more than you do. And you both know the same thing. He smelled good. I didn't realize I said it aloud.

He laughed. "I do?" His smile was sexy.

Dear God, when you're my age, do you still see sexy in men? I searched my brain records again. My grandma. A little tiny woman I thought was beautiful. She was part Indian. Had beautiful eyes and a wondrous smile. When we saw a man or she was describing a good looking man, she always said, "He's a pretty man." Even when she was the age that I am now. Did she mean sexy? And she always commented on his perfume.

"It's a new after shave," he said. His eyes twinkled. He sniffed. "It's something about the sea. Real he-man stuff."

I smiled.

"Well, my husband died three years ago. I said it to the Schwann man... that he smelled good. And to a waiter. It just came out and I didn't know why. Then I realized I have been living alone for a while and I don't use scent anymore. My husband used after-shave, a little cologne, once in a while because we got him some for Christmas. But I hadn't smelled any in the house since then. In fact, that's when I quit using perfume. I can't tell when I have too much on." I was talking too much. It was just coming out, like when I said he smelled good.

"And the Schwann man?"

"Scared the hell out of him. The waiter, too. I mean, I really blurted it out to them."

"You didn't scare me." He bent closer to me and whispered. "I find it sexy to hear that from a woman."

I laughed out loud. Not a dainty lady laugh. A gut-busting laugh. "I'm glad," I said.

"So you like James Dean?"

I nodded. Just then the waitress brought our orders.

"I'm not supposed to eat like this except..."

"Once a year," we said together.

"Did you like the plays and skits?" he asked.

"Some were good and some not. I like the feel of the place, walking around, excited, and feeling young again. There was a thrill, an excitement about Dean. I guess it still lives inside some of us. You know, when he was killed, none of us believed it."

"Oh?" he asked.

"I've had this secret theory, for 60 years now, that his death was faked. That he was tired of the fame. He went somewhere."

"Where?"

"Never-never land." I shrugged. "He wanted to get away from it all. To rest. He had all the money he needed. One of his secrets was his money and how he stashed it away. Maybe he reinvented himself. Well, he did. I think he's playing repertory. He was a Brando. Silly, I guess, but some people have to be on stage, to act. It's not fame. It's just..."

"The magic of the theater," he said.

I nodded.

Then he asked, "How do you know he had all the money he needed stashed away?"

"I looked it up. First in the library, newspapers, trade magazines. Research is my specialty now. It took a few years to verify it."

He smiled.

"Then came the Internet. I looked up more. It confirmed my first research."

"You were very thorough."

"I was. Damn, I should have written an article. I always do that. After I research and satisfy my curiosity, then I don't want to write about it. I love research. Part of my extra job is research."

"What would that job be?"

"Curiosity killed the cat." I looked at him. "And my story."

"Maybe that's why you understand his wanting a new beginning somehow." He stirred his soda.

We finished our meal in silence. I looked around the restaurant. It was as if I had stepped back in time. It was a 50's restaurant with James Dean stuff hanging on the walls. 1950 prices.

I looked at him for a long time. Then I took a deep breath.

"So, tell me," I asked, looking into his eyes. "Who was really driving your car that night on the California Freeway?"

AUTHOR'S NOTE

I think when you are young, heroes play an important part in the growing up process. You learn a great deal from studying how your heroes succeeded or failed. The secret is learning about the hero's journey to learn his faults, the price of trying to succeed, and finding a way not to fall into the darkness.

When I was young, I was totally enthralled by James Dean and wanted to write something about him. James Dean was not a bad hero. He worked hard. But his background or will wasn't strong enough to keep him on the path.

So a great deal of what I wrote was true. But I played "what if" for the restaurant scene. I wondered what if he had found his way. I thought what if he really loaned his car to someone and that person died. How that would have affected him?

Sherita Saffer Campbell

Tumbling Crows
N. W. Campbell

"Is this thing any good?"

She stood at the apron of her neighbor's garage, peering inside at him standing at the workbench, puttering with something or another. When he turned to look at her, she could see the little end table sitting on his workbench, a recent acquisition from a garage sale.

"Yeah, hey, lemme see whatcha got there," he said.

They had only recently become acquainted. Prior to Sheila moving into the community, Ralph spent most of his time puttering and casually volunteering his help to friends and neighbors. On occasion, he walked to the local brewpub for a beer and an opportunity to strike up a conversation with whoever happened to be there. His wife had passed years earlier and his kids had all moved out of state to chase their fortunes. Just about all of his neighbors in the condominium complex were retired like him, and many were gone at least half the year.

"It belonged to my granddad," Sheila explained as she held out the gun. "He was a farmer over in Illinois. He carried this with him on his tractor to shoot small game, varmints and stuff. Nobody else in the family wanted it, so I took it home with me. I came across it while I was unpacking and wondered if it still might shoot."

"These are good old guns," said Ralph, "I learned to hunt with one of these when I was a kid."

He took it from her hands and began inspecting it, turning it one way and the other to look for rust on the barrel and cracking along the grain of the wood stock. Then he slid open the action.

"I shot a lotta rabbits and squirrels with one of these. Bolt action, kinda slow, but if you're a good shot, it doesn't matter. One shot's all you need. Some guys could really work this bolt, though. Get that second shot off almost as quick as a guy with a pump. Say, if you've got the time, I could wipe it down a bit, check it out and then I could tell you if it still shoots or not. Okay?"

Ralph liked to volunteer his help to friends and acquaintances but did not want the responsibility of regular volunteer opportunities that frequently came his way. By all accounts, he was a naturally helpful type of guy, never destined to accumulate great wealth or power, or to captain great industry. His fortune lay in his innate abilities to be helpful and knowledgeable and to provide for himself and those around him. Loyal, faithful, steadfast, dependable. He was a good father, a good neighbor, a man who only married once in his life. Others turned to him when in acute crisis and left just as quickly when the crisis had passed.

When Ralph's wife died, his many "good" friends offered their condolences from afar. He would find messages on his answering machine.

"Hey, buddy, heard about your wife, so sorry for your loss. Hey, when you get a moment, give me a call..."

And there was the syrupy bargain greeting card, "Jesus needed another angel in heaven," with the sender's signature scrawled across the bottom.

Still, his instinct for helpfulness never dimmed, and led him out the door and across the drive the day Sheila arrived with her life's possessions packed in a small U-Haul trailer towed by her aging Chrysler. Two guys she paid from the local truck rental agency came over to help her unload and Ralph offered to join them.

"Hey, I got a little time if you can use the help," was how Ralph introduced himself.

Since the day they first met, they had become casually friendly. He would see her walking down the drive to retrieve her mail and wave to her. Sometimes she would stop and they would talk. She was thirty-ish, a bit plump, with nice, muscular legs and a habit of turning her head away slightly when she spoke, as though it was hard for her to look him in the eye.

One afternoon, mail in hand, she stopped and looked directly at him, standing in his driveway. "Come over for some coffee, won't you? I bought a coffee cake."

He agreed, and followed her into the townhome, just across the drive from his garden condo.

"Let me get the pot on. Have a seat in the living room. I'll be right out."

The townhome had been empty for months after the elderly woman who owned it died and her kids fell out over whether or not to sell. Finally, the eldest son decided to invest some money in the place and list it for rent.

Sheila came by the same afternoon the sign went up, walked through the place, paid cash for the deposit and the first month's rent and signed the lease.

This was the first time Ralph had ever been inside. There were no pictures on the walls. Some boxes sat in the corner, waiting to be unpacked. A little hallway ran off the foyer, to his right, into a bedroom. A set of stairs ran to an open loft on the second floor, which appeared to be empty.

In a moment, she came in, carrying two mugs of coffee, which she sat on a TV tray near the couch where he was sitting. She smiled and headed back to the kitchen for the coffee cake, two spoons, a small bowl full of packets of sugar and cream, and some paper napkins.

"Mind if we eat with our fingers? I'm still trying to unpack!" She giggled, with a little toss of her head.

She told Ralph she was from Illinois, a farm girl. She had a license and some experience working as a CNA in nursing homes. And Indianapolis had lots of places where she could find work. She didn't know anybody, although she had managed to land a job at a place nearby. She told him she was single.

"Never married? Really?" asked Ralph.

"Well, once, but that's over now, for me anyway. Just didn't work out, I guess." Sheila paused briefly, then continued. "I decided to stop running from my problems. Now I'm learning to face them head on, y'know what I mean?"

"Yeah," said Ralph, "good for you! That's the best way, for sure! A farm girl, hey? I grew up farming. South of here, a little place called Newburgh. Drove a tractor when I was a kid, hunted and fished, ran a trap line along Little Clifty Creek, did all the stuff farm kids do. Gave up hunting awhile back, eyes aren't as good as they used to be, although I could still handle a shotgun okay. It's gotten harder to pick up that bead front sight on a rifle, that's all."

"It's been years since I fired a gun," Shelia told him, "I used to be pretty good with one. My mother could shoot, too, raised on the farm like me. I just gave it up, when I wasn't a kid anymore and got married."

"Marriage changes a lotta things. So does losing someone like my wife. I'm getting over it now but it's tough to be alone," he said and paused, noting what he just said. "Well, you know that, I guess, don'cha?"

She smiled sweetly but said nothing. Ralph began to feel he might be wearing out his welcome. He thanked her for the cake and coffee and rose from the couch to go.

She rose with him, reaching out to catch his forearm with the soft palm of her right hand.

"Thanks, Ralph, for taking the time. Let's do this again!" she said with a lilt in her voice.

Their relationship grew warmer after that. They greeted each other every day, it seemed, and she always had a smile for him, no matter what she was doing.

The day she brought the gun over, she looked him fully in the face and smiled her prettiest. Ralph enjoyed being the guy for whom others would turn when they needed help, especially her. A short breeze caught her light cotton skirt and wrapped it tantalizingly around her legs, accenting her shapely thighs. She wore beige sandals with cork wedge heels that caused her calves to flex powerfully as she stepped into the garage to hand him the gun.

Ralph set the end table off the workbench and opened the shotgun's chamber. He slid the bolt back and forth a few times and noted that the weapon was unloaded and that the action was still smooth. With his right hand, he pulled the bolt back while he squeezed the trigger and held it with his left. He continued pulling on the bolt until it was free from the gun. He laid the gun and the bolt down on the bench and excused himself to go inside for a flashlight and a cleaning rod he hadn't used since he had sold all his guns to raise cash for his daughter's tuition. A moment later he was back with the rod and the flashlight and two small bottles, one of gun oil, the other labeled *Nitro Powder Solvent*.

"Gotta look down that barrel and see what kind of shape it's in."

He spoke over his shoulder, bent low over his work.

Sheila nodded, as though he could see it, and then acknowledged his remark when she realized he couldn't.

"I really don't know when that thing was fired last," she shrugged. "It might have been the last time Granddad let me fire it. He fell down the stairs at the farm shortly after that, and my dad had to put him in a nursing home. He didn't live long after he went to that home. He and I did everything together, back when I was a kid."

Her eyes took on an absent glaze, as she allowed herself a moment's daydream of an earlier, more carefree time with an elderly man she adored.

Her father did not share her love of her grandfather. He was so eager to get Granddad into a home it even shocked the home's administrators, though they went along with it. She had snatched up the gun to have something of her grandfather's that her father hadn't sold off in his frenzy to get as much from the estate as quickly as he could.

Watching her neighbor reminded her of Granddad. Both men moved the same when intensely involved in a project, their hands close, hovering near their work, talking over their shoulders, and casting a friendly smile now and again to assure her things were going just right. She needed a man like Granddad in her life.

"Your dad still alive? He's not interested in the gun?" Ralph asked over his shoulder.

Sheila thought about her family, and how her mother ran off with another man while she was still very young, about five years old. She remembered few things about her mother but she remembered enough to silently resent her father's ranting comparisons whenever she did something that angered him.

"You're just like that tramp mother of yours!"

The woman Sheila remembered was no tramp. She was tough enough to find a way to leave the house one afternoon after a bad beating and not look back. Her mother waited until Sheila's dad fell asleep on the couch, worn out from bourbon and from slapping his wife around, then gathered up little Sheila and headed for Granddad's farm. There, Momma hugged her little Sheila and made her a promise.

"Mommy's gonna get set up right, then I'll come back for you, you'll see. Be a strong girl for Mommy."

Her mother was tough but a poor judge of men. The guy she ran off with took her to Arizona, where, after a night of drinking, he managed to kill them both by running the car off the road and rolling it in the desert. Her dad gathered her up from her granddad, who had no legal right to keep her, and for the next ten years Sheila traveled back and forth from her father to her grandfather – whenever her father tired of her. When Sheila was with her dad, she bore the brunt of his abuse. Then he would send her out to "the farm," where her grandfather welcomed any opportunity to be near his dead daughter's only child.

Sheila's father eventually died of a heart attack, leaving her nothing but the house, a stack of unpaid bills and a jar filled with old coins. And she still had her grandfather's shotgun, a bolt-action Mossberg 190. She sold the house, paid most of the bills, kept the coins and the gun, and left town before the other creditors brought suit against the estate. There were some cousins on her father's side, but most of them were still friendly with her ex, just as her father had been.

"Coupla bad spots in there," mused Ralph, squinting down the barrel and listening for Sheila to answer.

Sheila barely heard him, her mind daydreaming through time.

Her father encouraged her to marry that man. Sheila was young at the time, much younger than him and too young to consent to marriage on her own. Her father gave his consent, without her ever asking.

"He'll be good to you, and God knows, I'm done doing for you. Go on now and start yourself a family. I got my own life to live."

Sheila's husband had a lot in common with her father. Both liked bourbon about as much as they hated women. He had been married before, and would not let her forget the infidelities of his first wife.

"She's a bitch who'd go with anybody, first time my back was turned," was his favorite description of her. "I'm not havin' any of that with you, now, am I? Your dad told me what kind of woman your mother was."

Sheila put up with fifteen years of that before her father's death gave her the courage and the opportunity to walk out.

Ralph asked again, "So your dad's not interested in the gun?"

This question brought Sheila back to the present. "No," she shrugged again, "Dad's gone, Mom's gone, I'm an only child. It's just me now."

Ralph nodded absently, intent on the firearm. "Barrel looks okay but there's rust in there. I've got some fine emery cloth that I can use to scrub those rust spots lightly to move 'em, then I'll go over all of it with this solvent."

He affixed a plastic eye to the end of the cleaning rod and slipped a strip of very fine emery cloth through the eye. "Normally, I wouldn't do it this way but that rust's gotta go, and this gun's not been cleaned in a while."

He ran the rod into the muzzle and stopped at the approximate point where he spotted the rust. He scrubbed back and forth slightly, then pulled the rod back out and replaced the emery cloth with a cloth wad soaked with the nitro powder solvent. He ran this the full length of the barrel several times, then pulled it out, checked it for dirt and rust, replaced it with another wad, and then ran the rod in again. He did this several times, checking and rechecking as each wad came out cleaner than the last.

She watched intently, carefully, rehearsing the lessons she had been taught years ago by her grandfather, who wanted his granddaughter to share his love of farming and guns. As she watched Ralph, she could see herself shouldering the weapon and swinging it toward the crows diving at Grandpa's corn, her finger tightening on the trigger, the flash of surprise she felt when the round went off, the punch to her shoulder and the tumbling crow dropping dead between rows of corn. Behind her, her granddad cheered.

"You're one helluva shot, baby girl! You shoot better'n your mama!"

With her mother gone and no divorce ever finalized, executorship fell to her father, Granddad's son-in-law and only surviving adult relative. Sheila's father wasted no time cashing in. He placed the old man in a nursing home to die, sold the farm and paid off his own house. Then he proceeded to accumulate more debt, which he passed to her when he died but not before telling her husband that he was leaving his daughter a pile of cash.

"Hell, that jar of coins alone's gotta be worth a fortune."

The memory brought her back to the present, where Ralph continued working over the gun.

The final wad went in clean and dry and came out the same way. Behind him, Ralph heard a small sigh, like contentment. Like love, the morning after.

"That looks pretty good," Ralph said, reaching for a toothbrush. He turned the dry toothbrush to the open chamber, scrubbing lightly wherever he could reach to loosen grime and dirt. He did the same to the bolt. He wiped both parts with a solvent-treated rag and then wiped both clean with a dry rag. Once more, he took the rod, fitted it with a clean wad soaked in gun oil and ran the rod into the barrel. He soaked a clean rag with oil, and used it to wipe down all the exposed metal parts, plus the chamber and the bolt, which he dabbed with a bit of extra oil to ensure that the firing pin spring was lubricated. Finally, Ralph slid the bolt back into the gun and turned to face her.

"I'm gonna dry fire this once and listen for the click. Dry firing's not a good idea generally, but since there's nowhere to shoot this thing around here, I should be able to tell from the click whether the firing pin's still working okay."

"Sure," she nodded, "Granddad used to give me hell for dry firing a gun."

He stepped outside the garage and pointed the gun at the ground. "Just habit, y'know?" He smiled, a bit self-conscious that he was slipping into a lecture.

"Never point a gun…" he began.

"At anything you don't want to kill," she responded, with a grin.

"Your grandfather taught you a lot about guns, didn't he?"

Ralph pulled the trigger.

The gun responded with a loud *Click!* Both of them smiled with satisfaction.

"I think you're all right here," he gestured toward the bolt, while holding the gun in one hand, "You got the clip for this?"

Sheila looked at him briefly. Then her face brightened.

"Yeah, there's a coffee can full of stuff in the kitchen," she said and trotted toward the townhouse. She returned with the coffee can, which she handed to him. He picked through its contents and came out first with the clip, a two-shot magazine with a metal spring, designed to fit into a slot below the chamber and feed shells into the chamber with each working of the bolt. He set it on the bench and went back into the can to pull out four 16-gauge shotgun shells. He inspected each one and determined that all were fit for use.

"Lemme wipe off this clip for ya. It could use a bit of oil, too," he said before wiping. "This pops right in here, like this," he pointed and then slipped the clip into the slot.

He slid the clip out and then back in twice, to show her how it worked and how to fill it with shells. Then he pointed to the safety, a thumb-operated lever sitting above the pistol grip and just behind the bolt.

"Push it to the left, where that red button is there and the gun is on *Safe*. Push it the other way, toward that green button there and the gun is on *Fire*."

Ralph handed her the gun.

Sheila accepted it, nodding enthusiastically, her memory refreshed.

"Boy, it's been a long time since I used this thing! Granddad took me out to the cornfield and taught me to shoot crows with it. I was kind of a tomboy as a kid and he got a kick out of showing me stuff. Thanks a lot for all this. I had forgotten so much! Let me hug your neck!"

She threw her free hand around his neck and gave a squeeze. He grinned and hugged her back.

"Yah, it was fun, messing with that old gun. I used to hunt a lot with one of these when I was a kid. It was nice to handle one again. Nice keepsake. Listen, there's a skeet range out in Brownsburg, not too expensive I hear. Why don't we go on out there sometime and shoot this thing a bit? How's that sound?"

"We'll do it," she said cheerfully, "And we can stop for a bite to eat afterward and grab a beer. My treat. Just let me know when you want to go and I'll be ready."

* * *

Ralph smiled and watched her walk back toward the townhome, her strong legs caressed by her cotton skirt. He decided he was hungry. A beer and a burger would do. He walked to the brewpub, ordered a pint and a burger at the bar, and struck up a conversation with a neighbor, a retired cop named Bill.

On the overhead TV, a news commentator was talking about the big story of the day: the Barnes versus State of Indiana ruling and how it led to a revision of the Castle Doctrine that the Indiana State Legislature had passed just yesterday afternoon. All day long, reporters on television kept telling the same story:

In 2007, the Evansville police responded to a domestic battery 911 call at the Barnes apartment by attempting to enter the premises. The call was from Richard Barnes' wife. Barnes refused them entry and even pushed one of the officers against a wall. The police subdued Barnes and arrested him on charges of resisting law enforcement, battery on an officer and disorderly conduct. Barnes was tried and convicted. Many in the public criticized the ruling as a blatant violation of Fourth Amendment guarantees against illegal search and seizure. The court ruling was upheld. But just yesterday, the Indiana legislature responded to the public outcry by enacting a revision to the Castle Doctrine, which was enacted in 2006. This newly revised law was written to "recognize the unique character of a citizen's home and to ensure that a citizen feels secure in his or her own home against unlawful intrusion by another individual or public servant."

Ralph was getting tired of all the news coverage on it.

His friend, Bill, shook his head.

"The legislature is missing the point! What are the cops supposed to do with a domestic battery 911 call? Go in the door and get blown away?"

"Yeah, but we are talking about the Fourth Amendment here, Bill."

"What about Barnes' wife, Ralph? Doesn't she have rights? Cops go in to check on her welfare and get ordered out and assaulted by the guy who the wife says is abusing her. How can you win? With this law, if you want to kill somebody, just have 'em come over! Get 'em inside and BOOM! Castle Doctrine applies."

Bill threw up his hands in exasperation.

Bill's had a bit more than his share tonight, Ralph thought to himself.

Ralph shifted topics to the Colts' chances in the playoffs but Bill wasn't interested. Ralph tried talking about home improvement projects and shared lots of good advice. Bill had little to say. Then their conversation turned to fishing. Bill's eyes lit up. He spoke joyfully about reservoirs, ponds, lakes and streams, all just a short drive from town, where a man could lose himself for hours with a rod and reel and some decent lures.

As they talked Bill set his drink aside and it seemed to Ralph that Bill was actually sobering up a bit.

"Whaddya say we call it a night, Bill? You walkin'? I'm walkin'." Ralph said, gesturing toward the door.

The two men headed out of the bar together. The evening air of early spring felt refreshing after the closeness of the bar. Bill was quiet as they walked but eventually cleared his throat.

"There is just one thing we got," Bill slurred, still a bit tipsy, "If the aggressor backs off, the defender's supposed to stop shooting, or it's murder. Better kill the guy with the first shot. See what I mean?"

Bill gave Ralph a sly wink.

"Still a cop, hey Bill? Does a cop ever put away his badge?"

Both men had a good laugh at that and then they were at Bill's place. Ralph said good night to his neighbor and walked on home to turn in for bed. All in all, it had been a very good day.

Around two in the morning, Ralph heard a loud truck engine lumbering in the drive, followed by the crash of a bottle. He jumped up and stumbled barefoot to the nearest window. A man, powerfully drunk and obviously irritated, stood at the front door of Sheila's townhome, pounding with his fist. A broken fifth lay carelessly tossed in the yard and a pickup truck was idling in the driveway.

"Hey, Sheila, I know I'm late, honey, let me in."

There was no response from inside the townhome.

"Sheila, you goddam bitch, open up this door! You think you can ditch me? For Christ's sake, Sheila, it's our anniversary! Come on, open the door! I wanna talk, that's all!"

His voice trailed off briefly, and then he sobbed, he bellowed, he threatened.

"I know all about the money you got from the homestead! Alla' them damn coins! You plannin' on just taking off with it and leaving me with nothing? What the hell, Sheila?!"

As awareness dawned on Ralph, he thought out what to do: *Call the cops, get dressed quick, and then see if I can talk some sense into this guy.*

He dialed 911, gave them his name, phone number, the location and described the situation.

"Stay on the phone, Ralph." said the operator calmly, matching Ralph's name and number to his address and sending out a dispatch to the police.

"Okay but hurry!" He waited at the phone, now disabled by the 911 operator.

In a moment, the operator was back.

"Ralph, you still with me?"

"Yes!"

"Can you describe this man for me?"

From the window, Ralph saw the drunk lift a sledgehammer from the bed of the truck and quickly go back to the door and start pounding at the frame.

"Listen, I can't see this guy's face, but he's about six feet, dark hair, pretty well built and somebody better get over here quick, cause he's got a sledgehammer and he's busting down the door! I'm going over there myself, right now!"

"No, don't! You need to stay put! The police are on their way!"

The operator warned him twice but he struggled into a pair of shoes and headed for the door. As he reached for the knob, he heard a sound he immediately recognized – the short, loud, angry bark of a Mossberg 190.

Never point a gun at anything you don't want to kill.

He opened the door. Lights had come on all over the neighborhood. The front door of the townhome stood wide open, driven off its hinges. He heard the wail of a police siren as two cruisers drew near to the address given them. Warily, he stepped out into the dark night. He heard a man scream.

"Sheila, Jesus, NO!"

Ralph called out, "Hey, you need help in there?"

There was another angry bark. This time he could see the muzzle flash reflected against the hallway wall, coming from the bedroom. Ralph waited. There was only silence.

Better kill the guy with the first shot. See what I mean?

Soon, the cruisers pulled up. From the first cruiser, two police officers headed for the townhome, surveyed the entrance and headed inside. Ralph's eyes strained to make out their breast-pocket name tags as they turned toward him. Ralph saw one badge. The man's name was De La Garza. Two other officers came over to where he was standing.

Nichols, a slender black man, asked, "You the neighbor who called this in?"

Ralph hesitated, then mumbled a half-answer.

"I'm not sure what's going on. I just heard some commotion and figured I'd better get on the phone to you guys."

Curtis, a burly woman of about 30, grunted, then spoke in a low voice to her partner, "She called it in, too, right?"

Nichols nodded, then walked over to Sheila's door, where he looked inside and spoke briefly to someone. Then Nichols said something into his radio.

In a few moments, De La Garza was visible in the doorway of the townhome. Ralph could see Sheila standing beside him. Ralph heard De La Garza say to Nichols, "You two stay out here and wait on the emergency van. We'll be inside, getting all of this sorted out."

Ralph looked directly at Sheila. Her eyes said nothing.

Is this thing any good?

He thought he heard a sigh.

Thanks so much for all this. I had forgotten so much! Let me hug your neck!

Curtis, joined now by Nichols, spoke again.

"It looks like she shot twice. Did you hear anything between those two shots, like maybe one or the other of them calling out — anything like that?"

He remembered the man's final scream. And he remembered Sheila's smiles and the way her skirt caressed her strong thighs.

I decided to stop running from my problems. Now I'm learning to face them head on, y'know what I mean?

He stood silent for a moment...

Click!

And then he answered,

"No, nothing at all."

Both officers frowned.

AUTHOR'S NOTE

Tumbling Crows, my first published work of fiction, was inspired by my experiences as a pastoral caregiver to abused and neglected persons in congregations where I served. The story is set in the time immediately following the Indiana State Legislature's March 2012 revision to the Castle Doctrine law of 2006, which upholds a citizen's right to defend his or her dwelling and curtilage against unlawful intrusion by another individual or public servant. This revision, and the Castle Doctrine law itself, raise a number of ethical and legal questions for police, homeowners, and the judicial system. It provides a moral framework for the story.

N.W. Campbell

A Ring of Justice
Barbara Swander Miller

Even in his sleep, the musky smell immediately put Hank back in Mr. Salvo's classroom. A caricature of the teacher's nose evolving into an enormous rutabaga commanded the movie frame in his mind. The teacher's heavily accented monotone provided a background soundtrack.

Hank didn't hear the question. All he saw was Salvo's sneering face, those black eyes looking across his giant nose at his friend George's drawing. A knobby fist snatched the textbook from under George's slender hands.

"You! On the floor. Ten pushups. Now!"

George's wide brown eyes darted around at his classmates. Hank knew his friend's fear, could feel his own sour bile rising, burning, rising still and threatening to spew.

"What? Who, me?"

"Who me?" Salvo mocked, cocking his ear toward the boy, his craggy face and pores providing an ugly close-up. "Yes, you!"

George was on the floor, but Hank cringed almost feeling the cold linoleum and the grainy bits of dirt under his palms as George lowered himself into pushup position. On the floor, Hank could see the tiny balls of paper that had been rolled between someone's thumb and finger, then glued with someone's saliva before landing short of their target. He burned with shame. Why couldn't he speak up?

Hank felt the thin muscles in George's arms burn, quiver and give out.

"Keep going! Salvo ordered. "Six more!"

And then the bell rang.

* * *

Hank jolted up and instinctively pounded the alarm clock knob. His arms and chest were covered in sweat. Even the scalp underneath his brown crew cut was damp. "Damn that Salvo! He still gets to me, after all these years."

Next to Hank, Millie's heavy breathing irritated him. Why wasn't she tossing and turning? Philip's decision should have stolen her sleep. Eighteen-year-olds never made smart choices. Hank reached for his glasses and tumbled out of bed.

In the kitchen, he tossed the *Morning Star* onto the kitchen table. The headlines were worse each day. Even under the fold, the conflict was escalating.

U.S. Embassy bombed in Saigon.

The words were guaranteed to start another argument between him and Millie.

But this morning, Hank just didn't have the energy. Last night was the third in a row he had relived the worst parts of his life. He poured milk into his cup of coffee and flipped over the heavy paper to the banner. He set down the milk carton when he saw the bold type:

Skeleton found in high school

Jack Frederickson's byline was underneath the headline.

"Leave it to Jack to be in on something interesting," Hank thought. The rest of the article made Phillip's draft dodging plans evaporate from his mind. Despite his mood, he had to smile.

In three columns of half facts and half sensational guesswork, Jack wrote that the police were called to the local high school after construction workers had made a shocking discovery yesterday afternoon.

A skeleton was found in a rarely used vertical passageway created for accessing the heating plant some fifty years ago. The skeleton was fully dressed in dusty and moth-eaten clothes. The coroner was examining the skeleton and its effects for identification and potential foul play. The story ended with the police and school superintendent's lengthy speculations about the body belonging to a vagrant or a long-forgotten worker.

Well, Hank thought, this will keep Millie and me from arguing. He started reading Jack's article aloud as soon as he heard Millie's heels tapping their way down the hallway.

"For heaven's sake," she exclaimed as she patted her lacquered bob. She picked up the percolator and poured herself a cup as Hank finished. "I've worked at that school for twelve years. How could we not have known?"

She sat down and took a sip of coffee. "So Jack Fredrickson found this out? I might have known he'd be involved in some scandal."

Hank refused to take her bait, even though his longtime pal probably deserved her contempt. He stood up and headed down the hall for his turn in the shower.

Just as at home, the shocking find dominated conversation in factories and businesses and classrooms. Everyone at Hank's office had a theory. The perky receptionist was sure the skeleton was a suicide victim after a high school love affair had ended. The quality inspector figured the coroner would find some trace of murder, maybe poison or hack marks on the bones. The boss suspected the Chicago mafia had taken care of a local informer.

With his lack of sleep and all the gossip, Hank couldn't keep his mind on figuring timesheets. It was taking twice as long as it should have. By lunchtime, he had to get out of the office. He grabbed his tan windbreaker and headed out the door.

Hank arrived at The Oasis in time to see Jack across the dark room stubbing out his cigarette. Dressed in his usual black leather jacket, Jack sat in a booth near the kitchen door with a beer and a burger basket vying for space with the morning paper.

"So?" Hank asked as he slid his slim frame across the worn red vinyl.

His old high school buddy flashed a toothy white smile and pushed away the paper. He methodically spread mustard over the toasted bun and carefully arranged the lettuce and tomato on top of the thick patty. Then he upturned the catsup bottle and pounded out a blob onto the wax paper liner. Hank knew his pal's actions were calculated, even dramatic. That was Jack. From his dark, longish hair to his tight jeans and deep voice, everything about Jack commanded people's attention.

"It's developing, O. Henry. Looks like it might've been a kid. Body's too small for a grown man." Jack dipped three fries into the sweet red pool and crammed them into his mouth.

"Seriously? You just find that out?" Hank caught the waitress's eye and pointed at Jack's burger and beer. She nodded.

"Yep. Coroner just told me. Save it for my scoop, though. It's gonna kill." Jack winked and took a bite out of the juicy burger that had made them regulars at The Oasis ever since they had come back from Korea and needed to toss back a cold one after work.

"So what else? How did he die?"

"Don't know yet. Probably not a homicide. Maybe internal injuries. Coroner thinks the kid fell down the shaft."

Hank's eyes wandered, as Jack mopped a dribble of catsup off his chin. "That's so weird. I was dreaming of high school last night." Jack's words suddenly registered. "Shaft? You said 'passageway' in the article. Is it the one we were going to use?"

Jack didn't seem to hear him, his eyes following the waitress out of the kitchen and across the room. Even his eating had stopped.

"You know... for The Great Revenge?"

"Hmmm? Oh, I dunno. Guess I hadn't thought about it." Jack took another bite and talked as he chewed. "It might be. I haven't seen it yet. I'm hoping to eyeball it this afternoon, after school lets out."

Hank leaned in, elbows on the table. "Well... the only access to that shaft was from the roof. Remember how we planned it? You and me ... and George?"

"Yeah," Jack licked his fingers carelessly, his eyes following the waitress back into the kitchen. "Now that you mention it. You're the one who keeps all that high school stuff straight, O. Henry." He finally looked closely at his friend across the table. "Hey, you look like crap. You alright?"

"Yeah. Just not sleeping much. I..." The waitress interrupted Hank as she set down his burger basket but smiled at Jack.

"Okay." Jack shoved his empty basket toward the woman and slid across the banquette. "Gotta run, buddy. Just had a thought." He turned to the waitress and patted her behind. "Thanks, doll."

Hank finished his burger alone. Jack had certainly made a name for himself, at least in this part of the state. He was a local celebrity, a news reporter dedicated to uncovering the truth, however ugly it was and regardless of who was hurt in the process. Hank wondered who it would be this time.

When Hank got home that evening, Millie and her son Phillip were chatting in the kitchen. She was slicing meatloaf while Phillip cut lettuce into her new wooden salad bowl. Hank stood in the hallway hanging up his coat, watching and listening.

"But where did they find it, Mom?"

"Phillip, I've told you that I can't discuss it. It wouldn't be right. The next thing I know, Jack Frederickson will be calling me and asking about it." Millie smiled inwardly, thinking she might be part of the investigation.

Phillip tweaked her. "Righter says it was a kid."

His mother's smile disappeared. "Do you mean Mr. Righter? He has no business telling students what he thinks he knows. He's there to teach you facts, not gossip." She turned to the stove to spoon the potatoes out onto the platter.

Phillip had finished with the lettuce and leaned his lanky frame against the sink watching his mother. "Oh, Righter always says what he thinks. You know. He's the one who told us we have the right to resist the draft if our conscience tells us we should."

"So that's where you got the idea." Millie put down the spoon and turned to her son. "Phillip, I thought this was something you believed. I didn't know that Mr. Righter put you up to it. Maybe Hank is right about you after all."

"He didn't put me up to it. I believe in resisting the draft. I'm a conscientious objector." Phillip popped a carrot slice into his mouth and grinned at his mother from under his long blonde bangs. "Besides, I have to do what I think is right, right? No matter what you or my stepfather say."

From the hallway, Hank had heard enough. He stepped into the room. "When's dinner?" he grumbled.

Phillip's smile vanished. He looked at the floor, mumbled something about not being late for work and headed down the hall.

That was just like Phillip these days, Hank said to himself. Phillip didn't care what Millie or he thought any more. He and

Phillip had gone fishing almost every weekend that first summer after the wedding. But during the last six years, they had gradually drifted apart. They never talked these days. They just ignored each other.

Phillip claimed that if he was old enough to die for his country, he should be old enough to drink a beer if he felt like it, or grow a beard without getting his parents' permission. The boy had no respect for how he had been raised, Hank thought. What do eighteen-year-olds know about life?

Hank sat down at the table and tried to push aside his irritation. Millie was full of gossip from school. Her face lit up as she chattered on.

Hank finally interrupted her. "Jack says it might have been a kid, Millie. Did you hear anything about that?"

"Jack says?" Millie pushed her bangs back and frowned. "When did you see Jack?"

"Uhh. We had lunch today. Burgers... at The Oasis." Hank fidgeted in the captain's chair at the small maple table. "Anyway, did you hear anything about who it might have been?"

"Nothing definite. Everyone's talking about it, though." The two sat and ate in an awkward silence, their forks tapping the orange Melmac plates. "I just don't see how it could have been a student," Millie finally ventured. "Surely someone would report a student missing."

After a long pause, Millie went on, "I mean, like I told Mary Ann, it doesn't seem very likely. An adult, a hobo, during the Depression, maybe." Millie speared a potato chunk and paused, considering her words. "I'm afraid you might have been right, dear. About the draft dodging, I mean. Philip's history teacher apparently suggested it."

Hank frowned. "Sounds like the Commies are still in the classroom. Same old story, huh?"

"Well, let's hope it doesn't end the same way as it did with your Mr. Salvo."

Hank bristled. "He wasn't *my* Mr. Salvo."

"I didn't mean it that way," Millie trailed off. The silence separated the two even further. Then the door slammed and they heard the rumble of Phillip's loud muffler.

181

In bed, around midnight, Hank tossed off the chenille bedspread. He hiked up his leg and pulled his arm underneath his pillow. As he drifted back to sleep, images began to flash across his mind, just the same as if he had sneaked into the Sky Hi Drive In to watch Rita Hayworth with the guys.

* * *

He and Jack were jogging down a darkened Elm Street to George's house. The stained, uneven sidewalk went on and on, and the boys couldn't figure out which house was the right one. Finally, they saw George's rusty bicycle leaning against a shed, the one he used to deliver papers. This must be it. The front door was huge, grotesquely oversized for the small bungalow. Hank knocked and Mrs. Faulkner came to the door in a red and white kimono, the flowers too large to be attractive. She took up the entire doorway, her hip jutted out to one side and one hand steadied herself on the peeling paint of the doorframe. Sultry music wafted from a radio inside the dark living room.

"Yeah?" she asked when she saw them both.

"Where's George?" Jack demanded. "He wasn't at school."

Mrs. Faulkner took a drag on an overly long cigarette and pushed back her shiny auburn hair. She exhaled slowly, eyeing them both. "He run off," she replied, coolly.

"But..." Hank started, but the woman had taken a step back into the tiny house in response to a voice. She turned back to them and waved them off with the smoldering cigarette.

"He done enlisted. In the Navy," she said. "That's what he wrote in his diary, anyways." She turned again toward the living room, "Yeah, baby. I'm coming." And she closed the door.

Hank felt his gut turning sour. He wanted to vomit.

* * *

The ache in his stomach woke him up. Hank pulled his legs toward his chest to make the churning stop. His mind was churning too.

That same question nagged him. It had for years.

Where was George?

He didn't enlist. His bout with polio would have made him 4F. Hank and Jack both knew it. George had run away, ashamed of his cowardice. That was their Great Unspoken. Their tacit agreement. After George disappeared, Hank and Jack graduated, enlisted and then served their time overseas. By the time they returned and used up their G.I. benefits for college, they didn't talk about George anymore, as if he had never existed.

Hank threw off the sheet. The bedroom was mostly dark, only thin strips of light appearing above the curtains. Millie was breathing regularly, so Hank grabbed his robe and stole out to get the paper and make a pot of coffee.

It took a full ten minutes to make a decent pot of coffee. The water had to boil, causing the grounds to percolate. Hank filled the pot with cold water and scooped out half the usual amount of Yuban. Lately, Hank had begun using less coffee and even adding milk to reduce the acid that constantly churned in his stomach. He stood at the sink looking out the window and gently rubbing his stomach as he waited on the pot. The craggy outline of the apple tree near the back fence was just becoming visible in the dawn. Hank thought about how he and Phillip had designed a tree house after he and Millie married. He had wanted Phillip to have the kind of fun he had when he and Jack and George were kids.

* * *

Hank muttered, "We oughta get that Salvo," as he plopped down on the plank floor.

"Yeah," George continued gently lowering himself onto a bench, "we should let the air out of his tires, or something like that."

"How about a potato in the tailpipe?"

"No, let's poison that crap he calls lunch, the Commie." He took a jackknife from his jeans pocket and stood scowling as he carved a crude poison sign into the soft wood of the walls.

"Only if you could stand to smell it," George laughed. He rubbed his hands together, as he often did before drawing. Then he opened a cigar box and took out a short pencil and a piece of paper. He began sketching.

"Well, we could put tacks on his chair. That would get a rise out of him," Hank smirked. The other boys groaned.

"I've got it," said Jack excitedly, turning to his buddies. "Chickens! We can get chickens from Uncle Elmer."

Hank and George looked at each other.

"We'll fill his room with chickens. Georgie, you're small enough. We'll fill a bushel basket with a bunch of chickens and then lower you into his room. You could push them out through the cold air return vent. The whole room'll be filled with chicken crap. Nobody'll ever know we did it."

George's pencil stopped moving. "I don't know, guys," he said.

"You're not chicken, are you? After what he did to you?" Hank asked.

"It'll be 'The Great Revenge.' We'll show him. It'll be the perfect prank before we enlist," Jack said.

* * *

The coffeepot began spurting, bringing Hank back to the present. He turned off the burner as his subconscious assembled the pieces. A new and disturbing picture was emerging: Maybe it was his fault that George had run away.

Hank had known that Salvo was a bully. How fair was it to pick on a boy who had suffered polio? But it wasn't all Salvo. Why didn't Hank have the guts to defend his friend? To say something? Put an end to it? He was old enough to know what was right. And bullying your friend into getting revenge wasn't right.

Jack, for all his antics, at least was loyal. After Salvo's cruelty, Jack was the one determined to save face for Georgie after he left. He concocted the story about Mr. Salvo that cost him his teaching job. No parent wanted a Commie teaching their kids. At least Jack did something. Jack ruined a man, and then just as quickly become a big shot writer in the Army.

The coffeepot quieted, and Hank poured a cup. He took a sip of the scalding liquid. Why didn't he insist on seeing the diary, see where George had actually written down his plans to enlist in the Navy back when it happened? Why hadn't he tried harder to trace his old friend over the years? Was he part of the reason his friend disappeared?

With a stiffening neck and a burning gut, Hank got the milk out of the refrigerator. He forced himself to sit down and then mindlessly opened the newspaper as distraction. Jack's story today gave few new details about the school mystery. The coroner confirmed there was no foul play but no cause of death had been determined. Officially, it was listed as "death from natural causes."

There were a few interesting facts about the clothing. The plaid shirt and blue jeans were too common to date. But some jewelry had been found on the floor near the bones.

The phone interrupted Hank's thoughts. He stepped into the kitchen to pick up the receiver before Millie woke up. It was Jack.

"Did you read it?" he demanded.

"Slow down. I just got up," Hank replied.

"Get dressed. I'm coming over."

In ten minutes, Jack was standing in the living room. His eyes darted from place to place, never settling on one specific spot. Hank's stomach was on fire.

"You read the article, right?"

Hank nodded.

"Well, it's the jewelry," Jack went on. "See, it was a ring. A class ring."

The wave of acid moved from the pit of Hank's stomach up through his esophagus and into his mouth. His gut knew where Jack was going and it was more than he wanted to admit. The pieces fit perfectly. He knew exactly what that class ring looked like. It looked like his own. And Jack's... And Georgie's.

"Don't you want to know what it looks like?" Jack pressed on.

Hank shook his head, "I already know, don't I?" He collapsed on the sofa. "All these years, we said George enlisted. But we knew even from the start that it wasn't true. Didn't we?" Hank looked at Jack for an answer that didn't come. "But I mean, why did he kill himself?" Hank squirmed at the thought of his pal throwing himself down the shaft to escape being called a coward. Maybe to get back at him. But it was crazy.

"Honestly, I don't know. It was almost twenty years ago," Jack returned. "But if it was Salvo that pushed him over the edge, he paid for it. We made sure of that, didn't we?" Jack began backing out the door. "Hey, I just thought you'd want to know."

Hank had to get some answers. He called out to Millie and grabbed his jacket. The sky was overcast like in his dream, but this time the sidewalk wasn't so long and he was alone. He parked two blocks away, in case he lost his nerve. The neighborhood had deteriorated since George's time. North Elm Street was all rentals now, bungalows with sagging porch roofs and aluminum siding that was hanging loose and chalky from being painted too many times. There were too many plastic toys in the dirt-covered, fenced-in front yards with too many growling dogs keeping watch over something. Or nothing.

Hank walked up to the Faulkners' house. No dog in the front yard, but when he tapped on the door, he heard a yapping inside. A faint voice called, "Just a minute."

Hank waited several minutes. He had no idea really what to say or what to ask. Earlier, when Jack was at the house, Hank felt filled with righteousness. He wanted answers. But now, waiting on the rotting front porch, with neighbors peeking through their curtains at him, his bravado was gone.

Finally, the door opened slightly. An old lady, her back hunched from too much work and age, looked up at Hank. Her face bore a slight resemblance to the woman who had answered the door so many years ago, but her gray hair was flat and dull. Her eyes were red-rimmed and watery. She held a dingy handkerchief in her hand. A little brown mutt pushed its way forward and sniffed at Hank's feet.

"Mrs. Faulkner?"

"Yes. What do you want?"

"You probably don't remember me. I'm Henry Gossage. Hank. I was a friend of your son George in high school."

The old lady straightened her back and peered up at Hank. Her chin stuck out a little and suddenly she looked twenty years younger.

"I remember you. You and another boy come here looking for Georgie, didn't you? That day he run off."

"Yes, you told us he enlisted in the Navy."

She looked down at the scruffy little dog and used her foot to push him back into the house.

Hank's courage was building. "Honestly, ma'am we never believed it. Not with his polio and all. And now... maybe you know this already... they've discovered his body. The one in the papers, at the school."

Her shoulders sank, her body deflating. The dog was back, trying to lick Hank's shoes. She turned back into the small, dimly lit house, but the door stayed open. Hank followed her inside.

Without a word to him, she picked up the mutt and disappeared into another room. Hank's eyes adjusted and he studied the tiny living room. So this was Georgie's house. Or had been. Had it changed? Light filtered through the dingy lace curtain that covered the only window in the room, creating lacy patterns on the tablecloth between the newspapers and glass knickknacks. An ugly crocheted coverlet neatly lay on the back of a worn upholstered rocker. Between it and a stiff armchair was a doily-covered end table, where a brown and faded rose gathered dust in a milk glass vase. Three steps away, next to a brown Zenith tabletop radio, a lone school picture of George smiled down from the mantel. No wonder Georgie had never invited him and Jack to his house. The place was suffocating.

The dog scratched at the bedroom door as Mrs. Faulkner shuffled back into the room. She had something in her hand, but she did not meet Hank's eyes. "I didn't know much back then. Thought I did, though. Been thinking about it all morning." She glanced at Hank and then looked away. "I thought any man was my ticket. Humph." She handed Hank a small book, its cover plastered with faded newspaper comics, and then she turned to her chair. "Men, you can't count on. But your son'll always be your son. Even if he don't love you."

Hank watched her lower herself into the threadbare rocker. Did she realize what she had done to her son with all her male friends in the house? What did this book have to do with anything?

Hank ran his hand across the rough newsprint cover. It had to have been Georgie's. A Superman picture plastered on the front and a Charles Atlas advertisement on the back. He flipped through book. Faded pencil lines half-filled the brittle, yellowed pages. He moved closer to the window for more light. On one page was a U.S. Navy insignia, its roped circle carefully shaded. On another the caricature of Mr. Salvo.

"Georgie was a good boy. Never complained. I was just so tired," she said. "I needed time to be young after nursing him through the polio." Mrs. Faulkner leaned anxiously toward Hank, hoping for some sign of forgiveness, but he was too absorbed by the book's contents to respond.

The pages softly fluttered as Hank thumbed through the sketches. There was the treehouse, and Jack, his nose proudly in the air turned away from the chicken he held by its neck. Next was Hank, wide-eyed and holding a potato. Finally, there was a caricature of Georgie holding a basket. From under the basket's covering, a rooster's head peered out. Underneath the caption read "The Three Caballeros."

Hank felt his eyes begin to burn. He turned to the last drawing. It was a box with an opening, like a trap door. Underneath, penciled in gothic letters were the words "The Great Revenge." Hank was confused. He looked up from the book at Mrs. Faulkner who had shrunk into her chair and was mumbling.

"I guess Georgie wanted to get back at me by running off," she said. "He told me if I wanted to ruin my life, he wouldn't stop me. I made up the story about the Navy when he didn't come home that night. I saw that emblem in his diary and just figured it was true. Got easier to tell as the years went on. And he was eighteen, so no one cared. I never really believed it." She sniffled. "All these years, I thought he run off and was punishing me. He never called, never wrote."

Hank cleared his throat and stepped towards her to get her attention. She looked up startled but ready to confess to someone. Her voice began to catch. "Then the police come here today. They told me the truth. He killed himself. At the school. The coroner says other things was found with him. They say he didn't run off after all." Her voice rose in pitch and she began to tear up. "And it's all my fault." Hank heard the tiny dog whimper and whine from the bedroom, its scratching becoming frantic.

Hank set down the book on the end table next to her, his eyes squinting at this shrunken, tiny woman who had once made him cower. She pulled herself out of the chair and stood. Hank's voice gently asked, "Other things? Like what?"

The old lady didn't hear him as she headed to the bedroom mumbling to herself. "It can't be true. Maybe he was just hiding down there. Until I felt bad and come looking. Maybe he was trying to make me sorry." She wiped her eyes. "I shouldn't have ignored him. No, I should've listened." She opened the door and the scratching stopped. She picked up the pitiful little animal and stroked its wiry coat.

Hank followed her to bring her back to the present. In a firm voice, he asked, "Mrs. Faulkner, what other things were found? What did the police say?"

"What?" Mrs. Faulkner turned to Hank. "Other things?" Her eyes began to focus on her visitor. "Why, strange things. A rope, a basket, a dish rag."

Hank was puzzled. Who would run away with those things? He supposed any food in the basket would have decomposed but why a dish rag?

The old lady went on, "They said they found chicken bones, too. That was Georgie's favorite. Fried chicken legs. Do you know what it means?" she pleaded.

Hank walked to the window, his mind trying to fit together the pieces of the blurry puzzle. Suddenly shafts of sunlight darted through the lacey panel. Hank finally understood. Everything fit: The sketches, the chicken and the rope. Even the dishrag. All these years, everyone had it wrong.

Georgie hadn't run away because he was afraid of their prank. He hadn't run away because he'd been bullied by Hank and Jack or even angry at his mother. He hadn't run away at all. Instead, he had run into the danger. Hank saw it all in his mind.

After the boys had planned the prank in the treehouse, Georgie had gone to practice, to prove to himself that he could do it. Georgie must've lowered himself into the metal shaft with the live chicken in a basket covered by a dishcloth to keep it calm. And once he got into the shaft, he couldn't get out.

Hank pictured Georgie's slight frame attempting to climb back up the rope. His arms were wiry but strong, far stronger than his crippled legs. What had happened? Did the rope break? Did it come loose from where it had been tied? Did Georgie pound on the walls to get attention? Or cry out in his thin voice? Hank shivered when he thought about the closeness of the space. Of the eerie silence and the silent waiting until suffocation or hunger overpowered his little friend. And what about the chicken? Had he killed it and eaten it raw?

It was too much for Hank to dwell on. The horrors that Georgie faced were far worse than anything he ever imagined from his wartime clerk's office where he just processed endless supply requisitions. Or even from Jack's office where he wrote light articles to entertain the troops. Even though Georgie had never enlisted, never served his country, he'd done something far braver. Opening his eyes wider to hold back a tear, Hank turned to the door.

Mrs. Faulkner was suddenly beside him and the dog was tugging at his pant leg. She grabbed his windbreaker sleeve to keep him from leaving. "Tell me. Tell me what happened. You know, don't you?" the old lady begged.

Hank turned back to face her, blinked and sighed. He picked up the tiny dog and patted it. "Let me pull up a chair," he said. "And then I need to get home to talk to my son."

AUTHOR'S NOTE

As a high school teacher, I was incredulous when I heard the urban legend about a skeleton being found in a heating shaft at Muncie Central High School. When I learned that it wasn't mere fancy, I couldn't get enough information. I peppered Bearcat alumni with questions. When did this happen? Who was it? How did this person gain access? How was the body found? Why didn't anyone know?

Everyone seemed to have a different answer. Some thought the body was that of a vagrant. Others told me the vagrant was *another* dead body found, a homeless man who had been living between the roof and the fourth floor in a tiny crawl space. Some said the body was a student. Some said it happened in the 1950's. Others said, no, it was in the 1930's. No one had any definitive answers.

My fictional tale draws on research of the time periods as well as my knowledge of schools and weak teachers I have known. Hank's life revolves around being a stepparent, a situation I also know well. He is trying to help raise a young man in a time of radically changing values, particularly troubling because of his own wartime experiences and beliefs. Today, I sometimes feel that tension with my students. Our values simply don't mesh.

I hope that I can learn, as Hank does, that some aspects of the past should simply be honored and then put to rest to successfully move forward in a new era.

Barbara Swander Miller

Miss Hattie Mae's Secret
MB Dabney

Miss Hattie Mae farted.

Often.

When anyone mentioned the flatulence, she'd blame it on the dog. She blamed most things on the dog. Only problem was, Miss Hattie Mae didn't have a dog, hadn't for years.

What Miss Hattie Mae did have, in addition to poor eyesight, was a secret – one that spanned decades. The secret was like a respectful traveling companion: generally silent but always present. She was one month shy of 96 and the secret had come to define her life for more than eight decades.

Raising her cane, she tried to tap her eight-year-old great-grandson, who was just out of reach and playing some game on the wooden porch. "Boy," she said, mauling her gums and repetitively licking her lips in the manner common in old people who weren't wearing their false teeth. "Step on dat dere ant."

The child looked in the direction the old woman pointed her cane. He reluctantly but without complaint got up to do her bidding. So she remained seated, somewhat bow-legged, in a well-worn house dress and with stockings rolled up to just below the knees.

A cloudy film coated Miss Hattie Mae's left eye and she had trouble with the other. So it amazed her family – and everyone else, for that matter – that she could actually see small ants on the porch or tiny pieces of lint on the rugs inside the house. But her family obliged her in addressing the occasional ant or speck of lint whenever she demanded.

A floor creaked as Miss Hattie Mae moved back and forth in the old rocker on the wooden porch, a seat she inhabited most of the time when it was warm outside. Negligible healthcare should have claimed her life decades ago, and would have except for her cursedness. That, and the fact that despite being a church-going, Bible-toting, God-fearing woman, Miss Hattie Mae liked to 'lace' her coffee with a little whiskey, starting with the second cup she had in the morning. As the day wore on, there'd be a little less coffee and a little more whiskey in each cup. By late afternoon, as it was now, the cup on the porch railing beside her rocker contained virtually no coffee at all.

Her small, five-room dwelling had a distinctive, although not all together unpleasant, aroma from all the years Miss Hattie Mae had lived, cooked and farted in the house. She was born there, lived there most of her life (even after she married), and raised her children under its leaky roof.

Hattie Mae's father Ezra Reeves built the house right after he moved to the area with his new bride Ruth the year before Hattie Mae was born. At the time, the house sat at one end of their land, which stretched 40 acres. Over time, and with hard work and careful buying, Ezra's property grew to more than 200 acres on which his extended family farmed cotton and soybeans. A small portion of land, the part closest to the house, also held apple and peach trees. Her mother's apple pies were legendary in the small black community outside of Clarksville, Tennessee. When she wasn't forced to work in the fields when she was growing up, Hattie Mae liked to play along a line of oak trees visible at the other end of their property.

The house, now sitting on a small parcel of land, was all the property she had left, though it wasn't her only financial asset. In truth, Miss Hattie Mae was a millionaire, a recent development she cared little about.

Last year, the federal government used eminent domain to take most of her land – and paid her handsomely for it, which explained her wealth. Plans were for the expansion of a four-lane highway for traffic heading to and from Clarksville. Large land movers arrived last week to start tearing down those oak trees and reworking the property in preparation for the highway construction.

But the land held secrets; long buried secrets that were about to be exposed for the first time in decades.

Miss Hattie Mae's eyesight was poor, but she could still distinguish the flashing lights atop the police cars among the land movers at the edge of the line of oak trees.

"Boy," she said, her tongue licking her lips, "Betta go tel-ah-phone yo pappy."

Earlier that day, Sheriff Jeremiah "Big Joe" Pittman looked down at the report the young man laid on his desk minutes earlier. The young man stood quietly and waited for the sheriff's response.

"You sure 'bout this, deputy?" Pittman said, scratching the microscopic stubble on his chin. It was something he often did when he was nervous – or held a bad hand at poker. It was a gesture his card-playing buddies were glad he was unconscious of.

"Yes, sir. There wasn't much there 'cept the bones. The skull was smashed. But the ID was positive," the young man said, remaining ramrod straight, hands behind his back. "How you wanta proceed?"

Pittman scratched his chin a little more and then rose from his chair. The report was in his hand as he walked around his desk, passing his deputy. He headed for the door.

"I'll handle it myself," he said.

* * *

"Hattie Mae, call ya lil' sista on in here for suppa. And Daddy, too," her mother said. "Cornbread's gonna get cold."

The screen door slapped the door frame as Hattie Mae, all long legs and 12 years old, ran out of the house.

"Dadd-eee," she called at the edge of a field of cotton. "Time to eat." Turning to her sister Beulah, a light-skinned girl like her mother who would need four years to catch up to Hattie Mae's age, she said, "Stop playin' in dirt. We gotta go wash up for suppa."

The house was small, had only gotten electricity the previous year but still had no running water. A trip to the well out front was Hattie Mae's first chore every morning, regardless of the season or the weather. There were no rugs or carpet covering the unpolished wood floors. A potbelly shove in the living area provided the only heat in the house in the winter, other than whatever came from cooking in the kitchen.

Despite the harshness of everyday existence, suppertime was filled with family laughter. And afterwards, Hattie Mae and her sister would sit and read before heading to bed, where they'd giggle and play until their parents made them quiet down.

The aroma of fried chicken still filled the air in the house long after the meal was completed that summer evening. And the girls had just gotten in the bed beside the open window which permitted a gentle cooling breeze in from outside. "Daddy's gonna come in there an' give you girls a whuppin' if you don't settle down," their mother admonished. But everyone in the house knew that was a lie, for Ezra Reeves was a hard-working but gentle man who wouldn't harm anyone.

The comforting smell of a country summer drifted in through the open windows, but there was no comfort for what was coming.

With the lights out in the bedroom, it was Hattie Mae who first saw the lights outside of the approaching car. And once the car stopped in front of the house, she knew who it was, even before he got out.

"The sheriff's back," Hattie Mae called from the bedroom.

In the far reaches of the poor black rural community, the only whites who ever showed up at the house were men because mingling so closely with coloreds wasn't something a proper white woman would do. And when males came at night, it was rarely good. Fear and apprehension came with them. And even at age 12, Hattie Mae could read that on her parents' faces.

Ezra was at the screened front door as Sheriff Jim-Bob Muller reached the top step on the porch. The buttons on his tan-colored shirt strained to contain his belly, which overwhelmed the belt holding up his dark pants. He staggered a little, grabbing the rail post to the porch to steady himself, because he had just finished off a jug of rot-gut moonshine in his patrol car.

When he got to the door, he flung it open as if he owned the house and everything inside, including the people.

"Sheriff, please," Ezra protested.

"Out of my way, boy," the man said, pushing him aside with such drunken force that Ezra nearly tripped over a sturdy chair.

Sheriff Jim-Bob Muller had made it clear in the previous fall's county elections that he hated blacks and would treat them harshly whenever they stepped out of line, which meant if they did anything other than what he told them. He WAS the law in Montgomery County and dared blacks to step out of line so that he could exact white-man's justice.

Ezra and Ruth knew that and, being law-abiding citizens, had no reason to encounter him, and would have avoided him if they had reason. But one day, Jim-Bob saw the attractive, light-skinned Ruth in a general store on the main road in Woodlawn, outside of Clarksville. He took an instant liking to her. After that he made numerous trips to the house when he was drunk, waving his gun around and threatening anyone who might object to his forcing himself on the helpless woman.

He always came for Ruth. But she knew, in time, it would be for Hattie Mae, who was showing the first outward signs of womanhood.

"Come here, you coon bitch," the sheriff said as he started to corner Ruth in the kitchen. She backed away, shaking her head, tears welling in her eyes.

Then something happened that hadn't happened before. Ezra grabbed the sheriff's arm from behind and turned him around.

"No. Not this time," Ezra said.

Sheriff Jim-Bob shoved Ezra back again and reached for his revolver. It was out of his holster amazingly fast and pointed at Ezra when he fired. Intoxication spoiled his aim but he still managed to hit Ezra in the chest, dropping the man to the floor in full view of the girls, who had gotten out of bed.

Ruth and the girls screamed and Ruth started for her bleeding husband, not sure if he was alive. But the sheriff took her arm before she reached him.

"He made me do it," the sheriff growled.

Ruth swung her arm, hitting him. "You bastard. You killed my husband."

Enraged, Sheriff Jim-Bob pistol-whipped Ruth in the face, knocking her to the floor. He reached down and took her wrist, pulling her barely to her feet and dragging her from the kitchen toward the bedroom. She kicked and tried to grab ahold of anything but it was no use. Once in the bedroom, he grabbed both her arms and lifted her up, throwing her violently onto the bed. She backed away from him but, with her back up against the metal headboard, there was nowhere to go. She cried and kept holding down the hem of her house dress. It had, unfortunately, been of little use in the past.

"Shut up, you black bitch. I'm going to teach you a lesson," he said as he unzipped his pants and started pulling them down. His back was to the door, so he did not see Hattie Mae come into the bedroom from the kitchen, though her mother did.

"Hattie Mae," her mother screamed as the girl hit the man in the back of the head with a large black frying pan that her mother used earlier to fry the cornbread. Dazed, Jim-Bob fell onto his hands on the bed, then turned to see the girl. He got up to reach for her and she quickly backed away. But in his anger and haste, he forgot his pants were down below his knees. With Hattie Mae out of reach, he lurched forward and fell face down on the rough wood floor.

Jim-Bob started yanking up his pants as a hatred played across his face. It was an image that would haunt Hattie Mae's dreams well into her adulthood.

"I'm goin' kill all you niggers. Just you wait and see. Y'all dead," he yelled as he struggled with his pants.

Those were the last words Sheriff Jim-Bob Muller would ever utter. And probably the last thing he ever saw was the skillet Hattie Mae raised and brought down hard onto his face. She hit him again and again and again, not stopping until long after he stopped moving.

Hattie Mae's mother was shaking when she eased off the bed and over to her young daughter, who was trembling. She finally dropped the skillet.

Mother and daughters stared down at the dead white man on the floor. His head was a mess, one bloody eye still open.

It took a while but Ruth regained a degree of composure. "You go fetch yo Uncle Roscoe, Hattie Mae. Now."

The girl ran in the pitch dark to the shack down the road.

"What you sayin', girl?" he asked as she tried summon the words to explain what happened. But Roscoe didn't wait to understand his young niece. He just pulled his suspenders up over his dirty, sweat-stained t-shirt.

"Oh my Lord Jesus in heaven," Roscoe said once he reached Hattie Mae's house and saw his brother-in-law shot on the floor, Ruth kneeling beside him and cradling his head. "What happent here? Hattie Mae said sum'ung 'bout the sheriff shooting sumbody."

"Erza's still breathin', Roscoe. I need help," Ruth said, her voice shaking. Ezra took short, rapid breaths. Beads of perspiration formed on his forehead and his eyes stared with little focus on Ruth, who stroked his pale face with one hand as she pressed a towel to his upper chest just below the collar bone with the other hand. "In the bedroom," she said to Roscoe, adding to the children, "Mae, you and Beulah stay in here with me."

In the bedroom, Roscoe got the biggest surprise of his life. But to his credit, he took charge, which was good. All their lives depended on it.

"Hattie Mae, run back over to da house and have yo Aunt Edna and yo uncles bring the truck over. Hurry now, Hattie Mae," Roscoe said. "Beulah, you go stand over there."

Roscoe's three brothers and his wife Edna arrived presently with a pickup that had no side rails. The first thing they did was lift Ezra onto the back and drive him to Roscoe's house where Edna and Ruth cared for him overnight, cleaning and dressing his entry and exit bullet wounds, keeping him calm and comfortable, and praying that he'd survive the night. If he did, there was hope.

"You caint tell nobody never, Hattie Mae," her mother entreated as they waited and prayed that night for Ezra's survival. "Ya hear me, girl? Never."

Calmly, Hattie Mae agreed.

Roscoe and his brothers wrapped Sheriff Jim-Bob's body in an old quilt, then lifted the body and carried it through the cotton field lit only by the silent stars and a quarter moon. They dug a grave and buried him along the oak trees. Roscoe took the sheriff's car to the next county over and drove it off a narrow, wooden bridge and into a raging river, ever thankful for a heavy rain the day before. By the time Roscoe got back, the first rays of orange-yellow sunlight were on the horizon.

Though the car was discovered about a week later, no body was found. Officials in several counties searched of any evidence as to what happened to the sheriff but, since no one knew his whereabouts just prior to his disappearance, none was ever found.

His disappearance was a mystery.

* * *

Rumors and stories circulated for years throughout the county about the disappearance of Sheriff Jim-Bob Muller but no one knew what happened to him. That is, no one knew until human bones were found buried on Miss Hattie Mae's land more than eight decades later.

Officials were first puzzled when the bones were discovered but quickly made an initial ID determination based on other evidence from the site. While human tissue and most of the victim's clothes had long since decayed, a few fibers of cloth, some hair on the skull, the buttons of Jim-Bob's uniform and his sheriff's badge survived.

A cloud of dust accompanied a line of police patrol cars on the dirt road leading up to Miss Hattie Mae's house. Sheriff "Big Joe" Pittman was in the first car, and was slow to get out once he stopped in front. He would later say his slowness in exiting the car was because he wanted the dust to first settle, and not due to a general reluctance to carry out a duty he knew would be difficult.

He may have been right. It's hard to tell.

Miss Hattie Mae, as most people called her throughout most of her adult life, had been Big Joe's nanny growing up. She virtually raised him. He had memories of her gentleness, her kindness, from as far back as he could remember. She was like a surrogate mother to him, having out-lived both his parents, who had left most of his privileged upbringing to Miss Hattie Mae.

Sheriff Pittman rounded his car but never took his eyes off of Miss Hattie Mae, who was still sitting on the porch in a chair, He paused at the bottom of the steps, as he overcame the last of his reluctance, then headed up the five wooden stairs. She greeted him with a calm composure, never ceasing to rock in her chair.

"Miss Hattie Mae, we need to talk," Pittman said in the most gentle of tones. But he stopped as the screen door opened.

"Sheriff, I don't think my grandmother has anything to say," said a sharply dressed young man in a blue business suit and white shirt.

Pittman turned to face the man. "Kyle..."

"Counselor," the young lawyer corrected.

Miss Hattie Mae might intimidate Pittman but the county's leading assistant prosecutor did not.

"Kyle, I know she's your grandmother but there are questions that need asking and it's my duty to ask them. There was a skeleton found out there on her property," he said, then corrected himself, "Or what was once her property. It looks to be the skeleton of a former sheriff who disappeared."

"I don't know anything about that," Kyle said.

Looking at his former nanny as he raised a finger, the sheriff said, "But she probably does."

There was a pause, which Kyle broke.

"Then let's go inside to talk," the young man said. He looked at his grandmother, who hadn't said a word, and the men walked inside in the house.

"Boy," Miss Hattie Mae said to her great-grandson, pointing with her cane. "Step on dat dare ant."

In her mind, the mystery of Sheriff Jim-Bob's disappearance was resolved decades ago. So she just rocked in her chair, sipped her coffee and farted.

AUTHOR'S NOTE

While this story is fictional, the main character, Miss Hattie Mae, is drawn directly from my maternal great-grandmother. Minerva Marshall, or Gaga as we called her, was born in 1881 – and unfortunately died long before I was old enough to stop hating her. I was only 10.

My greatest memory of Gaga is of her forcing my older sister and me to step on ants on my grandparents' porch or to pick up pieces of lint – bits, as she called them – from the rugs inside the house. Given her poor eyesight, I wonder how she managed to see any of it.

As an adult, I still may not have liked her but I certainly would have understood her better.

In my lifetime, I have endured racial discrimination, both implicit and explicit. But slavery ended four score and seven years before I was born, and I never faced the sort of Jim Crow hatred and soul-crushing, life-threatening racial segregation and oppression that was a daily reality for my ancestors.

This story was my chance to allow the Miss Hattie Mae's of my real and fictional life to say, "No."

MB Dabney

BIOGRAPHIES

N. W. Campbell: Norm has been a writer his entire adult professional life, first as a technical writer, then as a United Methodist pastor, and as an adjunct instructor of college English at the University of Florida, the University of Missouri-St. Louis, the University of Indianapolis, and Ivy Tech Community College--Indianapolis. He is a summa cum laude graduate of Northeastern University (Class of 1979), and holds graduate degrees in English studies, divinity and leadership development.

Sherita Saffer Campbell: Sherita practices and teaches a form of Guided Meditation that she engages in before she begins writing or while searching for new ideas. She believes it is a way for the writer, reader, teacher or anyone to reach the creative mind which enables the practitioner to formulate new ideas for poems, short stories, and novels.

Sherita was a feature writer for both the former *Muncie Star* and also for a weekly paper edited by Patricia Mills.

Sherita writes mysteries and has been published in *Alfred Hitchcock Mystery Magazine*. Her story "One Last Picture" was included in the Alfred Hitchcock Mystery collection *Garden of Deadly Delights*. Other publications include *Fate Magazine*, *Branches, Sage Woman*, and poetry books from the Humpback Barn Festival, where she was a member of the festival committee. She has had stories published in three earlier Speed City Indiana Chapter of Sisters in Crime publications – *Bedlam at The Brickyard*, *Racing Can Be Murder* and *Hoosier Hoops and Hijinks*.

Diana Catt: Diana has had pretty good success with short story publications in multiple genres: "Photo Finish" in *Racing Can Be Murder*, Blue River Press (2007); "Evil Comes" in *Medium* *of Murder*, Red Coyote Press (2008); "Slightly Mummified" in *A Whodunit Halloween*, Pill Hill Press (2010); "Boneyard Busted" *in Bedlam at the Brickyard*, Blue River Press (2010); "Au Naturel" in *Patented DNA*, Pill Hill Press (2010); "And Through the Woods" in *Back to the Middle of Nowhere*, Pill Hill Press (2010); "Salome's Gift" in *Murder to Mil-Spec*, Wolfmont Press (2010); "The Art of the Game" *in Hoosier Hoops and Hijinks*, Blue River Press (2013); "Raspberry Summer" in *Distant Dying Embers*, Four Horseman Press (2015).

Diana is married with three mostly-grown kids. She enjoys her laid-back cat and accepts the challenge of her stubborn dog. In her day job, Diana is an environmental microbiologist who teaches microbiology and hunts in scary places for mold.

S. Ashley Couts: Ashley, who lives in Greenwood, Indiana, holds a BFA in painting from Indiana University, Herron School of Art and Design and is a fellow of the Indiana Writing Project. Her life experience has given her grist for the writing mill, and she has worn many hats from grocery clerk to police dispatcher to middle school art teacher. Her writings in fiction, non-fiction and poetry have appeared in local, regional and national publications. Her most recent short stories are "Lady Luck" published in *Bedlam at the Brickyard*, Blue River Press and "The Freak Faire" published in *Unreal City* by Das Krakenhaus Press.

MB Dabney: Michael is an award-winning journalist whose writing has appeared in numerous local and national publications. Born and raised in Indianapolis, Michael spent two decades as a reporter in Philadelphia, working first as a business correspondent for *Business Week* magazine, and later as a reporter for United Press International and the Associated Press. As an editor at *The Philadelphia Tribune*, the nation's oldest continuously published African-American newspaper, Michael earned national and state awards for his editorial writing.

Michael annually writes a novel in November during National Novel Writing Month and plans to independently publish *An Untidy Affair*, first written in 2009, in the next year. He has been a member of the Speed City chapter of Sisters in Crime since January 2008 and currently is the chapter's vice president, a fact for which he is very proud.

The father of two adult daughters, Michael lives in Indianapolis with his wife, Angela, and their dog, Pluto.

Sarah Glenn: Sarah specializes in stories involving out-of-the-ordinary heroes and circumstances, usually with a sidecar of funny. She has a BS in journalism from the University of Kentucky. She also did some graduate work in ancient languages, which helps her immensely with crossword puzzles. She belongs to the Short Mystery Fiction Society, the Historical Novel Society, and Sisters in Crime: the Speed City Indiana Chapter and the Guppies Chapter. She contributed "New Age Old Story" to *Fish Tales*, the first Guppy anthology.

S. M. Harding: Suzanne has had two dozen short stories published in various crime fiction publications, both on-line magazines and in print anthologies and magazines. Two of the most recent include "A Winter Story" in *Wicked Things* and "Spirit of Christmas Past, Christmas Future" in *Unwrap these Presents*, both from Ylva Publishing.

Her novel *I Will Meet You There* will be published by Bella Books in August of 2015.

She teaches classes at the Writers' Center of Indiana and participated in panels for their annual Gathering of Writers, also at Indy Author's Fair, Magna Cum Murder and various local libraries. She edited and contributed an essay to *Writing Murder*, a collection of essays by Midwestern authors about writing crime fiction. You can find her blog at storytellersfire.wordpress.com and her Facebook author's page at S. M. Harding.

B. K. Hart: B.K. is an avid reader, sleuther of facts and exaggerator of those facts. Writing is the perfect complement for the skill set.

Previously published short stories appear in three separate horror anthologies. This debut short story is the fascinating foray into the realm of mystery publication.

B.K. is a member of the Speed City Indiana Chapter of Sisters in Crime.

Gwen Mayo: Gwen has a BA in political science from the University of Kentucky and is a history junkie. Her writing is steeped in the rich history of her native Kentucky. *Circle of Dishonor*, her first novel, and upcoming sequel *Concealed in Ash* are set during the turbulent political upheaval of post-Civil War

Kentucky. Gwen is a member of the Historical Novel Society, the Short Mystery Fiction Society, and Sisters in Crime: the Speed City Indiana Chapter, and the Guppies Chapter. She is currently the president of the First Florida Chapter of the Historical Novel Society.

Barbara Swander Miller: Barb is in her seventeenth year of teaching high school English to students at all grade levels and abilities. Primarily a writer of nonfiction, teaching materials, grant proposals, and blogs, Barb began writing short stories to feel the struggle her lower level students felt when they were asked to write anything. It worked. After slogging through many iterations of her fictional pieces, learning, revising, reorganizing, and editing, Barb appreciates how difficult writing can be for anyone. "A Ring of Justice is her second story written for Sisters in Crime.

Barb currently teaches high school English at Yorktown High School and also teaches a literature methods course to pre-service teachers at Ball State University. Barb also coordinates professional development programs for Indiana Writing Project, a teacher support organization affiliated with National Writing Project.

When she is not teaching or writing, Barb enjoys traveling abroad with her husband and spending time with their five grown children.

Elaine L. Orr: Elaine is the Amazon bestselling author of *Trouble on the Doorstep* and other books in the Jolie Gentil cozy mystery series, which includes eight books and a prequel. She wrote plays and novellas for years and graduated to longer fiction. *Biding Time* was one of the five finalists in the National Press Club's first fiction contest in 1993, and *Behind the Walls* is a finalist in Chanticleer's 2014 Mystery and Mayhem Awards.

Elaine regularly attends conferences, such as the annual Midwest Writers Workshop in Muncie and Magna Cum Murder, and conducts presentations on electronic publishing and other writing-related topics. Her non-fiction includes carefully researched local and family history books, and *Words to Write By: Getting Your Thoughts on Paper*.

Elaine grew up in Maryland and moved to the Midwest in 1994.

Claudia Pfeiffer: Claudia wrote in her youth and teens, then quit for nearly fifty years to work in her husband's law office, raise her family, and paint landscapes. Now a widow, she lives in Indianapolis with a married daughter and her family. Her two other adult children live in distant states.

In 2010, Claudia bought a computer and began to write again. She is addicted to writing, spending eight to ten hours a day (and night!) in this endeavor. Her genres are mystery, romance, and juvenile. When she grows up, she hopes to be published.

C. L. Shore: Cheryl grew up in Wisconsin before attending Indiana University and becoming a Hoosier. She received her Bachelor's Degree from I.U., as well as a Ph.D. Between these two degrees, she attended University of Iowa and obtained her Master's Degree in Nursing. Currently a nurse practitioner, she practices in a rural clinic for the medically underserved.

Cheryl has authored multiple academic articles about family coping with epilepsy. She published *Seeker of Truth*, a mystery novel, in 2011. Her second novel, *Titania's Suitor,* was published December 2014. She's currently working on the prequel to *Seeker of Truth*, as well as short stories in the mystery, inspirational, and horror genres.

She currently serves as president of the Speed City Indiana Chapter of Sisters in Crime.

Andrea Smith: Andrea, a native Chicagoan, holds a Bachelor's Degree in journalism from Northern Illinois University in DeKalb, Illinois, and a master of arts in novel writing and publishing from DePaul University in Chicago. Smith managed corporate communications for companies such as Eli Lilly and Co., Kraft Foods and Ameritech where she directed staffs in producing global employee communications, product communications, media relations, annual reports and executive speeches.

Following her career in corporate communications Smith owned two Subway restaurants and taught English as an adjunct professor.

Andrea has published four short stories featuring Chicago Police detective Ariel Lawrence, including "A Lesson in Murder," featured in the mystery anthology *Women on the Case*, edited by Sara Paretsky and published by Delacorte. The story earned this praise from Alison Burns, Highbury and Islington Express, United Kingdom: "Of the writers introduced for the first time, American Andrea Smith stands out with her sharp plotting and terrific new Chicago police woman, Ariel Lawrence."

Andrea's other short stories featuring the tenacious Chicago detective include: "Fatal Flaw," *Mary Higgins Clark Mystery Magazine*; "Elected to Die,' *Mary Higgins Clark Mystery Magazine*; and "Race to the Rescue," *Racing Can be Murder*, Blue River Press. Another short story "Tarnished Legacy," *Bedlam at the Brickyard*, Blue River Press, features a female racing team.

Andrea is the membership chair for the Speed City Indiana chapter of Sisters in Crime and coordinates the national Sisters in Crime's We Love Libraries! Program. She lives in Indianapolis.

Victoria Stewart: Vicki is a longtime member of the Speed City Indiana Chapter of Sisters in Crime and has managed the chapter's website for several years, which she says has been a wonderful experience.

"Lesson Learned" is her second published short story, with the first being "Picture Perfect," which was published in the chapter's June 2010 anthology, *Bedlam at the Brickyard*. She says the thought of being paid or acknowledged for 'telling tales' has always been intriguing.

Vicki has been married for more than forty years and has six children.

Vicki makes the point that Violence is NEVER the answer. Domestic Abuse is rampant. If you are or if you know of someone who is the victim of domestic abuse please call the National Domestic Violence HOTLINE at 1-800-799-7233 or visit the website at thehotline.org. Domestic abuse can take many forms, it can start with belittling angry words and easily and quickly escalate from there. Please get help.

ABOUT THE SPEED CITY INDIANA CHAPTER OF SISTERS IN CRIME

Sisters in Crime was founded to promote the professional development and the advancement of women crime writers to achieve equality in the industry. It has evolved to an organization of supportive women and men writers. The Speed City Indiana Chapter of Sisters in Crime has members from many Indiana cities. It meets monthly, and new members are welcome. Feel free to visit our website, www.speedcitysistersincrime.org or email us at Indychapter@speedcitysistersincrime.org